Just Act NATURAL

GENNY CARRICK

Cover illustration and design by Melody Jeffries

Edited by Cindy Ray Hale

ISBN (print): 978-1-957745-15-2

ISBN (ebook): 978-1-957745-14-5

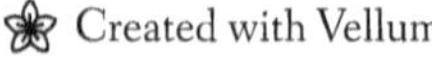 Created with Vellum

To everyone who would rather stay home with a book than go on a hike.

WHAT TO EXPECT

This book includes a cinnamon roll hero, fake dating, swarms of bugs, a critical ex, an unfortunate incident with a fish, distant parents, and talk of leeches. It also includes a very mild fade to black, but only kisses are shown on the page.

ONE

GRANT

ONLY MY YOUNGEST brother would call on the first day of my vacation. My phone lights up with Rhett's name as soon as I drop into a chair at the coffee house where I'm killing a little time this morning. I haven't been out of Texas for twenty-four hours. For someone who shuns responsibility whenever he possibly can, he's sure pretending he doesn't know what time off means.

"The store had better be on fire if you're calling me already."

"It's almost like you don't trust me." He sounds way too happy. Usually, that means he's up to something.

"I didn't accuse you of setting the fire." Although, with Rhett, I can never be too sure.

"Well, good news—there's no fire. Obviously, you got to Oregon okay."

"My plane got in late, but I've been awake since four." Which explains the large coffee in front of me—the house special with thick cream and entirely too much brown sugar. It's almost undrinkable, but with the barista right here watching while he wipes down the counter, I don't want to just throw it away.

"You should have given yourself an extra day to adjust to the time like I said."

"You are the paragon of good planning and responsibility in this family." I take a heftier gulp of the sweet coffee. Normally, I'm at my best first thing in the morning, but I'm not normally running on less than five hours of sleep.

"I know my place." Rhett might as well be preening, he sounds so chipper. "Youngest, troublemaker, best looking. The works."

"Most humble," I add.

"Nah, can't infringe on your territory. Are you heading out this morning?"

"In a few more minutes." As soon as I finish this cavity-inducing coffee, I'll grab my duffel and meet up with the guiding company. This café is right across the street from Horizon Hikes's green awning and their windows plastered with fliers, detailing the trips they offer. Somewhere on there is one for the easy five-day walk I'm about to go on in the nearby National Forest—the perfect start to my month off.

"Cool beans. How's the hermit cave?"

"I'll check in to my *cabin* after I get back from the hike."

"Cabin at a lodge on the outskirts of nowhere. I've seen the pictures. That's where people go to write their manifestos."

"It's a high-end lodge." Not that I know much about fancy accommodations. Most of my vacations have me sleeping on a mountainside, not luxury resorts. This place has a king-sized bed, a private hot tub on the back deck, and a fluffy white robe hanging on a hook somewhere. But if I talk it up too much, Rhett might pass on my managerial responsibilities to someone else and swing into town to crash my party.

He fakes a sneeze that sounds suspiciously like *hermit cave.*

"Fine. It's remote. That's why I booked it." A little cabin in the woods right on a river sounds just about perfect to me. My youngest brother, who would rather act like he's fifteen instead of thirty, would never understand the impulse. "I promise to keep the manifestos to a minimum."

"Seriously. A month off, and you go into the woods like Henry Flipping Thoreau. Your priorities are all wrong."

"A literary reference? I'm impressed." And may have downloaded *Walden* onto my e-reader in case I want a re-read while I'm in the cabin, but I won't give my brother that much ammo.

"Your stress levels would be better served by *more* social interactions, not less. If you know what I mean."

I'm surprised he doesn't verbally add *wink wink*. He's had no subtlety with his opinions ever since I announced my intention to take a month away from our family's business. He sent me links to singles' cruises, cities around the world with reputations for the best nightlife, and several hotels with swim-up bars.

None of that has ever appealed to me. Usually, my trips are centered around my next mountain summit, and truly, aren't all that relaxing. Weeks of prep and planning for a grueling climb? While it's worth it, I want something different this time.

As soon as I saw the lodge's website and that cabin, I knew I needed to stay there. It planted a restless itch beneath my skin that feels less like *escape from* and more like *run to*, even though I've never been here before. But Rhett wouldn't understand or sympathize with that kind of woo-woo explanation.

"Did you call just to roast my choices or was there something else?"

"No, just that. How's the town? Any chance you'll actually get out into sunny *Sunshine*?"

That's right. I'm sitting in a town called Sunshine, Oregon. It's like visiting a town named Dry Heat, Texas. But the cloudless June day defies the state's reputation for gloomy weather, even if the thermometer won't break eighty.

"It's a lot like home." Right down to the cheery bakery and the group of older men gossiping on a park bench. The only real difference are the mountain peaks standing like sentinels in the distance. Texas has a lot fewer of those. Here, I've got ten mountains to choose from within a two-hour drive. If I really wanted to take a rest from climbing during my sabbatical, I probably should have found a place without so much temptation.

The word "temptation" still rattles around in my head when the very definition of it walks through the café's doors. A dark-eyed brunette strolls across the shop toward the lucky barista, a metallic purple roller bag gliding smoothly behind her. Her smile is like staring into a solar eclipse—I'm blinded by the force of it, but I can't stop myself from looking.

Rhett keeps talking, but I don't hear a word. My focus is stuck on her.

"I think you know why I'm here, Troy," she says to the barista. I can't see her smile anymore at this angle, but it shines through her voice. It has a smoky quality that brings to mind late-night conversations, like it wouldn't take much for her to get me to bare my soul.

He nods, giving her a friendly wink that cuts an irrational jolt of jealousy through my gut. Suddenly, I can think of a few things I might put in a manifesto—banning flirty baristas being right at the top.

"Brown sugar milk tea with tapioca pearls, coming up."

He gets to work making something behind the counter. Meanwhile, she shimmies her enthusiasm in a way I should not be watching as avidly as I am.

"You're an angel. You saved me from having to drive into Bend every time I get a craving for boba tea."

He glances at her over his shoulder. "It's catching on. We

should probably offer you free drinks for giving us the great idea."

"Don't do it. I would put you out of business so fast."

Her laughter skates up my spine like a hand trailing a warm caress, and I smile like an idiot.

Am I having a sugar-induced daydream? Did I make her up? It must be real—in a fantasy, I'd get to see her face the whole time.

This isn't me. I don't get infatuated from seeing a woman's great smile or hearing her speak a handful of sentences. Not anymore. Yet here I am, wanting to bask in her presence for as long as I can just to store up this stretching, all-too-aware sensation aching through my chest. It's been years since I felt anything like this, and my impulse is to hold the feeling tight and not let go.

It's a moronic impulse, to be clear, but still undeniable.

"Are you even listening to me?" Rhett barks into the phone. "Did I lose you?"

I swivel away from my view of the gorgeous woman. Feels wrong to turn my back on her, but this ache in my chest feels wronger.

What did I say about being a moron? I've been aware of her existence for less than five minutes, and I've already lost my grasp on the English language. High schoolers who just discovered girls have more sense than I do right now.

"I'm here," I say, keeping my voice low. "Cut out there for a second."

"Then I'll say it again and get right to the point—do the stupid thing."

I freeze. Is Rhett in this café with me? Can he hear the jumble of thoughts careening through my mind?

"What stupid thing?" I say carefully.

"Any of them. All of them. I know you've got your whole month's itinerary planned out down to the last hike and climb."

He's not entirely wrong, but this area has plenty of outdoor sports to keep me busy. "It's more of a loose to-do list than an itinerary—"

"Exactly." A wrapper crinkles on the other end of the line.

"Could you wait to eat whatever that is until we're off the phone?"

He sighs as if I asked him to give up video games for the rest of the year. "My point is, don't keep yourself so busy you forget to relax. Don't do the Grant thing this trip. Do the stupid thing. Have fun."

I don't even want to know what he thinks of as a *Grant thing*. Probably anything not involving an out-of-control party or a few hundred feet of bungee cord. I climb mountains, I don't jump off them.

"You're making me sound like an old man. I'm thirty-six, not a hundred."

"If the loafer fits."

"I have f—"

"You should have *stupid* fun."

My youngest brother, everybody. Champion of good sense and wise decisions.

"Is that the extent of your advice?"

"Basically." He starts crunching on whatever energy bar he has on hand, ignoring that I don't want to listen to him chew. "You've been keeping the business together forever. You keep Dean and me in line, and you make sure Mom and Dad don't work themselves into the ground. You deserve to do something for yourself."

"Why do you think I'm taking a sabbatical?"

"From the looks of your cabin, it's not to have a good time.

In the unlikely event you get the chance, please don't take a woman there. It has creepy stalker vibes all over it."

"I'm starting to think you never looked up the cabin." The pictures on the website look nicer than Rhett's apartment, but that's a pretty low bar to hit.

"I filled in the blanks from how you described it. But my point remains: do—and I cannot stress this enough—the stupid thing."

"Thank you for your wisdom. I'll see what I can do." Can't really imagine what kinds of stupid things I'll encounter on my quick hike followed by three weeks relaxing at a remote cabin, but if something comes up...who am I kidding? Taking Rhett's advice is never a smart move.

Whatever he's chewing muffles his laughter. "I'm only here to serve."

"I should go check in."

"Stupid thing! Stupid thing!"

"Goodbye, Rhett."

He continues chanting until I thumb off the phone. If our middle brother Dean had called, he would have encouraged me to make an even more detailed itinerary for my trip. He's a big fan of numbers, schedules, and calendars. Only Rhett would consider stupid choices something to be indulged in.

Then again, Dean has loosened up quite a bit since he met his wife. Maybe he would have joined in Rhett's chant, after all. His wife absolutely would have. Eliza proves daily that she doesn't believe in letting fun opportunities pass her by.

I finish the last of the too-sweet coffee, grab my bag, and stand to face the counter. My gorgeous temptation is still chatting with the barista, her back to me as she tells him about other tea drinks she'd like to see on their menu one day.

I have a sudden interest in fruit jellies and taro slushes, whatever those are.

Approaching her would absolutely count as a stupid thing. Rhett's rash pep talk has me half-convinced to do it, but I hesitate. At most, I'm in town for a month. And she sounds like a local, but she's also dragging rolling luggage behind her. She's on her way somewhere, too.

Chatting up a strange woman in a strange town, knowing we're both here temporarily? That's never been my style. But I start leaning her way anyhow, as if my body's ready to test out Rhett's advice. What's the worst that could happen?

The answer to that thought pops into my head, showering icy pellets over the warm fuzzies this woman brought out in me. There's a good reason I haven't dated seriously in almost five years. Ever since Kelsey burned down our relationship, I've kept my distance from flames.

This woman is a four-alarm fire.

I toss the empty coffee cup into the trash as I push through the café door, telling myself that by the time I'm done with this hike, I'll have forgotten all about her.

Even if her smile is etched into my retinas.

———

Inside Horizon Hikes, I meet up with the owners-slash-guides, Deena and Mitchell Choi, and finish signing the waivers for the trip. They introduce me to the other hikers: two couples who are also good friends who meet up every summer for an adventure. Brian and Cindy Monroe, and Scott and Shannon Allen are celebrating turning sixty this year with our hike in the National Forest. They're giddier than kids getting ready for summer camp.

I expected it to be a small group, but I didn't think I'd be fifth-wheeling this trip.

"This must be a nice change for you," Shannon says to me.

She's leaning on her hiking poles like she's ready to head out the door and straight into the woods. "Getting to see some mountains and a break from all of that humidity in Texas."

She fans herself as though the weather followed me here.

I can't say she's wrong about the humidity—we're already in peak summer mugginess back home—but I don't correct her about the mountains. Sure, Texas is pretty flat, but I'm an avid mountaineer and have summited peaks even taller than the ones around here. I always feel like a jerk when I point it out, though. I don't want to be that guy who says, "Well, actually…"

"I'm looking forward to seeing a little bit of Oregon." Even if it will only be forests and mountains, it works for me.

"After, you should head up to Portland for a night or two," Brian tells me. "There's a pub crawl down Mississippi Street that'll knock you out even better than this hike."

It's not lost on me that a man my father's age is suggesting I relax with a pub crawl, while my vacation plans can best be described as "hermit-friendly."

"You don't have to go that far," his wife Cindy says. "We had a *very* good time in Bend the last time we passed through."

"I regretted it for a week, though." Brian taps the side of his head. "Too much craft beer."

"What about here in Sunshine?" I ask.

Cindy's mouth twists, giving me my answer. I guessed as much when I drove in this morning. It's a nice little town, but it's quiet. Probably not the best bet for anyone looking for a night out, but it's the perfect choice for my month off the grid.

"There's some shopping here," she says. "And a couple of good restaurants, but I don't think it has much in the way of nightlife. We never stay in town, though."

"I can give you better options." Brian's smirk is too much like Rhett's flurry of emails full of wilder alternatives for how I might spend my vacation. "Sunshine isn't really the place to go if you're looking for something unexpected."

The door behind us chimes, and a woman says, "Is this the right place for the wilderness adventure thingy?"

Her voice dances through me like a sparkler, and I spin around slowly. Now this *is* unexpected.

It's *her*. The woman from the coffee shop, complete with glittery purple roller bag. She's all bright smiles and eager eyes, standing there in black leggings and a blue plaid camp shirt. My chest warms, flickering to life against my better judgment. If this is still some sugar-induced fever-dream, I don't want to wake up.

"Lila! You're just in time." Deena leads her closer to our small group for quick introductions. Everyone welcomes her to the party, shaking hands all around. By the time she gets to me, I'm smiling like a dope, staring at this glorious vision like it's the only thing my half-functioning brain is capable of doing.

"Hi." She slips her hand into mine, and I'm done for.

Five days in the wilderness with her? Rhett's mantra echoes in my head until it's a deafening chorus. *Do the stupid thing.*

Don't mind if I do.

Then I remember just how stupid I've been in the past, and my smile comes crashing down.

This could be a problem.

TWO

LILA

I'M off to a great start.

Turn up late to a trip I don't want to take? Check. Meet the hottest man I've seen in eons? Check. Feel an absurd zing shiver across my skin when we shake hands? Double check.

Watch as his smile turns from friendly to frosty in a matter of heartbeats? Also check.

I smile even wider. I got used to being dismissed by the tech bros I used to work with and my ex-fiancé, who was their king. The key to dealing with it is to never let them know when they get to you. So when this guy's smile does a disappearing act? I don't even notice.

Even if a tiny little worm of insecurity wriggles around inside me, reminding me that I do, in fact, notice.

Honestly, he's a very noticeable guy. Tall and broad, with wavy dark hair that just kisses his forehead, sky blue eyes that seem designed to see straight into my soul, and an actual dimple in his chin.

Oh, and also? He's watching me with his mouth tugged down like I just ruined his vacation. The moment doesn't last, and he smiles at me again, but it's not the same.

"Grant Irwin, from Texas," Deena had said. Well, Grant Irwin from Texas, you can go jump in a lake.

Considering the trip we're about to go on, he would probably love to do exactly that, but whatever.

I try to put the guy out of my head—no small task—and turn back to Deena. "Did I miss anything?"

What I want to say is, *"Can I miss everything?"*

The closest I get to "outdoorsy" is driving around in my Honda Accord blasting *Folklore* with the windows rolled down —exploring the woods has never been on my list of to-dos.

Not that I would complete a to-do list if I ever made one.

But if I want to turn my part-time job as Sunshine's special events planner into a full-time job as their tourism coordinator, I need to get familiar with the woods, and fast. Everything else around town, I've got covered—where to shop, where to get the best meals, where to stay—but when it comes to all the outdoorsy stuff people might come here for? I've got nothing. Thus, the five days ahead of me pretending to be a Girl Scout.

It's fine. It's all going to be fine. This is just a little adventure. True, my adventures usually spin more toward *populated* places and five-star hotels, but I can work with this.

I kind of have to.

"We're just about to load up our packs."

Deena leads me to the back wall where six backpacks and a dizzying array of camping gear are laid out. Their storefront is mostly an empty room. Posters of people on mountaintops or rafting down rivers line the walls, blasting their inspirational messages. A counter sits near the door where someone could theoretically greet walk-in customers, but it's pretty clear this place is just a staging area for their trips.

Never in my wildest dreams did I imagine going on one of them semi-willingly.

Mitchell explains that this will be a light hike—we'll only

walk five to seven miles per day. I exhale the tiniest of whimpers. He adds that this is the trip they take families with little kids on, so nothing should be outside of our ability. Feels kind of pointed, to be honest.

Since we're going backcountry camping, we have to carry all of our supplies with us. Everything is already divided according to individual essentials and group necessities, with color-coded patches on each pack so we know which one is ours. I walk over to my section, and I think my eyes fall out of my head. They're making a whole lot of assumptions about what we can carry, that's all I'm saying. God gave us luggage with wheels for a reason.

"Don't some companies have alpacas or donkeys to carry all of the supplies?" I say, staring at everything in front of the pack. I don't even know what half of this is, and I have to lug it around for a week?

Mitchell's good-natured laugh rumbles around the room. He's very unassuming, even though he's low-key ripped for being in his fifties. Like a hot dad in a K-drama who turns out to be a mob boss. "As much as Deena would love to own an alpaca, we don't have one."

"It's something to consider. Backpacking with alpacas could be a big draw." I can see the website updates now, with a picture of one happily toting everyone's supplies on the trail. His name would be Jean-Pierre, and he would relish the attention.

If only.

"Alpacas might not get along so well with the bears."

"The couples share tents," Deena says before I can ask for bear-related specifics, "so we have room to carry more food supplies than the singles do."

My eyes dart to the only other single's wide shoulders. I bet Grant can carry a lot of food. Maybe not as much as Jean-Pierre could, but he would have no problem bringing the groceries home, that's for sure.

"And Mitchell packs the camp toilet," she adds.

I hold a breath. Here I was thinking bears would be the worst this conversation had to offer. "The what?"

"Camp toilet." She says it again as though those words make any more sense the second time around. "It's a collapsible chair with a bag underneath filled with a drying material. Kind of like cat litter."

Can you feel it when all the blood drains out of your face? Is that what this creepy-crawly sensation washing over me is? I'm not even going to try to imagine what she's describing. That could only compound my horror and embarrassment. In all my research, in all my prep for this trip, never once did I consider that there would not be *toilets* available.

Why wouldn't they put that right on the website home page? *Five days exploring the best the National Forest has to offer. Hey, also, you'll be peeing in a cup. Sign up now!* There. Fixed it for them.

"Don't worry," one of the other women says. Shannon, I think. They both wear colorful bandanas to keep their chic gray hair out of their faces, so I'm not entirely sure which is which yet. "You'll get used to it."

I really, really don't want to get used to a cat litter toilet.

"You also have the option of digging a hole every time," Mitchell points out. "The camp toilet provides a more comfortable experience if you want it."

I clamp my mouth shut on every retort about the definition of comfort. They're comping my spot on this trip in exchange for some social media promo. Whether I have a good time this week or not, I'm technically here on a business arrangement. Complaining about the "amenities" wouldn't be a good look.

No matter how justified.

"For what it's worth, our camp toilet is pretty nice."

Not exactly unqualified praise. Reminding myself to focus on the positive, I make a pathetic sound of agreement.

For some reason, my gaze meets Grant's across the room. His eyebrows tick up in amusement, like he knows exactly what I'm thinking. Well, why wouldn't he? What sane person *wants* to use a toilet like that? If you have to use more than one word to describe it, it's a bad toilet. If it's the next step up from a literal hole in the ground, it's a *very* bad toilet.

I tilt my chin at him in defiance and spin back to the gear on the floor. I force a smile as I take it all in. Smiling when you don't mean it is supposed to reduce stress and instill feelings of happiness. I don't know if I can reach "happiness" after hearing about the bathroom situation, but a little stress reduction would be nice.

I never really managed it at my last job working for my ex-fiancé, but I'm nothing if not optimistic.

"Go ahead and start loading your packs, everyone. The water reservoirs are already filled." Deena slips closer to me, and her eyes dart down to my roller bag as if I might have an alpaca in there. If only I'd known it was *BYOA*. "I think you might have overpacked. Did you get the list I emailed you?"

Everyone else seems to have a small duffel bag or a tote for their clothes. My bright, shiny luggage is doing its job, and then some—it stands out in a crowd. A plastic grocery bag would have been less conspicuous here.

"I used the packing list, but this is the smallest bag I have."

"Let's take a look at what you brought and see where we can pare down." She kneels right by my bag, waiting for me to open it.

Everyone else is loading their backpacks, but careful side-eyes shoot my way. This is worse than when TSA flags my bag and paws through it looking for the six ounces of vitamin C serum I forgot I packed.

I get on the floor with her and unzip my bag. Deena doesn't paw, but she assesses everything in a single glance.

"You've got a few too many things here." Her smile says she's trying to be sweet, but her volume says she doesn't care who hears this conversation. "What you've got on and a single change is enough."

"For five days?" I manage not to screech, but barely. That can't possibly be right. We'll be sweaty and dirty from hiking every day—of course I'll need more clothes than that.

"It's a relaxed trip." She shrugs as if that's explanation enough. When I go on staring at her, she adds a little more. "By the end of the hike, you'll be happier to have a lighter pack than clean clothes."

I try to keep my smile in place as I look over everything I brought. Following the packing list she emailed, I'd carefully selected my clothes: light layers, a warm fleece jacket, a raincoat, athletic shirts, long sleeve camp shirts, thick socks, an extra sports bra, and several sets of undies. Just to be safe, I also packed flannel pajama pants, fuzzy socks, a swimsuit, and a cozy sweater, but thankfully, she isn't making me inventory my luggage.

"Doesn't it get cold at night?"

"You've got room for the fleece and the rain jacket, and a pair of long underwear to sleep in. Bring the lightweight shorts and a tank top if you think you'll want to swim. Leave everything else but one extra shirt behind. We can put your bag in the office until we get back."

Having said her devastating piece, she gets up to check in with some of the others.

What did I do to deserve needing to alternate between two shirts for five days? I haven't committed any heinous crimes lately. It's been at least eight months since I bumped another car while parallel parking. Maybe seven, but it's up there.

Cindy leans my way. "Don't worry. Everyone winds up smelling equally ripe on a trip like this."

I try to laugh but just make a sad seal sound instead. Arguing about my clothes seems pointless, since I can't take anything with me besides this backpack. I pull out the two warm layers, an extra pair of socks, and the overly optimistic swimming gear. Checking that Deena's not looking, I grab all the underwear like a raccoon scooping up forbidden trash. I'm sure I can handle carrying a few extra ounces for the comfort of wearing clean underpants every day.

Following a helpful diagram on the wall, I load everything into the pack. First goes the sleeping bag and the sleep mat, both stuffed into tinier bags than seem possible. Next, the spare clothes and secret underwear, plus an abysmally thin camp towel and my extra-small toiletry bag. I predict a tween-level zit breakout in my future after a week of minimalist skincare, but if Deena thinks underwear is too much, I'd hate to see her reaction to my usual intensive routine.

The other containers and bags they've set out are a mystery to me—and an even bigger mystery is when I manage to get it all in the pack. I give the straining backpack a test heft, and can't help the little whimper I make. Why did I sign up for this again?

Right—to prove to Mayor Martinez and the town council that I'm serious about championing Sunshine's many outdoor activities, as well as our restaurants and shopping scene. Which I am...I'd just prefer to do it from a distance. I can encourage everyone else to get outside without having to experience it myself, can't I?

Mitchell double-checks our packs while Deena wheels away my rolling luggage in an embarrassing display. She disappears into a back room, and I long for my extra changes of clothes.

"You look like she just kidnapped your baby." Cindy doesn't do a good job of containing her smirk.

I clear my face of whatever pathetic thing it's doing. "It's just clothes. Who cares what I look like on this rustic adventure?"

This is another "fake it til you make it" type thing. I always care.

Shannon just grins. "You lose your pride pretty quickly on trips like this."

"Especially when you have to carry a personal trowel for digging private holes," her husband butts in.

A shudder wracks through me, crumbling my bravado. If that's the upside I have to cling to this trip, it's going to be a rough five days.

Meh. I always knew it would be a rough five days. Still.

"Do you go on trips like this a lot?" I ask them.

Cindy gestures between the two couples. "The four of us have had a backcountry adventure every summer for the last fifteen years."

"You might say we're professional outdoorsmen," Scott says. I don't think that's a thing, but he beams like he's just itching to point out a plaque with his name on it somewhere. "We can guess already that you're new to this, Lila."

Heat creeps up my neck at his patronizing tone, but it's not like he's wrong. My sparkly luggage probably gave me away the minute I walked through the door. "Pretty new."

"What about you, Grant?" Brian asks. Everyone swivels around to look at the guy hovering by his neat pack in the corner. "Professional outdoorsman?"

He could be one, given his build and the way he looks like he just walked off the pages of an LL Bean catalog. Somebody get this man an ax and a tree that needs chopping, stat. Dismissive eyes or not, I'd watch that show.

His gaze skates over the couples and lands on me. He shakes his head, but a smile touches his mouth. "I'd say I'm an amateur outdoorsman."

The prickle of heat crawling over my skin blossoms into something much more pleasant. I shouldn't feel good that he doesn't know what he's doing either, but it's a relief I won't be the only clueless person on this trip. Grant and I can stumble through it together.

Not *together* together. Just in the same vicinity. Obviously.

Deena returns from wherever she hid my roller bag and heads straight for me with a weird light in her eyes. Can she sense the extra underpants in my pack? Is she going to make me surrender them?

"Before we load up the van and head out, do you mind if I take a quick picture with you?" Her smile turns awkward. "Normally, I wouldn't ask, but our daughter Skye is out of her head with excitement that *Genuinely_Lila* is coming on one of our treks."

"Of course." I'm not really at my best in my athleisure and a high pony, but hopefully Skye won't mind the departure from my usual *Genuinely_Lila* aesthetic. Deena leans in close and takes a few pictures before doing something on her phone, her grin back to full wattage.

"Genuinely Lila?" Shannon asks. "What's that?"

I pull a face, hoping she'll let it go. "It's just a social media thing. Are we ready to be outdoorsy or what?"

I bend over and grab the top strap of my pack but can barely straighten up again. My attempt at nonchalance isn't going so hot. I'm *all* chalance.

"Lila's a local celebrity." Deena's fake whisper carries remarkably well. "She has thousands of followers."

My smile feels a little too thin. People in town have an image of me, probably fueled by my mom's constant stream of praise, that I'm this amazing success both on- and off-line. I was for a while in Seattle, but here in my studio apartment, scrambling to get a full-time job, that label doesn't fit anymore.

Plus…my followers have no idea I'm still using old pictures and B-roll videos from my life in the city more than six months after everything turned upside down. Social media followers don't exactly stick with you after your fiancé cheats, you end things with him, lose your job, and move back to your small hometown to restart your life.

Basically, *Genuinely_Lila* is a big old fraud.

"Are you one of those influencers?" Brian's mouth twists as though the word tastes sour.

"I'm more of a content creator." Most people don't know either definition anyway, but they're far more forgiving of content creators than they are of influencers.

Scott waves his hands across his chest in a big X. "I do not give consent for you to use pictures of me. I don't want my face all over the internet."

"Oh. I wasn't going to—"

"Like anybody wants to see your big mug," Shannon says with a laugh.

"I'm just here to enjoy the views," I tell them. "Nobody has to worry about non-consensual photographs."

The two couples look me over like I'm a particularly precocious child who's been indulged too long. Even Grant's expression turned to mild curiosity when the word *influencer* was tossed around.

So yeah, off to a great start.

THREE
LILA

THE HORRIBLE WHEEZING FOLLOWING me around would be the perfect soundtrack for a horror movie if I didn't know it was coming from a short, harmless woman's pathetic lungs.

Mine. My lungs are making the awful sound.

We've been walking for hours at what Deena assures me is a leisurely pace. We've paused regularly to admire the views, but I'd give anything to sit down somewhere. I'll take the dirt at this point. Shannon was right—my pride has abandoned me in the literal dust.

My thighs ache, my lungs ache, and don't get me started on my back. I'm in pretty good shape, but I've never gone through a yoga class with twenty-five pounds of gear strapped to my back like I'm relocating a comatose bear cub.

Yeah...no. I probably shouldn't think about bears too much. Mitchell said sightings on this trail are rare, but I'm sure the more we talk about them, the more likely we are to jinx ourselves. I don't want to run across a bear mafia looking for a fight.

I've snapped dozens of pictures of forest paths and soggy meadows to use for the website mock-up I'm making, but so far,

I haven't witnessed the wonders of the great outdoors. Maybe that's more of a third-day sort of thing. Wouldn't want to just hit me with it on the first day and leave me in awe the whole trip.

That won't stop me from finding a way to write some enticing copy when I get home. Something like: *Come to the wilderness. We have bugs!*

I think the stitch in my side is affecting my brain. I pause on the trail to dig my fingers just below my ribcage.

Grant stops a pace behind me. "Doing okay?"

Since the couples are up ahead, laughing over all the impressive hikes they've been on and stunning mountains they've climbed, Grant's become my default walking buddy. I wish he weren't—back here, he's got a front row seat to all the sweat pouring off my body and the excessive panting I'm doing. Plus, I can't forget the way his smile vanished off his face when we were introduced.

But for now, I'll focus on the fact I'm not alone, and therefore less vulnerable to the bear mafia.

"I'm good." I flash a big smile, still hoping for the shot of faux happiness that's supposed to come with it.

A little line cuts across his forehead. Even that stupid line is attractive on him. "You're wincing. Do you want to stop?"

"Me? No way. This is the face I make when I'm enjoying fresh air." I take a deep lungful to demonstrate my enthusiasm for it, but the pain in my side ramps higher. "That's crisp."

His low chuckle does criminal things to my insides. Doesn't my body know it's in distress out here? I could be dying, and it's swooning over angular jawlines and pillowy lips. Get your priorities in order, body. Survival first. Then, if we're lucky, comfort. Somewhere way down the line is reacting inappropriately to strange, egregiously handsome men while in dangerous situations.

I start walking again so we don't get too far behind. Deena

and Mitchell check in on us periodically, but I don't want them to have to halt the whole procession for us to catch up. Especially since *us* means *me*. If Grant really hasn't been on a hike before, he sure doesn't seem to be feeling the effects of his first one. I'm halfway tempted to ask him to carry me.

I *wouldn't*.

But I bet he *could*.

"It should only be another two miles to the campsite."

If I don't die from exhaustion, this man is going to kill me with his soft Texas accent. *Campsite* doesn't sound like a place where teens go to get murdered when he says it.

"And that will take us...?" I rasp.

"Longer than average."

I can't argue there. We're dragging, and we haven't been out here all that long.

"Especially if we see any more birds," he adds.

I would stand up straighter to glare in his face if I didn't have a million-pound pack on. When this trip is over, my spine will be so compressed, I'll be an even five feet tall. I can kiss those extra four inches goodbye.

"Birds are freaky. You saw how close the last one came to me."

"Yes, I saw." He's trying not to smile, which just emphasizes his full lips, and I hate it.

"They have bony feet and sharp claws, and zero reservations about drawing blood." I shudder as if a creepy little bird just strutted all over my grave.

"Do you get into a lot of fights with birds?"

I purse my lips. "Just once or twice."

His head dips down as though he's trying to draw my eyes to his. Ha. No, thank you. I'd be safer with the bloodthirsty birds.

"Once or twice?"

"Birds are territorial! That's a scientific fact." Probably.

"And?"

I barely have enough oxygen to keep walking—should I really use up my precious reserves to tell him about this? Yes. Because talking about old humiliations might distract me from my current humiliations.

"The first time was in a zoo aviary. I was ten. My mom had braided a sparkly ribbon into my hair, and one of the birds wanted it. Not the best day at the zoo."

Beaks and claws filled my nightmares for weeks afterward. Needless to say, I never wore a ribbon in my hair again.

"Sounds pretty scary for a little kid."

"Having a bird bigger than my head claw at my scalp unlocked a core memory." Birds are evil, end of story.

"What about the other incident?"

I guess if I'm going in, I might as well go all the way in. "I was at a home improvement store a few years ago, and two starlings attacked me in the garden center."

"Out of nowhere?"

"I didn't start it, if that's what you're asking. They probably had a nest in one of the displays or something, but the experience kind of killed gardening for me."

And was deeply mortifying as I ran around screaming trying to bat off the tiny things, but that part goes without saying.

"Your grudge against birds is understandable. I'll keep an eye out for you."

"If you see one coming, you have my permission to throw me to the ground. Just knock me flat. Don't even ask."

"I hope it doesn't come to that."

Far ahead, just before the trail disappears between the trees, Mitchell turns back to watch us. I wonder if he's got a timer set to remind him to look for us every twenty minutes. He raises a hand in the air, our Trail Dad making sure we're okay. I wave back, indicating we're not dying yet, and he continues on.

"Kind of nice of them to keep checking in on the slow-pokes." Even if my all-clear wave feels overconfident. A lot could happen in the next hundred feet of trail. I squint into the nearest trees, refusing to think about how many winged menaces might be hidden in there.

I live my life ribbon-free now, but I'm sure a bird could find something offensive about me if given the chance.

"Wandering off the trail and getting lost is a bigger danger for us than even coming across a b—"

"Ha ha, it's hilarious I'm afraid of birds. I get it." I scowl at Grant. He doesn't need to throw my well-earned phobia in my face.

He's quiet for a minute as we trudge on, that crease stuck on his forehead. "I was going to say, 'if we come across a bear.'"

"Oh. That...makes more sense." I've done that once already —I expected him to have something cutting to say, so I beat him to it. Guilt digs into my stomach along with the backpack strap. He's not the one who deserves to be on the receiving end of my pent-up retaliations. Three years with an increasingly critical ex has left me a little testy. "Sorry. I think I'm getting hangry."

Grant stops and gestures at his pack. "There's a granola bar in the side pocket."

"I don't want to take your food." I didn't even think to bring extra food. Horizon Hikes' website makes a big deal about providing all of our meals from scratch. No single-serve dehydrated meal packets here. But we're not having lunch until we get to our first campsite. I passed on snacks before we left, and am only now realizing what a mistake that was.

"You need to eat. Please. Take it."

I stare at the little zipper on his pale brown pack, debating whether or not to accept his offer. It's not like there are extras out here if he runs out. My stomach growls its vote, and Grant's head tilts down, his eyebrows lifting in an "I told you so" move.

"Listen to your body and give it what it needs. You'll feel better."

I finally cave and unzip the pocket. He's got five granola bars squirreled away in here. At least it's not a single solitary bar, but he probably brought one for each day because he knew he'd need them.

My hand freezes mid-air. "I don't like cutting into your supplies. I'm really fine."

"Lila." His voice hits an unexpectedly stern note. "Take the granola bar."

It's probably unwise to argue with him...and I don't really want to, anyway. With snackies in sight, my stomach is growling worse than ever. "Do you want one?"

"No thanks, I'm good."

My hand finally darts into the pocket to grab a bar. I zip the pack back up, and we continue on. "Thank you for sharing your loot. How did you get away with bringing extra food, anyway? Deena didn't even want me to bring underwear."

"I didn't tell her."

"You're such a rebel," I tease.

His wide grin holds a hint of mischief. "Bad to the bone."

I can tell already Grant Irwin is not the bad boy type. He's more of a Clark Kent, minus the glasses. Even his granola bar flavor of choice fits the persona: vanilla. The bright yellow label says it's high-protein and gluten-free, a very sensible option on the trail. If I'd brought snacks, they would have been the kind slathered with chocolate that probably sap your energy more than they replenish it.

I take a bite and chew. And chew. And chew some more. His gaze is heavy on me as I try to choke down the snack he so generously offered.

"You don't like it?"

"It tastes really healthy." It might be the driest thing I've ever eaten. But I need the calories, so I keep swallowing it down.

Grant chuckles. "You don't have to finish it."

I cover my mouth so I don't spit sawdust at him. "I don't mind. It's good."

"Your face tells a different story."

That story is probably titled *I Deeply Regret Putting This in My Mouth.*

Even with a little bit of food in my stomach, I've lost what scrap of enthusiasm I had for the day. Especially when I have to fumble around with my hydration pack's bite valve every time I want a drink of water. Who thought using SCUBA gear the wrong way was a good idea?

He notices me sucking away at the dumb thing, but I throw a hand up between us. "Please. This is humiliating enough without an audience."

He averts his eyes. "It can be a little awkward."

"A little? It's like a bunch of guys sat in a room and said, 'What's the least-convenient way to drink water?'"

"Maybe, but it's the most convenient way to carry a large volume of water in a backpack." He takes a sip from his own hydration pack as if proving his point. The long tube snakes from the large water bladder hidden in his backpack to where he bites the end with his white teeth.

I should not be noticing this guy's mouth so much. My eyes are constantly either on his lips or that dimple in his chin. You'd think I haven't been around a man since I moved back to Sunshine six months ago.

After the way things blew apart with Josh, I haven't been looking. Dating's a risky road I'm not ready for yet. But it's hard not to be at least a little bit interested in a guy with a perfect dimple in his chin and a secret snack stash, no matter how disgusting the snacks are.

No. This line of thinking is unproductive. In five more days,

Grant Irwin from Texas will be heading back home. There's no point in thinking a single one of those thoughts.

Except...okay. The dimple *really* does it for me.

"Is it bad that I'm glad I'm not the only newbie?" I blurt out just to shut up my racing brain. I stuff the granola bar wrapper into my pocket to dispose of properly later. "I was afraid when I signed up for this everyone else would leave me in the dust with their amazing survival skills."

"You're making light of my survival skills after I gave you a clandestine granola bar?"

See? Only Clark Kent and his newspaper reporter vocabulary would throw out the word *clandestine* when talking about snack food.

"I'm just saying, I wasn't sure anyone else would be new to all of this. I'm happy that it's not just me out here taking notes on how the outdoors works."

"You're taking notes, are you?"

"Oh, yeah. Rule number one: always accept offered snacks."

Eventually, we see Mitchell waiting on the trail for us. When we get closer, he waves us toward a small path off to the left and passes us each a baggie of trail mix.

The trail mix includes chocolate candies. Bless him.

"Campsite's this way."

"Best words in the English language," I say with a heavy sigh. Sleeping on the ground still sounds awful, but it will get me off my feet, and that's not nothing.

We follow him along the spur path well off the main trail to a clearing where everyone else has pulled off their packs and found spots to sit down. For turning sixty, every last one of them looks way more spry than I feel after hours of hiking. Deena and Mitchell are probably a bit younger than the couples, but since they chose to do this as their job, their enthusiasm for it makes sense.

Quickly unbuckling my chest and waist straps, I start to slide the heavy pack off my shoulders. As soon as the weight shifts, I lose my balance and almost tumble sideways into the dirt.

"Here."

Grant's voice is at my back. Suddenly, my body feels like it could float into the sky. I can't help the little groan of relief I make as he lifts the weight off my shoulders. It's a better rush than any massage. I spin to find him setting my pack down next to me.

"I almost landed on my face." Truly, my conversation skills with this man are unmatched.

He's already abandoned his pack a few feet away. I would ask how he got out of his monstrosity so easily, but the answer is pretty apparent beneath his slightly sweaty shirt: big old muscles. Which I try not to ogle like a weirdo, but my eyes have minds of their own.

"The extra weight makes it easy to get off balance." He offers me a small smile that starts that floaty feeling all over again.

Nope. I'm going to chalk that up to the fresh mountain air. I turn around to search for the best spot to sit down. This is technically a work trip, and I need to stay focused. I'm here to learn about outdoorsy stuff, not get all moony over Grant Dimplechin and his amazing voice and uncanny ability to lift heavy packs like they're nothing.

"How's our caboose holding up?" Scott's perched with his wife on a fallen log, grinning at us between handfuls of trail mix like he's hoping I might break down in tears.

I find a dry, smooth rock and sit down. My butt's probably going to go numb in about two minutes, but at least my feet can relax. I'm immensely grateful I took Mitchell's advice and walked around in my hiking boots every day after I signed up. My feet still ache, but they're not covered in blisters.

I don't think. Kind of afraid to check.

"We're doing great," Grant says.

"Totally invigorated." I sound like a goof, but they already know we're on the struggle bus. No need to indulge his morbid curiosity.

Mitchell's sprawled right in the dirt with his elbows on his knees. "After we set up our tents and have a quick lunch, there'll be time for a short hike with good views of the Three Sisters."

"It's one of my favorite spots on this trip," Deena adds. "It's also one of the last spots where there's reliable cell service. If you need to check in with anyone, I would advise you to do it there."

I pretend to be engrossed in picking through my trail mix, searching for the chocolate candies. We've barely sat down, and they're already talking about heading out again. There's no way I have the desire—or, maybe more importantly, the energy—for an optional hike just to see the nearest mountain peaks I've seen a thousand times in my life.

But…if the views are as good as they say, pictures would be useful for my website proposal. If this were any other type of company event, I would want to get the full experience so I can market it properly. Ugh. I should go with them. Even though nothing sounds better right now than taking a nap in my tent. Which I hope is self-assembling or something because I don't have the first clue how to set one up.

I barely listen to the couples talk about Yosemite, the Tetons, and other places they've explored across the country. Mostly, I'm thinking about how sweaty I am, the total lack of shower facilities, and how gross I'll be by the end of the week. I kind of need Mitchell to set up our horror show of a toilet, too. I am *not* going the personal-hole route.

My attention focuses when a big black ant crawls across my leg. I flick it off. Then I notice a second one. And a third. Looking down, I freeze as my brain catches up to the fact that I'm covered in giant ants.

I shriek, shooting to my feet. Ants rain onto the forest floor as I run my hands down my legs. Spinning in a circle, I swipe at everything I can. My skin tingles as though they're *everywhere*. They really might be. I start breathing too fast, sweeping my hands over myself again and again, but they keep marching on.

Someone's saying something, but I can't focus. My brain's too busy with the very important task of getting these bugs off me.

Grant catches my forearms, his eyes snagging mine until I stop squirming. "You're okay. I've got you."

My instinct is *not* to believe him—I'm swarming with bugs—but he's so calm and collected, I can't help but trust him. I nod, not even sure what I'm agreeing to.

He brushes quick swipes down my back and legs while I try not to completely lose my mind. His hands dust over my butt, and even in my freaked-out state, I can tell he's being totally clinical instead of taking advantage of the situation. His touch ghosts over the front and back of my clothes in swift motions.

"That's it," he says. "They're gone."

My heart's racing, and my skin isn't convinced yet that there's no more threat. Adding to my embarrassment, my hands flutter between us like I've had five cups of coffee. Grant's steady presence is comforting, though, and something inside me starts to settle down.

"Think that will go on her blog?" one of the men says behind him. Low laughter hums through the group, and I kind of want to crawl into a hole somewhere.

Except, of course, that hole would probably be filled with more ants.

For just a second, something very *non*-Clark Kent-like flashes in Grant's eyes. It's angry and protective, like it's costing him not to turn around and say something back. But it's gone again in a moment as he ducks his head to inspect me, nothing but concern in his expression now.

"Are you okay?"

Other than the racing heart and slightly shaky hands, there's no harm done. The ants didn't bite, thank goodness. "I think so. Thanks."

His smile just might be my undoing. "In some cultures, black ants are lucky."

"Why do I feel like you just made that up?"

He smiles, leaving me hanging on whether or not I can expect good luck on my trip out here. We draw apart, and I skim my hands down my legs again, just in case. Pretty sure I just unlocked another core memory. Thanks very much, wilderness.

"Whether you're setting up your tent or finding a place to sit, it's smart to check your surroundings." Deena launches into a tip I wish she'd offered *before* we got to camp. "You probably sat down in the middle of their trail to food. Ordinarily, that's all they're after."

She's right. The scattered ants have already formed back up into a long line winding its way past the rock I'd opted to sit on. I shuffle around, looking by my feet, half-expecting the forest floor to be crawling with more bugs, but I don't see anything.

Doesn't mean they aren't there, though.

Eventually, I pick a safe-looking section of dirt and sit down again to comfort myself with the last of the chocolate in my trail mix. My heart rate's finally back to normal, but my skin keeps crawling as though tiny feet are walking all over it.

"So," Scott drawls, "how are you enjoying yourself so far?"

Honestly? I already regret this trip.

FOUR

GRANT

I ALREADY REGRET THIS TRIP.

I should have just checked straight into the hermit cabin and holed up like I'd originally planned. Mountain biked during the day and sat on my tiny porch every evening watching the stars come out. Ignored Rhett's calls and tried to pin down what's had me so restless for the last several months.

But this backcountry trek had offered a closer look at the national forest without the hassle of arranging permits and renting gear, and I'd signed on without a thought. It was supposed to be easy and low-stress.

Now, I'm here in the woods with a woman who unknowingly makes everything difficult for me, and I am *stressed*.

The shiver of awareness that shot through me when Lila and I shook hands hasn't gone away. If anything, it's intensified with every scrap of conversation, every glimpse of her smile or her expressive brown eyes. I'm buzzing like a live wire, and I can't decide if I should give in to the spark, or keep doing my best to douse it.

It makes no sense to get caught up in someone I'm only going to know for a handful of days. Doesn't mean I can totally shake Rhett's mantra from my head, though. Every time she smiles at me, stupid things spring to mind.

Then I remember all the reasons following Rhett's advice is a terrible idea, and I slam back down to reality.

I arrange my gear in my tent, trying not to listen to the commentary buzzing around camp as Mitchell helps Lila with hers. He explains everything to her in a patient, fatherly way, and that alone will make me rate this trip five stars when I get back home. Nobody should ever be made to feel stupid when they're trying something they've never done before.

If only someone would tell Brian and Scott. They're not completely malicious, but they're not going to let Lila forget her newness out here either. Even their applause when she finally gets her tent up seems more like mockery than good-natured cheering.

One of the key traits I've insisted on from new hires in my family's outdoors stores is that there's no such thing as a dumb question. Everybody who comes into our store is treated the same, no matter what their skills or interests might be. Our goal has always been to encourage people to get outside and enjoy whatever activity they like best. No judgment, no snobby elitism, no dreaded mansplaining.

I would never hire these guys, is what I'm saying.

After a quick lunch of bean and cheese burritos, we head out on the day hike. Deena said it's only a mile each way, but it leads to clear views of three of the most prominent mountains in the area. I was in Oregon a few years back to climb Mount Hood, but I've never seen this part of the state. It's the same mix of pine forest and volcanic rock from ancient lava flows that runs from Northern California up through British Columbia—and comfortably familiar, since I've summited several of the peaks in the Cascades.

"What do you think?" Scott says to me. Our group has

shifted somewhat for the shorter hike, with Scott and Brian lingering in the back with Lila and me. Their wives are up front with Deena, and Mitchell ambles along between us. "Is hiking growing on you?"

"It just might." I've been systematically crossing U.S. mountain peaks off of my bucket list for almost two decades, but I get the feeling he wouldn't like to hear that. He wants to be the one offering advice, and I don't mind letting him.

"We know it isn't winning over Lila." Brian tosses a smirk at her over his shoulder.

She throws a bright smile right back. "I'm not rushing out to book a second trip."

"It's only been a day." My comment's pointed at the two men, not her. They're writing her off too easily, and it doesn't sit right. Giving her a hard time will only crush whatever tiny interest she might otherwise have had. "That doesn't seem like enough time for us to decide."

"Oh, I've decided," she mutters under her breath.

I stifle a laugh. I admire her self-acceptance, even if it undermines my defense of her just a touch.

"We climbed a mountain in Colorado last year," Scott says. "A fourteener. You might not be familiar with the term."

His superior tone pricks like a burr. Unfortunately, his attitude isn't all that uncommon in a group with a mix of skills and experience like ours. I don't really care if he aims it at me—I'm more than comfortable with my abilities—but it grates when he directs it at Lila.

I tell myself I would shield any other newcomers from the same condescension, but the urge has never been quite this visceral before.

"I know the term," I say. "Which fourteener did you bag?"

"Gray's Peak. There's no better feeling than standing on top of the world."

A bit of a lofty description for a relatively short day hike, but I'm not going to argue—the high of reaching a mountain peak is addictive.

"Congrats," I say, and I mean it. "Sounds like a good trip."

"Ranks right up there with the births of my kids."

Now I do want to argue. Lila and I share a brief look before I focus on him again. "I don't know if I'd mention that to your kids."

He laughs as though he didn't equate the arrival of his children with an afternoon hike. "You just haven't pushed yourself yet. When you've had enough of the beginner trails, you might want to try something more advanced. See what you're made of."

Brian's goading grin slides right off my back. Pointlessly competing with my brothers? Bring it on. Pointlessly competing with strangers? Not interested. I climb mountains to prove myself to exactly one person: me.

"What if he doesn't want to see what he's made of?" Lila pipes up at my side.

His expression falters as he looks from her back to me. "There's nothing wrong with a little challenge to test your mettle."

"Yeah, but there's nothing wrong with not testing it, too, right?" Her cheerful smile doesn't hide her annoyance. "What if he's fine with trails like this? Maybe Grant never wants to climb a mountain? That's his choice, right?"

Brian blinks at her like he can't quite figure out where he went wrong. And me? I'm way too flattered by how vigorously she's defending me. True, she's probably thinking of herself and her own choices, but I like the way she's speaking up.

Just ahead of us, Mitchell pauses on the trail. "I'm sorry— did you say you never want to climb a mountain again, Grant? You're giving up mountaineering?"

Here we go. Maybe I should have cleared this up sooner, but it felt like a harmless bit of conversation. Now, I'm not so sure.

"I said he doesn't have to try it if he doesn't want to." Lila swipes the back of her hand across her forehead, grimacing at the sheen of sweat that comes off. "Everybody has different tastes and likes different things."

She makes deliberate eye contact with me. "And that's totally fine."

I am loving her unequivocal acceptance. Her insistence that I accept *myself* is even more endearing. I just wish I could come clean to her without our current audience listening in.

"I didn't say he had to do anything." There's a note of laughter in Brian's voice, as though he's about five seconds away from saying, *"Calm down, little lady."*

Is it wrong I'd like to see her reaction to that? I have a feeling she would take him down in spectacular fashion.

"I only suggested he try something tougher than these entry hikes one day," he explains. "He might think about pushing himself with the kind of challenges Scott and I have been doing."

Mitchell looks at each of us in turn, confusion swirling in his eyes. "I guess I missed something. Why does he need the suggestion? Grant's summited half the mountains in this country."

In the silence his bombshell leaves behind, a bead of sweat trails down the center of my back. A chipmunk chitters somewhere close by. Everyone's eyes are glued to me.

Lila spins slowly to stare up at me.

"It's not half," I say.

Her eyebrows tick up, telling me the clarification didn't help anything.

"He's got more mountain certifications than I do, and I'm no slouch out here." Mitchell continues on, oblivious to the way the others are goggling at me. "Didn't you just climb Mount Whitney?"

"Last year. How do you know that?"

"Highest peak in the continental U.S. That's impressive." He glances around at us again. "I don't internet stalk our clients —it's a total fluke. I get magazines and newsletters from trail organizations around the country. Just part of the job. Your family was featured in one a while back. The name rang a bell when you signed up, so I dug around a little bit, and there you were."

"You were featured in a magazine?" Scott seems to view me more favorably all of a sudden, even though this tidbit means nothing. We could have been profiled as the laziest family in America, for all he knows.

"His family owns a chain of specialty outdoors stores in Texas." Mitchell's apparently become my one-man PR team, and is attacking his job like he wants a promotion. "The whole family's big on extreme sports. You could probably do this little hike with us in your sleep, couldn't you?"

I shake my head, ready for this Q&A to end. "You've put together a great hike. I appreciate everything you're doing for us."

"That's a relief. I'd hate to think I could be replaced by that alpaca Lila wants." Mitchell laughs and nods up the trail. "The view point's not far now."

He strides away, leaving me to face my bewildered companions.

Brian looks me up and down, his appraisal feeling just as accusatory as it did before he knew about my summits. "I guess you're doing okay out here, after all."

"Maybe we should be asking *you* for advice," Scott adds like he's ribbing an old pal.

Awkwardness hangs in the air, and they're quick to get moving behind Mitchell.

I stare at my hiking boots five whole seconds before I meet Lila's eyes. Her mouth forms a perfect pert frown. Probably not the best time for me to stare at her lips, but...I do anyway.

"You really climb mountains and stuff?"

"Yes."

"What was all that you said about being an amateur outdoorsman?"

I shrug. "There's always more to learn."

She gives me a full-body eye roll, shoulders slumping, a sigh heaving from her lips. "Right."

In a field that can get dangerous quickly, thinking you already know everything can be a deadly mistake. Not that my reasoning was so altruistic. I hadn't liked the look on Lila's face when they called out her inexperience this morning. Her smile had turned brittle, like she'd expected them to say something even worse. I'd wanted to make it better.

No way am I going to admit all that, though.

"I wasn't trying to deceive anyone. I just don't lead conversations with my accomplishments." I guarantee she wouldn't have liked that start any more.

"I guess that's something," she mutters. She turns to go but stops to narrow her eyes at me again. "That mountain Scott said they did—have you climbed it?"

I only hesitate for a second. Downplaying it now feels like a bad move. "Yes."

"Was it as life-changing as he says?"

That day on Gray's Peak in Colorado comes back to me, along with the views, the exertion, the thrill of accomplishment. "Yes. But I was in high school at the time."

She freezes, eyes widening. Then she laughs and starts

walking the trail again. "Scott had better call 911 to see about that burn."

Even when she's irritated with me, her laughter pings around inside my chest like lightning in a bottle.

She exhales a stuttering breath that's probably half exasperation, half actual exhaustion. "But ugh, all that stuff I said about us being morons on the trail together like we're newbie besties."

"I'll still be newbie besties with you."

My earnest offer doesn't land as well as I'd hoped. She fires an unimpressed glare at me as she stomps away.

Looks like I'm doing a great job following Rhett's advice whether I mean to or not.

FIVE

LILA

SO MUCH FOR Grant and I stumbling through this hike together. Turns out, the man doesn't need any help. Makes sense. He hasn't been bumbling through the day in the same way I have. I should have known this wasn't his first rodeo when he showed up with his own bear spray.

Hearing everything he's done, I feel like even more of a dummy. I kind of liked the idea of having a partner in ineptitude-crime for this hike. Now, it's just me, trying to keep up with everyone else.

Really, it's a good thing. I don't need distractions right now. Getting hearts in my eyes over Grant would make it difficult to focus on the awesomeness of nature. Which absolutely requires my undivided attention.

Because it's so compelling. Apparently.

I snap several pictures at the view point and make a few voice notes about where we are and what we're looking at to help me keep track for later. When I get back home, all of these trees and rocks will look the same, and I don't want to mix anything up for my presentation. Next month, I'll make a case to the town council to expand my responsibilities and go full-time, so I need to get all the details right.

After a few minutes looking at the views, we spread out to take advantage of our last blessed moments with cell service. I move closer to the nearest tree but manage to stop before my face lands in a giant spider web, complete with fat spider. My skin crawls as though phantom insects are doing the cha-cha on me.

So peaceful out here.

Steadfastly ignoring thoughts of giant arachnids, I make my call.

"Proof of life," I say when my sister answers.

Hope's laughter is surprisingly clear for the teeny tiny bar my phone displays. "Are you even out of town? You've only been gone a few hours."

"Feels like weeks."

"Where is your chipper 'what could possibly go wrong?' attitude?"

Usually, I would be the first to try something new. But those things are typically more along the lines of new fusion restaurants or a retro denim-on-denim look. I *want* to see this trip as an adventure full of opportunities for fun, but it's not giving me butterflies yet.

Well. It is. But not in any realistic or acceptable way. I need to squash out all the Grant-butterflies.

"That was the old Lila. The new Lila is bitter and jaded."

"Unlikely."

"Likely. The new Lila has already been covered in ants."

"What?" Her shock is deeply satisfying. When I was well and truly swarming with bugs, the rest of my group took it a little too calmly. Only Grant stepped up to rescue me.

Which I am totally not thinking about.

"I'm communing with nature." Lower, I whisper. "Please send help."

"Aww. You're going to have a great time."

"You and I have had very different experiences in the woods."

"Maybe. I mean, all of mine have been with Griffin, so…"

Neither of us spent much time outdoors growing up. I don't even remember making mud pies as a kid. Hope changed all that when her boyfriend—her fiancé as of a week ago—came along. Now, she's all about camping, hiking, and going feral in the great outdoors. She's even gone fishing with him a few times, and I can't decide if I'm more impressed or disgusted.

I barely even like to eat fish. I don't want to actually touch them.

I might worry my little sister was trying to change herself to suit a man if it weren't painfully obvious she truly looks forward to their adventures. The weirdo. Plus, he treats her like royalty and dotes on her as if the only thing he wants in the world is to make her happy.

Weirdos in love. Honestly, I'm here for it.

"I can see how a rugged mountain man might make the whole thing more appealing." My gaze darts to Grant because I am a ridiculous little bean. I can't help it—he fits the part. Luckily, he's on a call, too, and unaware of my Pavlovian response to the words.

"There are some benefits to having a rugged mountain man at your side."

"Mmm hmm." I'm not imagining benefits with Grant. That would be a mistake and inappropriate and absolutely magnificent.

But mostly a mistake. I spent way too much time trying to be what my ex-fiancé wanted. I can't start out at this kind of deficit with a guy—Grant's some kind of mountain-climbing expert, and I can't even take off my pack without risk of injuring myself. I probably sound like a dummy to him. I won't be in another relationship with a man who looks down on me.

Of course, Josh didn't start out that way. That's the tricky part—how do you know the guy who's showering you with affection now won't look right through you in another year or two? You don't. So, you focus on rebuilding your life from the ground up, with a move back home, an all-new job, and a vintage studio apartment that's at the very limit of your budget.

And by you, I mean me.

"Speaking of men, both rugged and otherwise..."

"Don't say it." I wince, preparing myself for the worst. "Please don't say it."

"Mom hasn't given up on setting you up with Dr. Brendan." Her sympathetic delivery doesn't make the news any easier to take.

As much as Mom loved my fiancé, after we broke up, she became my ultimate defender. We ate countless tubs of ice cream while I poured my guts out about all the red flags I missed until I was swimming in them. But now that I've had a few months to regroup, she seems to think it's open season on finding me a man.

Her man of choice: some pediatric dentist my dad knows in Bend. I've put her off approximately one thousand times, but eventually, I'm going to have to meet him. Unless I find someone on my own, which is unlikely.

If my gaze darts to Grant again, it's only because I enjoy his profile. That jawline should have songs written about it.

"She needs a hobby outside of our love lives."

Hope's sharp laughter cuts through the line. "You're one to talk. You got to avoid this for years when you were in Seattle. When it was me, you said I should indulge her and give the guys a chance. Funny how you're singing a very different tune now that you're the center of her romantic hopes and dreams."

"I was naive, what can I say?"

"All she wants is to steer a good man your way." Hope's sing-song voice is little sister perfection. "Like a pirate ship ready to plunder your seas."

"Ew, no. Terrible image. There are no marauding men on my horizon."

Inexplicably, Grant and I lock eyes. I freeze, a tiny woodland creature who just frightened herself. He's definitely close enough to have heard that, right? His mouth tugs the tiniest bit at the edges before he drops his eyes back to his phone.

Then, his mouth tugs up a tiny bit more.

Yeah. He heard it.

We can all agree this hike is turning out to be a funhouse trip called *Things That Make Lila Squirm*. I'd like to get off the ride, but I'm strapped in for the next several days.

"I should get going," I tell Hope. "There's probably a hornet's nest somewhere I'm scheduled to stumble over this afternoon."

"You're going to do great. Embrace the adventure."

"I would like to embrace a cheeseburger and air conditioning. Are you aware of the toilet situation out here?"

Her delighted laugh holds zero sympathy. "It's the wilderness, Lila."

"I don't even want to think about how comfortable you are with this." Do they dig their own holes when she camps with Griffin? I guess that's one way to bond with a guy.

"Then think about how you're going to rock your presentation and get that promotion." Her voice goes all rah-rah, cheering me on. "Tackle this trip as if it's any other challenge like the boss babe you are."

I stand a little straighter—which I can only do because

nearly all of the contents of my pack are back at camp. I am a kick-butt, thirty-year-old woman who will not be intimidated by the wilderness or any of the contents therein.

Mysterious mountain man included.

"I *am* a boss babe."

"Yeah, you are."

"I'm going to absolutely crush my presentation."

"Woo!"

"That promotion is mine."

She's going absolutely wild. "You've got this, Lila!"

I thumb off our call and take a couple more pictures of the mountains for good measure. Hope's cheer turns into a rallying cry in my mind. This boss babe can handle anything the wilderness throws at me.

As long as it isn't more bugs, please and thank you.

SIX
GRANT

"THERE ARE *no marauding men on my horizon.*"

I would love to say I'm not fixating on that sentence as we walk back to camp, but the damage is done. It doesn't even tell me anything definitive—it could be literal. Maybe she's been plagued by robbers and bandits lately. Doubtful, but probably more likely than the tantalizing possibilities swirling through my head right now.

I've fallen into my usual spot close by her. It's the safest option—we're walking in pairs this way. Plus, I have the bear spray, and animals can be unpredictable. But that's not really why I want to stay in her orbit.

It's not just because of Lila's wry enthusiasm for everything *except* this trip. She has no idea about my past. Living in a small town, my reputation is impossible to escape. But to her, I'm not *Grant Irwin, Guy Who Was Left at the Altar*. I'm the *Guy With the Bear Spray. Potential Newbie Bestie.*

I'm just Grant.

I didn't realize how much the gossip had weighed me down until I met this woman who doesn't know a scrap of it.

Unfortunately, Scott and Brian hang back with us, too, and

they're dominating the conversation. They've been grilling me on my certifications for ten minutes, trying to find something I don't have. It would be flattering if it didn't feel like a trap.

"What about ice climbing? Do you have that one?" Scott asks.

I nod. I might tell them about one of my ice climbs in Wyoming or Banff, but they probably just want the highlights.

Brian snaps his fingers. "Wilderness first aid?"

"That, too."

"You've been busy. How many mountains have you climbed?"

"I don't have the exact number." I do have it, but they're treating me like a minor celebrity even without the specifics.

"What was it like climbing Mount Whitney?" Scott wants to know.

"Did you do the day hike or two-day?" Brian asks. "We've been thinking about tackling it, ourselves."

"Did it in one day. But I applied to the permit lottery for four years before I got my chance."

"How'd you handle the altitude?"

"I hiked a couple of smaller peaks in the area first, and camped at altitude to acclimate."

"He climbs smaller mountains to get ready to climb the big mountain," Lila says next to me. "As one does."

I turn to her and drop my voice. "It's the best way."

She rolls her eyes, keeping me humble in the middle of my mini fan club meeting.

"What was the most surprising part of the climb?" Scott asks as he adjusts his sun hat.

It's like I'm being interviewed for that magazine article all over again.

"Probably the marmots." I know they want something technical—crossing the snow and ice at the top, dealing with the physical exertion, or the dangers of sudden bad weather. But I'm already enough of a spectacle as it is. I don't need to give them more fodder.

He chokes on a laugh. "Marmots?"

"They're a real threat. They'll chew up anything they find to get to food. One of the guys came back from Whitney to find holes in his tent, his pack decimated, and marmot poop everywhere."

Thousands of dollars in gear destroyed, all for the sake of a granola bar wrapper. Which reminds me—Lila's still got one in her pocket.

"Do they have marmots here?" Her question doesn't sound as casual as she probably intended. Maybe she's thinking about the wrapper, too.

"Big ones. And they're mean." Scott bares his teeth like a chipmunk and waves his crooked fingers as if he's clawing at her.

Four more days with these guys. He's harmless and only trying to joke around with her, but I don't like how she's become their punchline simply for asking questions.

I shift slightly in front of Lila, blocking her from his bad marmot impression. "I've never had issues with them in the Cascades," I tell her. "Deena and Mitchell would have mentioned it if they were a problem."

Any animal ransacking their camp would be worth a warning. They're not even using bear canisters out here, only odor-proof bags—we're probably safe from curious rodents.

"Do you have any marmot spray on you?" she asks.

I pat down my chest. "I left it at home."

"I thought you were prepared for everything."

"Not everything." I'm not prepared for her, that's for sure. I could stare at the curl of a smile along her pink lips for the rest of the trip. Shouldn't, but...could.

"What's your most memorable climb?" Brian asks. "What's the one that stands out the most?"

I know my answer before he finishes the question.

"Mount Katahdin, about five years ago."

"Really? Katahdin's not a technical climb. More of a walk in the park. You had a hard time on that one?" He looks like he's about to crow.

This is why I don't feel like giving them details. Guys like this only want to compare. Even when someone else comes out on top, they'll find a way to spin it in their favor. There's no winning.

"It's not memorable because of the challenge. I met a woman on that climb who gave me some much-needed perspective." The men bob their eyebrows, but I shake off their suggestive looks. "She was celebrating her cancer going into remission. She'd been battling it for three years, and finally got the all-clear. It was a special moment to witness."

I was still reeling from the shock of heartbreak when I tackled that mountain. I'd been in a fog of regret, and wanted the physical exertion to numb my emotions. That day, I didn't care about the sights, the experience, or even checking another mountaintop off my list—I wanted the mental escape.

But she conquered the climb as a testament to possibility, and how beautiful life can be despite our setbacks. She smiled the whole way, in awe she had the chance to experience it.

Watching her glory in being alive shook me out of my pity party. I'd gone up a heartsick fool, and come down...well, I like to hope a slightly wiser fool.

"You asked what stands out," I say. "That one does."

"Okay, what's your most *challenging* climb?" Scott asks.

I shrug. "Denali, I guess."

"Whoa."

Denali *is* an impressive accomplishment, but it doesn't

stand out in my mind like that day on Katahdin. Sometimes the heart of the climb is more important than the technical details.

"Here's a tip." Brian sounds like he's ready to whip out a whiteboard and teach a class. "Always lead with the more impressive one."

"He did," Lila says at my side.

I have to fight off a smug grin. I like her jumping to my defense more than I should probably say.

———

After eating our fill of Mitchell's surprisingly good pesto pasta, our group scatters to do our own thing as evening falls. Deena offered to initiate some get-to-know-you games, but the couples declined, on the grounds they've known everything about each other for forty years.

I sit not too far outside my tent, working my pocket knife against a dry chunk of wood. We can't have a campfire out here, so I have to use what daylight we have left.

"This many layers of bug spray can't be good for me." Lila rubs something into her neck from her chin down to the top of the pale blue fleece jacket she's thrown over her camp shirt. She sits at the other end of the fallen log I've commandeered—I already checked it for ants. "That's a lot of eucalyptus oil."

"At least you'll breathe easy all night."

"I guess that's a bonus." Her gaze skates over me. "Are you whittling?"

"Badly, but yes."

She scoots a touch closer. "I've never seen anyone whittle before. I thought it was a myth."

"It's more of a dying art form, which I'm currently bungling."

"What are you making?"

"I don't know yet. Something will come to me."

She squints at the chunk of wood as though she can decipher something in it. "Are you an artist?"

I can't help the laugh that barks out of me. "Not even close. It's just something to pass the time."

It's surprisingly relaxing on evenings like this. Soothes my mind when it would otherwise be consumed by technical details, route plans, and weather forecasts.

"See, my first thought would have been card games."

"Cards are useless weight. A knife can be used for a lot of things."

"One thing, really."

I pause. "Fair point. But it can do one thing in a variety of scenarios."

"Did they teach you how to whittle in all your outdoorsman classes?"

"I'm a self-taught whittler, specializing in the boredom technique."

Laughing softly, she watches me work for a minute. Then she swipes at a mosquito that hasn't caught wind of her eucalyptus aura yet. "There's really such a thing as wilderness first aid?"

"Oh yeah. Lots of things can go wrong out here, and it's not a normal emergency scenario if something goes sideways." Not that I should point any of that out. She's already out of her comfort zone, she doesn't need me outlining worst-case scenarios.

"I guess I'm safe in your hands, huh?"

Do not think about her in your hands.

That warning is several hours too late.

I meet her gaze, and a soft pink washes over her skin.

"You know—in an emergency. Obviously." Nervous

laughter bubbles out of her. "Do you have to take all those classes to climb mountains?"

My brain is still stuck on the idea of her in my hands, and it takes me a second to recover. "Not necessarily. A lot of peaks are just long hikes. But some involve ice climbing or traveling across glaciers, and you need to learn those technical skills first."

"Are you a mountain guide on the side or something? With all of those classes, it seems like you could be."

I focus on the wood in my hands and the knife slicing away each thin strip of bark. "When I was in my twenties, I had dreams of starting my own guiding company."

"What happened?"

"Reality happened. I took on more and more responsibilities with my family's business and had to make a choice."

"Oh. Do you still want to be a mountain guide?"

I look up to find her watching me with big doe eyes. "It's been a long time since I considered it. Most guides don't work past fifty, and nobody does it for the money. They do it for the love. This way, I can still climb and keep my family's stores running. Everybody wins."

It's what I told myself all those years when the choice still stung. Something in it feels like a lie, but I can't pinpoint what.

She zips her fleece all the way up. The temperature's fading along with the daylight. We might have to retreat to our tents before the sun is completely down just to cuddle up and stay warm.

I really shouldn't be thinking about *that*, either.

"What are your stores like?"

I summon my best impression of Dean. "When you walk into an Irwin's, you know everyone is there because they love using the gear, and know it inside and out. They answer customer questions from experience, not a brochure."

She stares for several beats before she bursts out laughing. "Why are you talking like that?"

"It's something one of my brothers said, and I never got over it." I close my knife and slip it into my shirt pocket. I don't need to put my first aid skills to the test out here. "We sell all kinds of gear for outdoor activities—camping, hiking, kayaking, you name it. Some stores are pretty small and niche, but most have sizable square footage. We want them to be warm and welcoming, no matter anyone's sport or experience level."

"Your family must all be outdoorsy nuts—I mean...*outdoors enthusiasts*."

I laugh. "We are outdoorsy nuts, but we come by it honestly. My parents met on a camping trip."

"Your parents met on a camping trip like this?"

I hadn't thought of it that way until exactly this moment. Huh. I swallow. "They fell in love that week."

I don't know why I added that last bit. I don't know if I've ever fully bought into the story.

"I guess that's romantic. If you can get past the camping parts." She smiles to let me know she means no harm. She has no idea how the simple gesture aches through me. "And your whole family works there?"

"My parents are co-presidents, and they handle all the biggest decisions. I'm the General Manager, my middle brother Dean is the Chief Financial Officer, and my youngest brother Rhett is our marketer and social media manager."

"And they're all...like you?"

I narrow my eyes on her in the deepening twilight. "Elaborate."

"You know. Outdoorsy. Accomplished. Handsome." She runs a hand over the air between us. "Big."

Her cheeks grow even pinker, and she tucks her hand between her knees. I can work with *handsome* and *big*.

"Big is a very interesting description—"

"Just tell me about them, please." She widens her eyes at me, practically begging me to end the awkwardness. I rather enjoy the begging, if I'm being honest.

"We're not all that alike. Rhett is thirty and possibly the most immature man I know, but he's great at what he does. He's a whitewater rafting nut. Dean is thirty-three, and the most serious of us. He doesn't do as much outdoors as he should."

"What does that mean? He doesn't do as much outdoors as he 'should'? Is it a requirement?"

I get the feeling she's ready to leap to Dean's defense from my unjust *shoulds*. "I mean, I think he needs the distraction. He's so caught up in our business, he doesn't take time for himself. He needs a life outside of work."

Hypocrite, thy name is Grant. Rhett wasn't wrong when he said I've been too busy to enjoy myself lately. Even my trips away have been more distractions than vacations. Plus, that characterization is unfair to Dean. He's created a work/life balance for himself these last couple of years that I envy. He took on our grandparents' house when our grandma downsized, and he's planning to fill it up with babies just as soon as Eliza gives the okay.

If any of us has a full life outside of work, it's Dean.

"Actually, that info's kind of out of date. He got married last year, and his wife has softened some of his rough edges."

"And you? Do you have somebody back home in Texas to soften your edges?"

"Do I seem like I'm rough?"

"I don't know, I've heard rumors about guys who whittle..."

I hold her gaze for a second. "I don't have anybody back home in Texas. What about you?"

"I don't have anyone, but my edges are already pretty soft,

so." She closes her eyes and shakes her head. "That's—pretend I didn't say that."

"I never disagreed with you."

She gives me an unimpressed look. "Well, it's getting dark. I guess we should probably go to bed. *I* should go to bed, I mean. You can whittle for as long as you want."

I'm loving the awkwardness. It gives me a stupid kind of hope.

"I really made an impact with the whittling."

"It's memorable. You're the whittling guy in my head now, I'm sorry."

"If that's what it takes."

She stands and dusts off her pants. "All right, Grant the Whittler. See you in the morning."

She scrambles away to her tent, crawls inside, and zips it shut.

I stay up way too late thinking about Lila's soft edges.

SEVEN
LILA

ADD another line to the list of things I am completely unprepared for on this trip: Sleeping in a tent. From being swaddled like a baby in a narrow sleeping bag to the general weirdness of having only a thin layer of fabric protecting me from the great outdoors, I didn't get much rest last night. I probably burned as many calories wiggling around trying to get comfortable as I did from yesterday's hike.

And don't get me started on the noises.

Every little sound had my eyes jolting wide open all night. They were probably just tree branches moving in the breeze or nocturnal animals inspecting our campsite, but it's hard to think rationally in the dead of night. Restless serial killers who prey on unsuspecting campers when they're at their most vulnerable probably would have made a lot more racket, but I didn't completely rule them out. I shivered in my little sleeping bag cocoon while my mind filled with creepy monster men.

I'm not usually a catastrophizer, but I've also never slept in the woods before. Looks like that's a package deal.

"She's awake!" Deena calls as soon as I crawl out of my makeshift cave.

It's barely seven, but I guess that's late in this group. The smell of pancakes cooking draws me closer to her propane stove.

She waves a spatula over her small griddle. "We're eating in shifts since I can only make three pancakes at a time."

The others are gathered in a circle nearby, but only Scott and Shannon are eating so far. Nobody else looks quite as rumpled as I feel. I guess sleeping outdoors is some kind of skill I haven't mastered.

"I don't mind waiting."

"If you need coffee or tea, we've got some mugs and a carafe of hot water over here."

"Ooh, yes." I sort through the selection of instant beverage packets and get a bag of cardamom cinnamon tea steeping in an enamel mug. It's cold this morning, and my breath puffs out in a little cloud. I'm chilled everywhere except the places my palms make contact with the mug. Not for the first time, I think wistfully of my purple roller bag and all the extra layers of clothes I could be wearing this very minute.

But alas.

I wander away from the breakfast line to enjoy my tea. It's probably best if I don't socialize until I wake up a little more. Honestly, I don't know if tea is enough to perk me up out here. These last twenty-four hours haven't been anything like a normal day. I went to bed before nine last night like an infant, for goodness's sake, and I still feel like two-day old pizza—stiff and unappealing.

"Good morning, Lila."

That voice rumbles through me like a cat's purr. My stomach goes weirdly fluttery. I'm going to think of it as the wonder of the great outdoors finally hitting me. Right in the fluttery feels.

I turn around, and holy moly, I am not prepared for the sight of Grant Irwin first thing in the morning. His hair is askew, dark stubble coats his jaw, and the hint of sleepiness in his eyes almost makes my heart hurt from cuteness overload.

Grant's definitely not having a two-day old pizza morning. It's disgusting how little effort men can get away with. His eyes could be crusted over, and I bet it would work for him. And me? I gave myself an even messier messy bun, swiped my face with a cleansing wipe, and pretended I didn't see the beginnings of dark circles under my eyes in my tiny travel mirror.

Take that, beauty influencers.

I mumble a close approximation of "Good morning" and sip at my tea.

"Not a morning person?"

"I'm more of a hurkle-durkler, myself." There's nothing better than snuggling back into bed after the alarm goes off. Sometimes I set my alarm early just so I can get cozy in the covers one more time.

He looks at me like I made that up. Grant must not watch TikToks about the joys of indulging in lazy mornings.

"No, I'm not a morning person." In absolute perfect timing, my mouth cracks into a huge yawn behind my hand. "Especially when I didn't sleep very well."

"Were you too cold?"

"The sleeping bag was the exact right temperature, surprisingly. I was as snug as a little burrito." I opt not to tell him how much the spooky sounds bothered me. "I just couldn't get comfortable. There was a rock under my mat, and it might as well have been in my sleeping bag for all the good the mat did."

"You don't like the sleeping mat?" His teasing tone says he knows very well there's nothing much to like. "It's the finest four-inch-thick mattress on the market."

"Anything that rolls up to the size of a Stanley cup can't possibly cradle my hips and shoulders the way I'm used to. I spent most of the night longing for my brand-new memory foam queen bed."

His mouth curls into a smile. "Are you sure it wasn't a pea underneath your mat, princess?"

I narrow my eyes into slits and take another sip of tea. I will *not* think about how much I might like that nickname if he said it under any other circumstances. No way.

"We can't all be experts at sleeping in gruesome situations." He's probably camped in all kinds of crazy places. Maybe even one of those trips where they sleep right on a cliff wall, and one wrong move means *splat*. Sounds about right.

"Is this a gruesome situation for you?"

I grumble some more. "So far, I've carried all my stuff like a pack animal, been attacked by an army of ants, and was forced to sleep on an *incomprehensibly large* rock all night. This forest has some room for improvement."

"The camp toilet didn't make the list?"

My glare turns murderous. "I am actively trying to block that from my mind. Please don't ruin it for me."

"My apologies." He holds eye contact with me a beat. "Any positives so far?"

He's not flirting, right? No. Maybe? The bigger question: do I want him to be flirting?

This guy? Who manages to be absolutely gorgeous first thing in the morning, is apparently more than capable in the woods, and when asked for his best memory on a mountain climb, responded with someone else's emotional achievement? This guy?

Magic Eight Ball says: *Ask again later*.

"Dinner was surprisingly good," I finally say. Nice and neutral.

And completely honest. My expectations were low, but Mitchell's pesto pasta might be the best I've ever had. That could have been the total-body exhaustion talking, but I stand by it.

"We need to find you a few more positives to add to that list."

Yesterday, I would have said it was an impossible mission. Now, I suspect Grant's up to the task.

———

This landscape doesn't look real. It's what I imagine whenever a sci-fi movie uses the word "terraforming"—a weird approximation of Earth.

Volcanic rock tumbles everywhere in bumpy mounds left over from the last eruption several thousand years ago. Every now and then, a skinny, bright green pine tree shoots up out of a rocky pile in a way that makes zero logical sense. Like nature saw this desolate landscape and said, "You're not the boss of me."

I take a few pictures, since the volcanic stuff has tourist appeal. People love looking at old rocks, right?

"Are the pictures for your social media?" Grant asks as he navigates some of the bigger chunks of rock that have made their way onto the trail.

I thought maybe now that his secret mountain-climbing talent is out, he would switch to the front of our group. Show off his skills and lead the way. But as soon as we had breakfast and packed up all of our gear—which, by the way, is a process I'm so excited to do every morning, yay for that—he was right next to me again in the back.

I tell myself it's just what good hiking buddies do, but I might be lying.

"No, not mine. I'll create some content for Horizon Hikes

that they can use on their own accounts, but my followers aren't really into this stuff."

I don't think. I've never posted pictures from first-hand visits to the woods, but it's not a safe bet. Being out here is about as far opposite as you can get from the city-centric lifestyle I used to feature every day.

"What is your account like? I don't have service, or I'd see what *Genuinely_Lila* is all about."

"That offer is weirdly flattering and mildly horrifying."

The sun slices through the sparse trees as we stump along the bizarre landscape. I slathered on sunscreen this morning, but the skin on the back of my neck is already cooked. Yet another thing I should have brought but didn't—some kind of sun hat. I feel like Deena's packing list could be expanded just a touch.

I would start with the freedom to bring underwear.

Grant chuckles. "Why mildly horrifying?"

"Mmm, I don't think it would be your thing. There's a lot of fashion on there, home decor, aesthetic pictures, and day-in-the-life stuff."

"I'd be interested in your day-in-the-life stuff. I wouldn't mind a glimpse at what makes Lila tick."

"What makes me tick is a steady stream of boba tea and chocolate."

"See?" He splays his hand at me. "That's great information. Is this a bad time to admit I've never tried boba tea?"

I stop dead on the track and throw out a hand to grab his arm. Um—wow. His biceps are delightfully solid, but not my immediate concern. "You've never tried boba tea? A life without boba is only half a life."

"It's that serious?"

With the utmost regret, I release his arm, and we continue along the trail, heading into denser trees. "It's the most serious.

You have to try it when we get back to town. I love it so much, I convinced one of Sunshine's cafés to serve it."

"I heard you mention that."

"Really? I don't think I've talked about Perk Me Up out here, have I?"

I do talk about boba tea a good percentage of the time. Specifically, whenever I don't have a drink in my hand, and I've been sadly bereft on this trip. But I haven't started jonesing so hard for one that I've whined about it on the trails yet. And I do mean *yet*. The time will come.

Grant's got this strange deer-in-headlights look on his face. "I heard someone say it."

"Huh." I'm pretty proud of the fact that I successfully swayed the owners to add it to their menu, but I didn't know anyone else talked about it. That's probably a good thing, right? Proving my support of Sunshine's businesses already. Even if by support, in this case I mostly mean I begged them to satisfy my borderline unhealthy addiction.

In the name of growing their business, of course.

"I'll have to try it when we're back in town." Grant sounds decided, and I like that. Score another win for me.

"I'll need a glowing testimonial afterward, please."

"No pressure."

"I have faith in your good taste."

"That might be unfounded, but I'll take it. So you're out here just to get content for advertising for Horizon Hikes?"

"Mmm, not really. I am doing that, but the bigger reason is that I'm trying to get a promotion. I work for Sunshine part-time planning events, but the mayor and a few council members want to create a full-time tourism position for me. Which sounds great, except there's a big chunk of Sunshine's tourism potential I don't know the first thing about."

I wave my hand at the freaky rocks and skinny trees around us.

"You're doing research?"

"I could just Google 'central Oregon hikes that make you want to pass out from exhaustion,' but I'm hoping the first-hand experience will provide an edge when I give my presentation."

"That's a good idea. What else is on your list to get first-hand experience with?"

"Just this." A five-day hike is plenty. Isn't it? I chew the inside of my lip. "Do you think I should do more?"

"Couldn't hurt. There's a lot in this area to enjoy. Mountain biking, fishing, kayaking, rafting. And that's just summer activities."

My hopeful little heart deflates. Arranging this hike had seemed like such a genius move a few weeks ago. Get a little one-on-one time with nature and prove to the council I'm committed to the cause. Now, I'm having second thoughts about how much difference a single hike will make. I don't know the first thing about any of that other stuff either, and my winter experiences aren't any better.

Unless sitting in a ski lodge sipping hot cider while the rest of your group tackles the slopes counts. Which I doubt.

"Hey, I didn't mean to criticize." Grant's got his look of concern on, like I'm covered in ants again. "It's a good plan. When do you give your presentation?"

"In three weeks."

"That's plenty of time to get a few more outdoor activities in."

I try to smile, but I'm not sure I manage it. "Yay, me."

"Is this your job focus? Events and tourism and social media marketing?"

"Basically, aside from the tourism. That part's new. I worked for a tech firm in Seattle for several years, but I moved back to Sunshine last winter." And...that's about as in-depth as I want to be. I'm really not in the mood to talk about Josh's business or my old role in it. There's no point in sharing how I sometimes worked sixty hours a week just to make his company look good.

Definitely don't want to mention how I was "downsized" within twenty-four hours of breaking up with him. I was replaceable in every way.

"Seattle to Sunshine's a big change."

"Yeah. I'm...adapting." I'm trying, anyway.

"What brought you back?"

"I missed my family." I refuse to tell him the truth: that the choice stemmed from a place of total humiliation and the utter loss of almost everything I'd valued in my life. I lost my fiancé, my job, my apartment, and my friends in one fell swoop. Just your average rom-com cliché. The only thing missing was my car breaking down on my drive of shame to my hometown and getting rescued by a lumberjack.

"Change like that isn't easy. I admire—"

He steps closer to me and throws an arm out like he's slammed on the brakes and he's the only thing stopping me from flying through the windshield. In the same instant, a shadow swoops low over us. I shriek and crouch behind him, clinging to his pack.

"What is it?" I whisper.

"Just an owl."

"But?"

"But...it landed right in front of us."

Slowly, I peek around the edge of his pack. Not fifteen feet away in the trees sits a massive owl. Maybe it's regular-sized, I don't know that much about my nemeses. Either way, my bird-fearing brain concludes it's massive, and that's really all that matters.

"It's staring at us." I barely make a sound. Am I clutching Grant's biceps again? Absolutely, I am. He's the closest thing to a lumberjack rescue I've got.

"It probably has a nest nearby."

"I know how this scenario goes. Up against a bird that big, we don't win." My scalp tingles with potential injuries.

"We're just going to walk by it slowly." He reaches across me until his hand hits my hip, like that would do anything to protect me against the bird's pointy beak and sharp claws.

Weirdly, it's still comforting.

"How did the others get by?" I hiss.

"It was probably out hunting then."

We take tiny baby steps along the edge of the trail. I'd like to scooch over and off-road it, but that would involve taking my eyes off the owl. It never stops watching us. I don't know much about wild animals, but I'm pretty sure sustained, direct eye contact is never good.

All my systems are malfunctioning: I'm shaking, my heart's going wild, and my lungs seem to be turning on and off again.

"I'm freaking out." Grant's probably aware of that, since my fingers are digging so deep into his arm I'm going to leave a bruise, but I can't loosen them.

"Everything's okay," he soothes. "He's not going to attack you."

"Do you have bird ESP? You don't know that."

"I'll protect you."

I really don't know how he could. Still, a tiny sliver of tautness inside me loosens. Not my fingers—those keep their death grip on Grant's arm. I don't take my eyes off the owl, either. I'm no dummy. It will strike the second I'm anything less than vigilant.

I don't take a full breath until we're out of sight of the great horned menace. I think. It could have better eyesight than I do, and it's still watching us through the trees.

Grant turns to me, and I finally release him. "I'm sorry about your arm."

"Don't be. Are you okay?"

My heart's racing, I think I pulled something in my Grant-gripping hand, and that owl will most likely visit me in my nightmares tonight.

"Pretty much. Can I ask you a question? As a professional outdoorsman?"

His mouth flattens, but he nods. "Fire away."

"Is there a part where this is supposed to get fun? People do this for fun, right?"

His smile chases away the last of my panic. "It's my new goal to show you something fun before this trip is over."

Past him, Mitchell appears in the distance for his check-in. About a hundred feet and one big bird too late. I wave at him, and he carries on again.

My attention refocuses on Grant. "You must like a challenge."

His eyes spark. "I love them."

EIGHT

GRANT

I DON'T WATCH reality shows. I don't like the concept of witnessing someone else's uncomfortable and embarrassing moments for the sake of my own entertainment. They have zero appeal, and I try to avoid even listening to recaps when coworkers chat about the most recent reality show disaster.

So explain to me why I can't look away as Lila prepares to learn how to fish.

We set up camp in a denser forest than we did last night, tucked away in the trees. Thankfully for Lila's sore back, we've left the lava flows behind for now, and our sleeping area should be relatively rock-free. We had lunch, explored the small lake, and are getting ready to catch dinner.

When Deena asked who wanted to fish, I expected Lila to decline. No part of what I know of her tells me she would enjoy either the standing around waiting or the end result of this endeavor. But she volunteered right along with the rest of us, despite the little curl of distaste along her mouth.

I admit, her physical beauty attracted me immediately, but her tenacity is knocking me out. She knows what she wants, and she'll do whatever it takes to get it, even if personally, the thought of doing it makes her want to run the other way. Failure's not an option for her. It's impossible not to appreciate that.

Mitchell and Deena set up the collapsible fishing poles and handed them out, leaving us to find spots along the rocky shore. We're using floats, both for the more obvious nature of them, and to try to keep the line out of the rocks in the shallows.

I'm absolutely delaying, fiddling with my reel while Mitchell shows Lila how to cast. She copies his demonstration in jerky motions, but she's starting to get the hang of it.

After an especially good cast, Mitchell cheers her on before moving along to check in with the others. She's white-knuckling the fishing rod like she expects it to fly out of her hands any second. Every now and then she gives the reel a turn to keep the float moving, but otherwise, she's as still as stone.

Good for not scaring fish away, bad for enjoying the sport.

"You're staring."

She doesn't look away from the float, which is a good thing. I *am* staring. I can't help it. I haven't taken my eyes off of her since she walked into Horizon Hikes yesterday morning. She's fascinating and gorgeous, and I could listen to her talk for days on end and...yeah. I *really* need to get this staring thing in check.

Soon.

"I want to watch a master fisherman at work."

That gets a laugh out of her, and her shoulders relax just a touch. "I'm available for private lessons."

"Where do I sign up?"

She shakes her head, but I'm pleased she's loosened her death grip on the pole. Now she almost looks like she's having a relaxing day on the lake. I'm not sure what will happen if she actually catches something, but fishing's ninety percent about the process.

"How do you even know the bait is still on there? Fish could have swung by, snagged the food, and taken off again, and I'd never know."

"That happens sometimes. It's good to reel the line in once in a while and cast again."

She drags her eyes away from the float to look straight at me. "Aren't you going to fish?"

I crack a smile. "In a minute."

She gives me a dirty look and turns her attention back to her line, but not before I catch a glimpse of the smile she's trying to fight.

I'm still watching a few minutes later when her float dips sharply in the water.

"I think something's happening." She sounds like she just unlocked a new fear.

The float dips again, and I set down my pole to move closer to her. "Looks like you've got a fish on the line. Reel it in."

"Uhh..." She starts spinning the reel, but when the end of the pole curves toward the lake surface as the fish resists, she shoves the whole thing toward me. "You do it."

I raise my hands in the air. "It's your fish, princess. You've got this."

"I don't know how!"

"This is when you learn."

She glares, but cranks on the reel, muttering something about mountain men under her breath. By the time it's close enough we can see the fish swimming in tight figure-eights just below the surface, Mitchell has joined us to offer advice.

I watch and wait, saying silent prayers that she doesn't accidentally lose the fish. This might be the win out here she needs. In another minute, Mitchell snags the fish out of the water right in front of her, deftly removing the hook with a small tool.

"Well done. Gorgeous rainbow trout." He offers it to her. "Do you want to hold it?"

She recoils as if he just offered her...well, a writhing fish. "No way."

"You sure?" He's unfazed by her disgust. "It's your first fish. Pretty big moment."

She hesitates. Then, she reaches out to run a delicate finger down the pink line that decorates the fish's middle. She shivers and wipes her finger on her pants. "Yeah, that feels like touching a fish."

A tiny smile graces her mouth, though. Like she's proud of herself against her better judgment.

"You want me to take care of it?" Mitchell asks.

"Uh, sure."

In one swift motion, he slams the fish's head against a large rock. The dull thud jolts through Lila like she's been shot, her gaze bulls-eyeing to the middle of the lake. Mitchell hits the fish against the rock a second time, finishing the stun job.

"Great work," he tells her. "I'll clean and gut it and take it to the stove for dinner."

She acknowledges him with a stiff nod, her lips tight between her teeth as he walks away. Otherwise, she doesn't move. I give her a second, but I'm not even sure she's breathing right now.

"Are you okay?" I ask softly.

She shakes herself like she'd forgotten I'm here.

"What? Yeah. That's just circle of life stuff." Her face twists as though my question is crazy, but she's gone so pale I worry she might faint. With all these rocks around, she could get seriously hurt.

"Maybe you should sit down."

"I'm going to go take a victory lap." She passes me her fishing pole and raises both fists in the air in a sad little cheer. "First fish!"

"Lila, wait." But she's already heading back toward camp.

"Everything's great," she shouts back. "This is totally going on my presentation. Yay, me!"

I don't know why she's so obviously lying, but if she needs a minute, I'll give her one. And only one. I gather up our fishing poles and take them back to camp before I go looking for her.

She's not hard to find, so that's good. She's on a fallen log with her back to me about fifty feet away from her tent. I'm careful to make a little noise as I approach her, and she sighs heavily when I close in. I round the log, dropping into a catcher's squat in front of her.

Her eyes are full of tears, stripes on her cheeks where they've already fallen.

My heart clenches in my chest. "Oh, princess."

"I know it's stupid," she whispers, batting away a tear.

"It's not stupid. Are you a vegetarian?"

She snorts. "No. I eat meat. I've just never been *right there* when the meat ceases to be."

"I understand. I went hunting exactly one time."

She tries to smile, but her chin wobbles. "That would be so much worse."

"It's okay if you need a minute."

"I mean, I knew it would happen somehow, I guess, I just wasn't expecting...*that*." She lifts her eyes to the sky as if she can make her tears drain away. "I've never killed anything before."

I set my hands on her knees. "You didn't kill that fish."

"Yeah, but it's my fault." Her gaze drops to meet mine. "I'm a fish murderer."

I let the tiniest smile peek out on my face because she's so adorable even when she's weeping over a trout. "You're not."

She swipes beneath each eye, catching the tears. "I'm the monster fish parents tell their fish children about at night."

I gently squeeze her knees, her skin warm beneath her

leggings. "I appreciate that you can quote the MCU through your tears."

She releases a long exhale. "I'm fine, I'm just...I feel like this is a sign."

"Of what?"

She spreads her hands out, gesturing at herself, the trees, me. "I'm not meant for all of this. This proves how bad I am at being outdoorsy. And I don't know if I can get this job if I'm this bad at being outdoorsy. And if I don't get it..."

Her shoulders hitch, worlds of worry in that unfinished sentence.

"I respectfully disagree."

She makes a dismissive sound, but I go on.

"I'm as big of an outdoors advocate as you'll find, but even I don't expect you to like everything you try. Nobody does. You just keep experimenting until you land on something that's a good fit for you."

Her mouth has a skeptical slant to it, but she holds my gaze. "What if I don't find anything? What if I'm just not an outdoorsy person?"

I'm not sure if she's asking what that might mean for her promotion opportunity or what that might mean for me personally. I can't say for sure how it would affect her job outlook, but I can say with confidence it wouldn't affect my opinion of her.

"You don't have to do anything different. You're wonderful exactly as you are, princess."

Her smile lights me up like a firework in the night.

She presses her palms beneath her eyes and nods once. "Okay. Enough mourning the fallen fish."

I stand and hold a hand out to her. She takes it, and I help her to her feet. "Ready to go back?"

"Meh. Then I'll just be around everyone else's dead fish." A fat tear pools in her eye and slides down her cheek.

I bet it'll be a while before she's ready to deal with that. "Need a hug?"

Her eyes brighten. "I would really like that."

She steps to me, and I fold her into my arms. Whatever I thought about shaking her hand, *this* is what will unravel me completely. How perfectly she fits against me, so warm and soft. Her hands pressing against my back, cuddling me close. An overwhelming sense of rightness I've never felt before.

She lets go first. I'm not sure it would have ever occurred to me.

"Thank you. For everything." She smiles again and heads back into camp.

I follow, surreptitiously rubbing my chest. I've been so careful not to get burned by relationships again, but Lila's tempting me to play with fire.

NINE
LILA

I DON'T HAVE MUCH of an appetite for dinner. I can barely look at the others as they savor their fish. Grant abstains from fish, too, the sweetheart. He'd looked pretty excited about fishing...right until I lost my mind when I caught one.

The risotto's good, though.

We ate later than we did last night, since the meal was dependent on successfully catching the ingredients. The daylight's already starting to fade by the time the last dish has been wiped, cleaned, and dried. Everyone's saying their goodnights, and it's only eight-thirty. I'm physically tired, but my brain isn't ready to shut off this early.

Only one person hasn't settled in for the night yet. Grant is sitting in his tent's vestibule, sort of a tiny three-walled garage, if you will. He's whittling. I don't know why, but I love that for him. It's an incredibly old-mannish thing for such a strikingly virile guy to do.

Virile, yuck. I never use that word. Still fits him.

"This is how you don't go insane from boredom, isn't it?" I'm standing to the side of his tent in my nighttime clothes, not quite ready to zip myself into my cocoon for the evening.

"Every little bit helps."

"Do you have a spare knife?"

He looks up at me. "Do you want to give it a try?"

I shrug. "Why not?"

"I don't have a spare knife, but you can use this one. Come here." He scoots over until he's right up next to the tent wall, leaving me just enough room to sit on the floor of the vestibule.

I fold myself down next to him, only moderately mortified by the smells that must waft off my body after hiking for two days straight. He demonstrates how to use the knife on the block of wood he's holding, and I swear I try to focus. But he's got really great hands. Strong and long-fingered, they monopolize my attention.

"You got it?" he says, incorrectly assuming I've listened to all of his instructions.

"It seems pretty self-explanatory. Wood—cut."

He chuckles and passes over the knife and wood. I make my first pass—and utterly fail to scrape off any wood.

I exhale a laugh. "The wood-cut process is harder than you make it look."

"I've had a lot of practice."

The second try, I get the knife lodged in the wood too deep to do anything and have to see-saw it out. "I didn't mean to do that."

"It happens."

The third comes a little bit too close to my fingers. "Whoops."

"Maybe it's getting too dark to whittle." He gently takes the knife away from me.

Seriously, good call.

"So this is the life of an outdoorsman?" I ask. "Exhaust yourself all day and let boredom put you to bed at eight every night?"

"What do you usually do in the evenings?"

"Take electricity for granted."

"Addict."

"I curl up in a blanket and read, mostly. I knew I should have finished the book I'm reading before the trip started. I gave myself a terrible cliffhanger."

The gargoyle has finally revealed himself to the human he's in love with, but will she accept a monster mate? Obviously the answer is yes, but I still need to know how it all plays out.

"What's it about?"

"Oh, uh...it's a romance." I'm not sure how cool Grant is with the genre. Josh always treated my reading habits as a dirty little secret. I don't want to give him too many details if he's going to be a pain about it.

"You can borrow my e-reader. I don't know if I have anything downloaded you'd want to read, though."

I clutch at him. It's happening a lot, and I should probably stop, but dang, dude. *Biceps.* "You brought an e-reader?"

"It keeps me from going insane from boredom."

"I thought that was the whittling."

"It's a two-prong approach." He unzips his tent, reaches in, and pulls out a naked e-reader two seconds later. He places it in my lap. "You can borrow it."

"You said cards are useless weight. What's this?"

"Vital to my mental well-being."

I grin at him and pick up the slim e-reader. "You'd really let me scroll through your book library? That's very bold of you."

"Why is that?"

"Oh, you know..." It occurs to me he actually might not know. He probably has perfectly normal titles on his e-reader, unlike some people in this vestibule.

His eyebrows twitch. "Wait, what's on your library you wouldn't want people to see?"

I make a face. "Nothing. It's all totally average and bland. Super vanilla."

He dips his face closer to mine. I...kind of need to unzip my fleece. Just got a blast of southern heat.

"What's on yours?"

He shouldn't be allowed to throw his sultry voice around like this. It could give people the wrong idea.

Hi. It's me.

"Just romances of different varieties."

"What varieties?"

"Totally regular stuff. Human stuff."

When he laughs, his breath ghosts over my cheek. "Human stuff?"

"Some of it is, yeah." It's a low percentage lately, but he doesn't need to know every detail. Or any detail.

"Now I'm dying to know what you read."

"That's too bad, because it's your secrets we're revealing tonight."

I push the button on his e-reader, and the screen lights up between us. We're crammed way too close together in this tiny space. My heart's racing a happy little beat, but I tell myself it's just because I'm about to see what Grant has on his library. Going through someone's books is a very intimate experience.

Maybe I shouldn't be thinking the word *intimate* right now.

I thumb to the library, and—huh. It's pretty normal. Extensive and full of classics, but all very respectable titles. "Oh."

"You're actually disappointed I don't have something scandalous on there, aren't you?"

"A bit, yeah."

His wide smile fills me with fluttering wings.

Then, fluttering wings land right on the e-reader. A giant moth practically covers the screen. A creaky gasp sticks in my throat. It's only my undying respect for books of all kinds that stops me from flinging the e-reader straight into the trees.

I make a pitiful sound while Grant shoos the moth on its way. He pulls the e-reader from my hands and turns it off again.

"Probably best to wait until you're in your tent, or you'll attract more unwanted visitors to read over your shoulder."

I close my eyes, calculating how close that thing must have been for it to reach us within seconds of the light switching on. *Very, very close.* I open them again to find Grant watching me.

"Why does everything out here have to be so…"

"Full of natural beauty?" he offers.

"Ha. I haven't seen much natural beauty."

"I have."

This close, his utter sincerity throws me. The moment slows, snags, halts entirely. I won't pretend I don't get compliments. I'm well aware of my face. But he's not talking to glammed-up Lila ready for a night out. He's talking to *two days out from a shower* Lila who isn't even wearing tinted moisturizer.

His compliment sinks straight into my bones.

I kind of seriously wish he weren't heading home to Texas in a few more days.

He passes the e-reader back to me. "Take it. If nothing else, you can scan my whole book library and discover all of my shameful secrets."

"You mean all the middle grade stuff on here?"

"They're comfort reads."

"Someone's very attached to Percy Jackson."

"Who wouldn't love to find out they're secretly a demi-god?"

Insert *You* look *like you're secretly a demi-god* joke here.

"I already took your snacks. I don't want to take away your entertainment, too."

His eyes drop to the device and back to me. "We could read something together. Or I could read aloud."

My heart stops. I think I just walked into every book-loving girl's dream come true.

"Really? You wouldn't mind?"

"It'd be fun. But we should move into my tent." He hitches a shoulder. "To avoid the moths and mosquitos."

"Right. I don't want any more moth buddies to find us." Going into a guy's tent after knowing him for two days? I should feel weirder about doing that than I actually do. Maybe because I have no context for it. I'd never been in a tent *alone* before this trip.

"Think of it as my reading nook. Forget my bed is in there."

There's the context. Now that's all I'm going to think about.

He unzips half the entrance and snaps on an LED light, then waves me inside. He slips off his boots to leave them outside, a habit I've seen the others in the group follow too. I do the same before I crawl into his tent. It's a two-person tent like mine, with enough space for both of us to sit comfortably without ever touching.

Or at least I think so, until he crawls in after me. He zips the door closed and sits at the head of his sleeping bag, folding his legs criss-cross. The mini lantern swings from a hook in the center of the ceiling, knocking against his head. He straightens it and shifts as well as he can.

You never realize just how big a *big guy* is until you're smooshed into a two-person tent with him. Grant is broad and muscular, and my heart might be racing for entirely different reasons if he weren't so totally unbothered. He's not acting like I've accepted an invitation into his lair. We're just chilling in his reading nook.

"This proves how susceptible I would be to kidnapping if given the proper lure."

He lifts an eyebrow. "That's concerning."

"I have a weakness." I look around the ultra small space. "It's neat in here. Very tidy."

When I get ready for bed, I'll have to shove the rest of my gear off my sleeping bag to get inside it.

"What are you in the mood for?"

"Well..." My gaze drops to his mouth. "I'm not sure..."

"Adventure, fantasy, sci-fi? One of the middle grade books you disparaged?"

My eyes snap down to his e-reader in my lap. Right. I am in the mood for reading. Obviously.

I switch it back on and scroll through the options. Something feels off, though, and it takes me a minute to realize what it is.

"How do you have all this extra stuff? The granola bars, the e-reader, the lantern. None of that was on the packing list."

His tent is fancy compared to my bare-bones version. I had no idea glamping was an option.

"I've been on a few hikes like this. I know what I want to have with me."

"Yeah, but you're breaking the rules." Generally, I don't care about the rules, but I had him pegged as someone who would.

But you know how first impressions can be totally deceiving? The mischief in his slow smile makes me realize that what I took to be an innocent, vanilla Clark Kent personality is just a mask. His All-American good looks make him seem mild and unassuming—the man underneath has a strong undercurrent of rogue about him.

"You learn the rules so you know how to break them," he explains. "If this were a more rigorous hike, I might be more cautious with the extra weight. But for a light walk—"

I scoff. "Excuse me, this is *not* a light walk for some of us."

"There's no reason I can't bring a few extra things," he finishes. "Plus, I know I can carry my extras."

"That feels a bit like a dig at me."

"It's not meant to be. I'm just well aware of my own abilities."

After Josh, excessive confidence became a turn-off for me. Being with a man whose ego required attention at all times got exhausting. But there's a line between confident and arrogant, and Grant never sticks a toe over. It's weird.

Weird and intriguing.

"Now." He points at the e-reader. "What do you feel like?"

I drag my eyes away from this mysterious mountain man and go back to scanning books. "You have a lot of Terry Pratchett on here. What are those like?"

"Fantasy and humor. Not much romance, but you might like it."

"Let's try one of those." I pass the device back to him.

He scrolls around for a minute. "How about we start at the beginning?"

"Where all the best stories start."

I'm a romance girl through and through, but with Grant reading the book and doing all the voices? By the time I slip my boots back on and scurry into my own tent a couple of hours later, he's won me over on fantasy.

Even if, way down deep, I still hope everyone gets their love story in the end.

TEN

LILA

"I'D KILL for an alpaca right about now." I roll my shoulders beneath my pack, wincing with every movement. It's not just the aches—after three days of hiking, everything feels gritty. Or, in the case of my hair, greasy. Deena said we get to swim-slash-wash today if we want, and all my clogged pores are crying out for relief. "It's normal to slip into a coma to get out of walking any more, right?"

We're hiking through dense forest, and by Grant's estimate, about halfway to our next campsite. We stopped thirty minutes ago at a stream to filter water for our hydration packs and secure snacks. Technically, it's been an easy morning, but I am over it.

I'm sorry, wilderness, but you're just too much for me to handle.

"Pretty normal," Grant says.

"Honestly—do you ever get sick of it?"

"I'm not sure how you're picturing me, but I reach my limit just like everyone else. I'm not Superman."

Too bad for him I've already imagined him in the costume, tights and all.

"And on this specific hike?"

He grins. "I'm not tired."

"Okay, Man of Steel. I'm definitely not Wonder Woman. At this point, the only reason I'm still moving is so I can prove to my sister that I can be tough like her. And also because if I laid down in the middle of the path, nobody would carry me home."

"I'd carry you. But then that post-hike boba tea would be your treat."

A sharp little pang pierces my heart. "Now I'm thinking about boba tea."

"Try to stay strong in these trying times."

"This hike is my villain origin story." I do sort of want to destroy the world right now.

It's pretty out here, though. Even I can't deny that. Especially today, when we passed a green lake tucked away in the woods—I can see the appeal. And I do mean *see only*. I would rather acknowledge it, take my pictures, and move on with my life than stay immersed in the experience for days on end.

I still worry just a little bit what this will mean for my promotion. If this trip will mean anything at all. Mayor Martinez knows I'm out here and why. If he asks how I liked it, am I supposed to lie? Rave about my uncomfortable sleeping mat and the lack of running water and the rabid owls? If I don't, will he find someone else for the tourism job?

Ugh. Now I want to cry myself into that coma.

Grant passes me his baggie of trail mix. It's all chocolate candies. There's a bright spot in my day, after all.

I stare at the multi-colored goodness. "Are you trying to seduce me?"

Now he's the one staring.

"Sorry, that just popped out. I meant to say 'thank you.'"

"Is chocolate the key to seducing you?"

Would he actually like to know?

"Probably." It's been a while since someone bothered trying

—which I'm just sensible enough not to say. I savor each piece, probably making scandalous sounds.

"Noted."

Grant Irwin, you flirt. If only he was staying in town for longer than a few days, maybe...

Heck, I don't even know what. I'm still a mess after Josh. I can just enjoy having a hiking buddy. It doesn't need to be more than that.

I slap at a mosquito sucking away on my arm. My eucalyptus oil shield isn't completely impenetrable. I've lost count of the itchy red marks I'm sporting. I look like I have some terrible medieval disease. It pairs nicely with my terrible medieval odor.

"Does the sister you're trying to show up live in Sunshine?"

"Yup. She's recently become an outdoors enthusiast, and told me about a million times how easy this trip would be." I exhale a soft laugh. "I think she knew if she said she could do it, I would feel like I have to prove I can, too. She set me up."

"A little sibling rivalry going on?"

"Always. I can't be mad at her, though. She helped me get my job here." I frown. "Actually, that should make me even more mad at her. I can't owe my little sister."

I'm joking. But also, I'm one hundred percent serious. If Hope hadn't let me work a little social media magic on her Christmas Festival this year, the mayor wouldn't have considered me for the events job. It's just one more thing that's completely upside-down in my life. I'm the oldest. I'm supposed to be the one she looks up to, not the one mooching off of her connections.

"I hear that. My brothers are dividing most of my responsibilities while I'm gone. I guarantee Rhett will use that as an excuse to slack off when I get back."

"Are you going straight home to Texas when this terrible ordeal is over?"

"Sometimes I get the feeling you're not enjoying yourself out here."

"Me? I'm having the time of my life. Look at all the…stuff." I gesture at the trees around us. My phone is crammed with pictures of them, all virtually identical pines just doing their thing.

"The 'stuff' is pretty impressive. But no, I'm not going straight back to Texas. I'll be around for a few weeks."

My heart does a funny little jig. "Oh? Are you doing another trip like this?"

"Are you looking for suggestions?"

"Heck no!" I would rather eat Grant's dry granola bars for a month.

"I'm staying at the Moonlight Lodge. This is as exciting as my vacation will get."

"Then we should change that." I'm not flirting, I swear. I only sound like I am because sometimes I talk before I think. Especially, apparently, with Grant. "You should come to the Fourth Fest. We're going to have a parade, a festival in town square with farmers' market booths and live music, and of course, fireworks."

His eyebrows lift. "That's you? The Fourth Fest? I saw the website when I researched my trip out here."

"That's me." I can't help my huge grin. I'm really proud of the work I've put into our town's Independence Day celebrations. I've done a couple of smaller events for Sunshine, but this is my first big festival. "No pressure if you already have plans, but it's going to be a huge hit."

"I was already planning to go."

"Really?"

"It's a good website."

I'm probably glowing, but I don't care. This is exactly what I love to hear. "Hopefully, my tourism website is just as good, and

I get this promotion. Otherwise, I'm going through a *lot* of eucalyptus oil for nothing."

"Is that the only thing that will make this trip a success for you? If you get the promotion?"

He doesn't sound like he's trying to be judgy, but his comment still hits something tender I don't want to look at too closely. "It is why I'm here."

On a normal day, I'd be sitting at my dining table, editing photos and planning social media messages about the Fourth Fest. I'd also be freshly showered and relatively free of bug bites.

"Sometimes I can plan for months for a mountain climb, but once I get there, I have to turn away before I reach the top because of unexpected bad weather."

Hmm. Feels like a *lower your expectations* speech. "Are you trying to tell me to prepare myself for figurative bad weather?"

"No. I'm saying, the outcome isn't always a guarantee. So it's good to find things you enjoy in the process, too."

Okay...he might have a point. I do sometimes get too obsessed on the end result and wind up losing focus on the middle bits. But this time around, it's like it's *all* forgettable middle bits. "You still owe me something fun."

He grins. "I'm working on it."

I'm still smiling like a fool when we catch up to the others. They're stopped at an overlook, gazing out at a huge blue lake. Pine trees grow right up to the edge of the water. In the distance, the Three Sisters mountain peaks complete the scene.

It's a great shot, and I have my phone out immediately, snapping pictures. I've been rationing the battery, but I'll need to plug it into my power bank tonight.

"Do you want some of you?" Grant asks. "For your behind-the-scenes, day-in-the-life stuff?"

I kind of love that he remembered that. A lot of people tune out as soon as I start talking about my social media. "Oh, no.

Even if my followers were interested in mountain lakes, they don't want to see me without makeup. The last time I posted an all-natural picture, my comments were flooded with helpful hints about the importance of concealer."

I force a laugh, but he just frowns.

"Then your followers don't know real beauty when they see it."

He holds my gaze, his compliment swirling through me, leaving glitter in its wake. For a laid-back mountain man, he sure can be a sweet talker.

"It makes it all worthwhile, doesn't it?" Shannon says to no one in particular.

I don't have it in me to come up with a snappy response. I *did* walk myself here. That's an accomplishment of sorts. And I can't deny the beautiful view. I soak it up, hoping for some kind of outdoorsy transformation. At least I'll have one moment of triumph to relay to Hope when we get back.

"That's our swimming hole today," Deena announces. "Trimble Lake. It might be brisk, but it's our best bet to avoid leeches."

I slowly turn to face Grant, who's watching me with soft amusement. Clearly, he's expecting a reaction. Predictably, I give him one.

"Leeches?" I mouth. It's more of a silent scream. He just lifts a shoulder like it's no big deal. Look, I like the man, but it's hard not to question a guy's life choices when the threat of blood-sucking parasites is such a blasé thing. No *Should I wear a wet suit to avoid infection?* No *Obviously we don't want to swim if it's only our "best bet."* Just a shrug and *What are you going to do?*

His unbothered attitude is strangely attractive.

"Did she scare Lila off the swim?" Scott's question is twenty percent curiosity, eighty percent glee.

"I'll swim if everyone else is getting in." If this is some hiker hazing ritual, then forget it.

"Oh, we're swimming." Cindy fans at her armpits. "It's time."

A chorus of agreement moves around the group.

Grant nods. "I'm swimming, too."

Great. Perfect. Bring on Leech Lake.

———

I do not want to swim in Leech Lake.

Everyone else has already trekked from camp down to the water and gotten in, but I'm still messing around in my tent. I'm decked out in my tank top and athletic shorts. I'm coated in sunscreen. I've got my paper-thin travel towel at the ready. The sun's sweltering enough that a cool dip will feel good, and I'm certainly smelly enough to need it.

But *leeches*. Even the slight possibility of them feels like too much.

I draw in a long, slow breath. It's either a quick dunk or live in my filth for two more days. How long could it take a leech to attach to me, anyway?

Forget that. I don't want to know.

I follow the path through the trees down to the access point. Pairs of hiking boots are tucked next to big rocks on the shoreline, along with camp towels and dry clothes. I slip off my boots, set my things aside, and inch into the cool water.

Then, I freeze. Did I hit my head on the walk down? Did I finally slip into that coma? Grant surfaces out of the lake several yards away from me, eyes closed, hands running through his hair as he gains his footing and stands waist-deep in the water. Droplets cascade down his bare chest to the top of his swim trunks. I knew the muscles would be there. I…was not expecting this much chest hair.

Also, he hasn't shaved this whole week, and the beard he's sporting does wicked things to my senses.

Before I can commit felony-level ogling, I drop my gaze to my feet. Focus on the pointy rocks covering the lake bed that are jabbing at my soles. Put that vision of manliness out of my head forever.

Ha. Unlikely. It's locked in.

"Don't hang out by the shore," Mitchell calls. He and Deena tread water about thirty feet away. "That's where you're at greatest risk of being discovered by our little bloodsucking friends."

Okay, *that* puts the vision of manliness out of my head.

I scramble deeper into the chilly water. Goosebumps break out over my skin as I submerge, but the sudden shock is the lesser evil here. While I can still touch the lake bed, I dunk my head under and rub my fingers over my scalp and through my hair. I can't use soap or shampoo, but after days of being covered in a fine layer of dirt, it's heavenly.

Treading water, I make my way closer to Grant. Naturally, I pretend I've only just now noticed him. *I didn't see you and your generous pectorals standing there.* "Is this the leech-free zone?"

"Should be."

"How can you tell?" Not that I don't trust his judgment, but more reassurance would be nice.

"It's not murky."

That's true. I can see his body pretty well from here. Not that I'm looking. *I'm not.*

"Wait, are you touching the bottom?" He's way too steady with the water at chest height, unlike the way my arms and legs constantly churn to keep myself upright.

"I'm a bit taller than you."

I stretch one foot down but can't reach anything. Then, a thought occurs, and I jerk my foot back. "Are there fish in here?"

"Yes."

"Big fish?"

He scans the lake. "Probably, given the size."

"*Biting* fish?"

One side of his mouth quirks. "A few things in here might be tempted to bite you."

That's it. Bath time's over. I start to turn back, but he gently takes hold of my forearm so I don't get far. He lets go again as soon as I pause my escape.

"I'm just teasing, princess. You don't have to get out." His giant grin isn't all that contrite. "It sounds like they swim in this lake every time they come out here. It's safe."

"If I see even a hint of fish fang or leech sucker, I'm out."

"That's fair." He rakes his fingers through his hair again, making it curlier than ever.

It's like this man was created specifically to throw me off guard. Not that it's just me. I'm sure women everywhere would have a similar reaction. So of all the camping trips in all the great outdoors, how did he wind up in mine?

I avert my gaze from the dusting of black chest hair, but my attention snags on something else. "What's your tattoo?"

He stills and lets me shift closer to get a better look. A black and gray mountain range cuts across the top of his right arm, but there's something more just beneath the water. I grab his elbow and lift it out to see.

"'Not all those who wander are lost.' Aww. You're a nerd." A mountain man with a Tolkien tattoo? He's so adorable.

"You know the quote." His eyebrows bob, telegraphing *takes one to know one.*

"Yeah, but you got it permanently inked on your body."

He looks sheepish but not entirely repentant. "I got it when I was twenty-four. I thought it was unique."

I spin in the water so he can see my right shoulder blade. "Tell that to my dahlia tattoo. It's not a butterfly on my lower back, but they're practically interchangeable."

It's a botanical design with a wash of maroon through the petals. I still love it, even though I saw something similar on every other woman I met in Seattle.

"It's pretty," he says as I paddle around to face him again. "Delicate. It suits you."

How does he have me blushing in borderline frigid water?

"Do you have any more tattoos?" I ask.

He smiles, looking ridiculously at home standing in a lake. "You mean, do I have any more tattoos for you to make fun of?"

"I'm not making fun. I think it's *precious*."

His laughter curls around me like the coziest blanket. "You sound like you want to get dunked, princess."

Half-laughing, half-shrieking, I splash myself away from him, but he immediately closes the distance again. He's super fast in the water, and he's got his hands wrapped around my upper arms in about two seconds.

"It'll be fun." His voice is all mischief and naughtiness.

"Not so close!"

He pauses, eyes searching mine, his hands loosening their grip as I bob in the water. I applaud his immediate response to my warning, but I might have reacted too strongly.

"I smell like a wet dog," I explain.

His gaze sparks. Warms. Heats up to inferno levels. Slowly, he leans closer, angling his face within an inch of mine until his nose brushes against my temple. He inhales. Now, I'm the one burning.

Nobody has ever smelled me before. If you'd asked, I would have said it's a weird thing to do. And yet, I'm responding to him as if he'd traced my skin with his mouth instead of the tip of his nose.

He pulls back just enough to meet my eyes. "You smell good."

Then, he lets me go and floats backward without a care, as if he didn't just *sniff* me. As if I didn't enjoy it. As if he hasn't seen me looking my worst, and still declared me beautiful. Amazing. Enough.

As if he isn't making me redefine exactly what would make this trip a success.

ELEVEN

GRANT

I KNOW this isn't my fault, but staring at the carnage that's descended at camp, I can't help but feel like I've jinxed Lila.

We hiked across an open meadow and over another stretch of lava rock on our last full day in the national forest. Around one, we set up camp, had lunch, and left our things behind for a short hike to a viewpoint. There, volcanic ridges covered in green pines stretched away in front of us, leading to three different mountain peaks from the ones we've seen at other points on the trek. It's a mountain lover's paradise out here.

But as soon as we returned to camp, evidence it had been ransacked while we were out greeted us. A scrap of blue fabric. A piece of red canvas. Lots and lots of scat.

"This is new." Mitchell tugs gently at the ground-level hole in Lila's tent. A six-inch tear has been chewed into it, and I think I can guess the guilty culprit.

Marmots. I've seen their work before. I'm not superstitious, but maybe it was bad luck to tell that particular story.

"We haven't had anything like this happen out here." Deena holds the piece of blue fabric.

I've memorized the shirt it came from.

Lila's face is as pale as it was when she caught the fish. "Do you think it's still in there?"

"Nah. There's an exit hole on this side." Scott's on the opposite end of her tent, looking at the damage like it's all part of the fun.

"There's one over here, too," Cindy adds from the back wall.

"Maybe there was more than one."

"More than one would explain all the poop."

Lila swats the side of the tent, watching the nearest rip in the fabric as though she expects several marmots to run out squealing. Nothing happens. She crouches to unzip the door, holding the zipper between her thumb and forefinger like it might bite. When she finally kneels inside, a sad little sound of dismay fills the air.

"My shirt...my extra socks...my leggings..."

"Did she keep any food in there?" Mitchell asks me.

"I don't think so." My thoughts head straight for the granola bar wrapper. I have no idea if she ever put it in one of the odor-proof bags. Judging by her wrecked tent, I have a sinking feeling she didn't.

Lila stands, shaking her head as though the scene is too unbelievable to accept. She puts her face in her hands, and her shoulders shudder. It's an unfortunate way to end her first hiking trip, but I hate to see her like this.

I move closer and slip a hand onto her back. I trace over her skin as though I can smooth out her sobs. "Hey. It's okay. It's just stuff. It can all be replaced. The important thing is, you're safe."

Not that marmots would have attacked her, but I can think of about a hundred ways this trip could have ended worse for her.

She pulls her fingers away from her eyes. Tears shine there, but...she's laughing?

"I'm cursed, aren't I?"

Her giggles make my heart lighter, easing away some of the guilt. "I wouldn't say *cursed*."

No better explanation comes to mind, though.

"I'm not meant to be a camper. Or a backpacker. Or a lake swimmer." She swats at the tears rolling down her cheeks, but she keeps on laughing. "I'm just a girl who likes to stay inside my cozy home and sip drinks while I read books. I want to move from one temperature-controlled room to another. I'm just not outdoorsy. I'm sorry."

"Don't be. I'm not."

Her wry expression gets lost in a fit of giggles. "There's so much poop in there. More than I think a marmot even weighs."

"They're magical creatures."

That sends her into another round of laughter.

"Let's air out your sleeping bag." Deena stoops to pull it from the tent, shaking marmot scat as she goes. Mitchell does the same with the sleeping mat.

As the tent flap flutters behind them, I catch a glimpse of Lila's clothes strewn around the floor. That marmot must have taste-tested everything in its effort to get to the wrapper.

"I checked the other tents," Shannon says. "No sign of any damage."

"Congratulations." Brian reaches across me to shake Lila's hand. "This is a badge of honor."

"An honor? Really?" She sounds like she's ready to collapse into laughter all over again, but she shakes his hand.

"Next time you're sitting around a campfire and somebody starts complaining about worst hikes, nobody's going to be able to top this story."

"I guess it's good to have bragging rights. Kind of."

"Only a small nibble in the sleeping bag," Deena says as she and Mitchell join the rest of us circled around Lila's tent. "I can patch it up when we get back."

"At least it happened on the last day," Mitchell adds.

"I'm so sorry. This is all my fault. I think it was after the granola bar wrapper I had in my pocket."

"I saw the shredded foil. It's all right. Things happen. We're just glad nobody got hurt."

"But we do need to talk about where you're going to sleep tonight," Mitchell says. "The sleeping bag will be fine, but the tent won't keep out the cold very well like this."

Lila frowns down at the open tent. "I didn't think about that."

"Grant has space in his tent." He sends a careful look my way. He's not quite offering, but it's clear he thinks someone should.

Lila's eyes also shoot to mine, brimming with questions.

"Of course you can share my tent." I've slept in two-person tents with strangers on trips like this before. This wouldn't be any different.

Except Lila's not a stranger. And I haven't been able to get her out of my head for four days. And having her so close just might kill me in all the best possible ways.

But I can set that aside so she can sleep in comfort tonight. Well—relative comfort.

"We would divide up so Mitchell can share with Grant, except we sleep in a two-person sleeping bag." Deena looks to the other couples, silently testing if either of them are willing to split up.

Cindy smiles but shakes her head. "I'm a really light sleeper. I don't think I would be able to sleep if I wasn't with Brian. Sorry."

"And Scott snores like a freight train," Shannon says with a laugh. "Unless Grant has heavy-duty earplugs like I do, he wouldn't sleep a wink if they paired up. I'm sorry, Lila. I think you'll have to go with Grant."

"It wouldn't be the first time she's been in his tent." Scott lifts his eyebrows, but looks away as though claiming innocence of what he just said.

I figured they'd noticed as much—there are no secrets on a trip like this—but I didn't think anyone would bring it up to our faces. Apparently, I gave them too much credit.

"We've been reading together." I read more *Color of Magic* last night until Lila could barely keep her eyes open, and she ducked out of my tent with a huge yawn.

He elbows his wife in the side. "I remember when we used to read in our tent."

I ignore his insinuations, and turn to Lila. "I don't mind sharing."

She drops her mouth open but snaps it shut again, like she's torn between two answers. Given the circumstances, there's only one feasible option.

"Okay. Thank you."

I'm not sure she's as comfortable as she's pretending to be, but I'll do whatever it takes to put her at ease. This is only about keeping her warm.

Even if I spend the whole night trying not to think about all the other ways I could do just that.

———

After dinner, Lila appears at my tent, toting her sleeping mat.

"I figured we should get everything set up before the sun goes down. We don't want to have to fumble around in there in the dark." She closes her eyes slowly and doesn't look at me when she opens them again. "You know what I mean."

"Go ahead." I unzip the door and hold it aside for her. I'd

already slid my mat and bag as close to the door as possible. There's enough room for her, but only just.

She crawls inside and arranges her mat. No matter how she pokes and prods, there's no space between them. "I'll go get the sleeping bag."

I stare down at the practically overlapping sleeping mats, trying to erase every single thought that crops up in response. I need to treat this like an emergency situation. I just can't think of what the protocol should be.

A minute later, she returns, bulky bag in her arms like a limp bride. "I'm so sorry. It still smells a bit like marmot."

"It's my fault. I should have taken the possibility more seriously."

"Yeah, but I still had the granola bar wrapper in my pants like a dummy."

"Who gave it to you in the first place?"

She rolls her eyes. "You saved everyone from a wretched case of the hangries. It was very noble of you."

It doesn't feel very noble now that it's led us to sleeping in the same tent. Not my end game, but I can't pretend I'm disappointed.

Before she can duck through the door, I stop her. "I don't mind sleeping in your tent tonight."

"What? No, it's ruined. You'd be too cold."

"That doesn't matter if you're uncomfortable with this. I can sleep in extra layers. Say the word, and I'll move my things."

"No." She stands straighter. "We're grownups. This is no big deal. We're just doing this to share warmth. Wait—" She slashes a hand through the air. "Pretend I didn't say it that way."

"I know what you meant."

She lays out the sleeping bag. I catch her trying to create any kind of space between them, but they touch.

It's going to be a long night.

TWELVE
LILA

"DO you want to read for a while?" If my voice comes out squeakier than usual, Grant doesn't seem to notice.

I might be freaking out ever so slightly over the idea of sharing a tent with him. He's been nothing but gentlemanly and kind, and I know he's not expecting us to get frisky in there. Still...my stomach's swarming with butterflies that aren't entirely the happy kind.

"Actually, I wanted to try one last time to show you something fun. If you're up for it."

In the fading light, Grant somehow looks more earnest than ever. Like he really, truly needs to help me find something good to take home from this journey. It's endearing and oh, so sweet. I get the feeling I could say yes to anything he suggested and be perfectly safe as long as he's right there with me.

"It's not a night swim, is it?" I tease. "I heard leeches like the darkness."

"It's not a night swim, but it does require the cover of darkness."

"Ooh, ominous. Is it a bird sacrifice?"

That throws him off. "You think I would kill a bird?"

"I was thinking the birds would sacrifice me."

He grins. "That doesn't sound like fun. I want to walk a little deeper into the woods and stargaze for a while."

"Oh. I've never done that before."

"I figured. You won't get a view like this in the city because of all the light pollution. What do you think? Join me?"

I look out into the trees. In our immediate vicinity, it's still twilight, but beyond our camp circle, it already looks pretty dark. My mind fills with creatures great and small. Most of them have fangs. "Is it safe?"

"We won't go far, and I'll have my bear spray at the ready."

"That wasn't a yes."

He tilts his head down, fighting a smile. "I'll keep you safe, princess."

A tremor runs through me, but I tell myself it's only because of the falling temperature. "I guess I'm up for it."

He looks me over. "Is this the warmest gear you have?"

I'm in my fleece-lined leggings, long-sleeved nightshirt, and fleece jacket. "You don't think it's enough?"

Crouching, he rummages around in the tent before reappearing with something in his hands. "Here."

He slips a knit beanie over my head. I've kept my hair in two braids since the swim yesterday, and after he rights the hat, he runs his hands over their ends. "That should help."

He pulls a similar hat down on his own head. Now he's all blue eyes, huge smile, and beard. I kind of miss the dimple, but the beard is winning me over.

"Wait—this is even more stuff you're not supposed to have!" I whisper-shout it, but I think he gets the point.

"And I regret nothing. You look good wearing my hat. Ready?"

I'm...flustered. Speechless. Delightfully warm.

He grabs a flashlight and zips his tent closed before heading along the path we took to find the mountain views this afternoon. The rest of camp is quiet. Mitchell's about to climb into his tent as we pass.

"Don't go too far," he says like a true camp dad.

Grant acknowledges him with a wave. "We won't."

The deeper we go along the path, the darker it gets. Soon, I'm struggling to keep from tripping over imaginary rocks and tree roots. "I can't see anything."

Grant stops and takes my hand. I cling to his arm, committing his biceps to memory.

"Sorry. It's not much farther."

He's right—my stomach's still soaring from the warmth of his hand and the press of his arm when we reach a small clearing. He leads us to a fallen log, and after checking it for anything unexpected, we sit down.

"Do you do this a lot?" I ask.

He flicks off the flashlight and turns to me in the sudden darkness. "Lead women into the forest?"

I nudge him with my shoulder. "Go stargazing."

He nods—I think. My vision's still swimming from the aftershocks of the flashlight glare.

"I noticed this spot on our walk. Seemed like a good place."

"How often do you go on trips like this?" Obviously it's a lot, if Mitchell's claiming he's climbed half the mountains in the country.

"A couple of times a year. I took a lot more when I was younger."

"How old are you? You keep talking about your younger years as if you're ready for retirement."

He turns his face toward me in the dark. I can't see his features anymore, only shadowy outlines of black on black. "Thirty-six."

"You're right, that is pretty old." I nudge him again because apparently, I can't stop teasing him. "I'm thirty, so I'm still in the prime of life."

"No argument there."

After a minute, he looks up at the sky, and I do the same.

My breath pauses on its way through my lungs. Hundreds—thousands—of stars spread over us like a glittery blanket. A lighter haze shines directly overhead creating billowy, glowing clouds. I don't have words to describe how beautiful it is.

"Is that the Milky Way?" I ask.

In my peripheral vision, Grant hums confirmation.

"I've never seen it before."

I stare at the sky as though I can drink it in. As though I need to memorize this view so I can carry it with me always. Obviously, I always knew they were out there. I've seen stars before. But I've never seen anything like *this*.

Something moves on my face, and I brush it away. It takes me a second to realize I'm crying. I laugh softly at my silly, over-dramatic response, but I don't take my eyes off of the stars.

"It's so beautiful." I barely whisper the words, because that's all I've got.

Grant's hand finds mine in the darkness again and holds tight. "The most beautiful thing I've ever seen."

I don't know how long we stare in silence. Long enough for me to count three shooting stars. Long enough for my shoulder to sag against Grant's. And long enough for me to get a really nasty crick in my neck, but it's worth it.

"Thanks for coming out here with me," he says. "I can't remember the last time I relaxed like this."

I drag my eyes away from the star-studded show above us. "But you do outdoorsy things all the time."

"I do. But sometimes all the hikes and campouts and mountain climbs are more of a distraction than something I truly experience."

"What are you trying to distract yourself from?" I ask softly.

He inhales long and deep. Somewhere in the darkness, crickets chirp. Maybe my question went too far?

But he finally answers. "A few years ago, I had a relationship that ended suddenly. Totally blindsided me. For a while after that—too long, really—I wanted to think about anything else. I climbed a lot in that first year, but I couldn't tell you much about what I saw or did. I only knew I needed to get out of my head."

"You really loved her." I don't even mean to say it, and I hope it doesn't sound like I want to pour salt in his wound. But just telling me a few quick sentences about it, I can hear in his voice how deeply this affected him.

Josh started dating again the same week I gave him back his ring. Considering the circumstances, I'm not sure he ever stopped.

"I thought I loved her. Now, I don't know if that was really love. I think I wanted it to be more than it was."

I understand that too well. For a while, Josh was everything to me. My favorite obsession who seemed equally obsessed with me. But now, I'm not sure that image of perfection was real love, either. Maybe it's been tainted by everything that happened afterward. Or maybe my feelings for him were never as deep as I'd hoped they were.

"I'm sorry." I squeeze his hand that still grips mine. "She sounds like she didn't know how good she had it."

I've only known him four days, but this is *not* a man you walk away from easily. I don't want to say goodbye to him tomorrow, and she dropped him after they were together who knows how long? Impossible.

Even in the darkness, his small smile stands out. "Thanks."

I turn my face up to the stars. "I didn't move back to Sunshine because I missed my family. I did miss them, but...I found out my fiancé was cheating. The old classic. He sent a text to me that was supposed to go to her. Rookie mistake."

Every other weekend after he proposed, he would send me to the spa for a massage or to get my nails done. My girlfriends were all jealous of how Josh spoiled me. I thought it was a sign of how much he loved me—I never dreamed it was an excuse to get me out of the house. Until the day I got the message he'd meant to send to her.

She's gone. We've got at least two hours. Get here as quick as you can, baby.

Baby. He'd never called *me* baby. Not that I'd wanted him to—it's not my favorite endearment. Even knowing that, I'd stared at the text message for agonizing minutes, desperate to make it mean anything else. My stomach had rolled and a sickness like I'd never known sank deep in my chest, but I couldn't bring myself to go straight home and catch him in the act.

"At first, he tried to deny it. I was reading it wrong, obviously the message didn't mean anything. Then, I think he just wanted me to accept it, you know? Like this was part of the package deal with him. 'All guys do it,' he'd said. So, I broke things off."

The break had been coming on for a long time, but I couldn't just smile and overlook cheating like I had for so much else.

"I was immediately replaced at my job because I was dumb enough to work for him. I moved out of his apartment and had to resort to couch surfing. And to make it even worse, most of my friends sided with him when the dust settled."

Of course they did. Everybody wants to be on Joshua Brandt's good side. Tech genius, media darling, one of Seattle's rising stars. Nobody was going to choose me in that scenario.

Grant's thumb traces patterns over the back of my hand, grounding me.

"It sounds so stupid, but a few months ago, I had *everything*. Now, I'm back in my hometown, trying to claw my way into a decent job, and wishing I could live up to the Lila everybody thinks I am. Sometimes I feel like a teacup that nobody realizes has been smashed and broken."

He lets go of my hand, and for half a second, fear worms its way into my chest. I've said too much. I'm too much work. He's going to walk away and leave me here in the wilderness.

But he wraps his arm around my shoulders, holding me tightly against him. "You're not broken, princess."

I stare at the stars and pretend the fresh tears falling down my cheeks are because of the night sky's overwhelming beauty instead of a very different sense of overwhelm.

"Sounds like he didn't know how good he had it," Grant says.

I sniffle but have to laugh, too. "That's not as comforting as I thought it would be when I said it."

"He sounds like a complete idiot who didn't deserve you. I'd like to meet up with him and say some choice words. Is that better?"

"That's much better." I lay my head on his shoulder and relax against him. "What are the choice words?"

"'I am going to punch you in the face.'"

"Eloquent."

We look at the stars for a while longer. I don't know why, but my heart feels a little bit lighter. Is that all it takes? Confessing my deepest hurts and humiliations to a mountain man? I've been carrying around all this guilt from the breakup, counting it as one more piece of evidence that I'm a fraud. That's not *gone*, but right here and now, it can't touch me.

"This is it," I tell Grant. "This is the good part of the journey."

Even if I don't get the promotion, this moment under the stars makes the whole trip worth it.

To be clear—I have no idea what I'll do if I *don't* get that promotion. But I wouldn't trade this moment for anything else.

He holds me tighter, and I swear his lips brush against my temple. "It's the good part for me, too."

———

I don't know if confessing our past heartbreaks makes climbing into adjoining sleeping bags an hour later better or worse. I shimmy into mine as quickly as possible, trying to make room for Grant to get comfortable, too. The *shh-shh* of our sleeping bags slipping against each other feels crazy loud in the stillness. We lie down as though it isn't thoroughly awkward to share this kind of space after knowing each other a handful of days.

Maybe it isn't awkward. Maybe co-ed stranger sleeping arrangements are normal on long hiking trips. It's just that *none* of this feels quite normal. But Grant's totally unaffected.

That's a good thing. He's not making this weird. Somehow, though, him being calm is just amplifying my weirdness. I can't explain it.

I watch him as well as I can in the darkness. "Are you facing me?"

"This is the side I sleep on."

"This is the side *I* sleep on." We're lying face-to-face in a tiny tent. Okay...that's not troublesome at all. "We're going to breathe on each other."

This isn't what I'm worried about, but it's not like I can just say, *Hey, what are the odds we wind up tangled against each other in the night?* Or, more concerningly, *What if sleeping cuddled next to you is exactly as cozy and comfortable as I imagine it would be, and it ruins all other sleeping arrangements for me forever?*

I've been doing a lot of imagining lately.

He chuckles softly. "I'm not worried about you breathing on me, princess."

"I get really bad morning breath."

"I'll survive."

He should really take the threat more seriously, but I guess that's on him.

"What if I have a nightmare and kick you in the night?"

A pause. "Do you get a lot of nightmares?"

"Mostly about birds." I chew the inside of my cheek. "If you hear any snoring, just assume it's all Scott, okay?"

The tiny little laugh I force out edges close to hysterical.

He props himself up on one elbow. "Would you feel better if I slept in your tent?"

"What?" I snake an arm out of my sleeping bag and pull him back down onto his mat. "No, I don't want you to go."

He settles back down again. "Then what's wrong?"

"Nothing's wrong." I snuggle myself deeper into my sleeping bag, grateful for the darkness. "You're just really unbothered about all of this."

"Princess." The nickname comes out in a low rumble. "I am anything but unbothered about sleeping next to you."

A glowing spark of adrenaline pinballs through my body. *Wow.*

"Oh. Okay, then." I duck my face into my sleeping bag, hiding the huge grin he can't see anyway. "As long as we're on the same page."

He exhales a soft laugh. "Goodnight, princess."

"Goodnight, mountain man."

THIRTEEN

GRANT

I'M HOT. Hot and surprisingly sweaty. And...deeply content?

It takes my morning brain about ten seconds to fully wake up and realize that the extra warmth surrounding me is from Lila's body tucked up against mine. My arm is wrapped around her, my hand dipped into the top of her sleeping bag to rest against her upper back. Her face is almost pressed against mine, her fingers twisted in my shirt.

I shift so I can see her better. She's still wearing my green knit hat, a fact that makes all of my nerve endings stop and pay attention. She's stunning like this, completely peaceful. I move my hand from her back to capture one of her braids, running my thumb over the plait.

This is just temporary. It can't last. Even if I weren't going home in a few weeks, this bubble Lila and I are in would burst one way or another. Still...I'm growing fond of the bubble.

If I were smart, I would extract myself from her death grip on my shirt and escape the tent. Make some coffee and let us start the day free of awkwardness. I guess I'm not that smart. Nothing's going to get me out of this position but her.

I breathe her in. Despite her fears the other day, there's nothing unpleasant in her scent. If I knew it wouldn't wake her, I would lean even closer and fill my lungs with her.

Way to keep things firmly on the awkward side of the line.

Eventually, she stirs, and instead of pulling away from me, she burrows deeper. Her hand in my shirt pulls me closer, her cheek grazes mine. I make a sound. It might be a groan, I can't say for sure. But that's what finally shakes her from sleep.

Where I woke up piece by piece, she wakes all at once. Her eyes fly open wide just a few inches from mine. She releases my shirt like it's on fire. Then, she covers her face with her hands and rolls until she's facing away from me.

"Grant!" Her hands muffle her miserable moan. "I'm so sorry! I didn't mean to do that!"

Not going to lie—an apology is the last thing I want right now. All I want is her, back in my arms. Immediately. It's this, even more than her embarrassment, that pulls me from the spell her snuggles had me under.

"It's okay, Lila." I sit up and run my fingers through my hair. Sleeping in my clothes had seemed the most convenient option last night, but it isn't the best look this morning. "I was about to go get breakfast."

"Right, just as soon as I finished pawing you." She drags her hands down her face, then rubs at her mouth. "Ugh, I've been *drooling*, too."

"I didn't see any drool."

She rolls enough to cut her eyes to mine. "We're going to pretend this morning never happened, right?"

I pause a beat. "Sure. You want some tea?"

Her eyebrows tug together like she's about to ask me why I'm so *unbothered* again. The truth is, I'm completely bothered. No way on earth can I pretend this morning never happened.

Waking up with her in my arms is burned into my memory. I'd like to relive it again, as soon as conveniently possible.

But since she's already asking me to forget about it, I need coffee. Breakfast. Anything to get me out of this tent.

"No, thanks. I'll just..." She looks around the tiny space. Finding nothing to occupy her, she sags deeper into her sleeping bag. "I need five more minutes."

"Is this hurkle-durkling?"

"Half hurkle-durkling, half dying of embarrassment."

"You don't have anything to be embarrassed about."

She laughs. "I practically drooled on your face."

"Very few men would complain about that."

She makes a sound like an angry bear cub and swings her hand over her shoulder, shooing me away. "Go get your coffee. Let me drown in regret."

"That hurts, princess." That word pinches something deep in my chest, but she doesn't need to know I mean it literally. Certain words and phrases become sore spots when you've been left at the altar. *Regret. Mistake. I can't do this.*

I love you, but I'm not in love with you.

I shake myself out of cataloging my trigger words and climb from the tent, leaving Lila to her regrets. I have none.

But if I stay in here any longer, I just might.

By design, the hike back to the pick-up point is the shortest leg of the trip. Lila gives no indication we woke up in each other's arms this morning. If anything, I get the feeling she's trying to distract me by giving voice to every thought that comes into her head. She comments on the clouds of bugs in the air, how lucky it is her hiking boots didn't give her blisters this week, and her plans for decimating Sunshine's water supply as soon as she gets home.

"I'm going to take a shower and use up all the hot water. When the tank warms back up, I'm going to do it all over again." She groans softly. "With *soap*."

"Soap? Aren't you fancy."

"Then, I'm going to sleep in my comfy, cozy bed. The refrigerator's ice maker clanging around will be the only spooky sound to keep me awake at night."

"You've been bothered by sounds out here?" It can take a while to get used to sleeping out in the open. I don't like the idea she was afraid in her tent and never said anything.

"There's a million things in the woods, and all of them make noise. I only slept well last night because—"

Her gaze darts to mine. She closes her mouth, clearly rethinking the end of that sentence.

"Because?" I prompt.

She shrugs. "It didn't feel as spooky when you were there."

My chest puffs up as though I actually defended her from wild animals.

When we reach the parking lot we started from a few days ago, the Horizon Hikes twelve-seater van already waits for us. A teenage girl jumps out of the driver's side and runs over to hug Deena and Mitchell.

"You're supposed to be at grandma's," Mitchell says.

"I know, but I figured I'd give Curtis a break." She's trying to play it cool, but she can't stop looking over at Lila. "Because I'm such a good employee."

Deena laughs. "You're on thin ice, miss."

The girl puts her hands together, silently pleading.

Mitchell opens the back of the van and helps load our gear while Deena leads her over to us. The teen looks like she might burst from glee.

"Lila, this is our daughter, Skye. She apparently only mostly-legally drove the van here so she could meet you."

"Oh, wow. I'm flattered you would resort to borderline crime, Skye." Lila's wide smile is all warmth, but she works to smooth out the hair that's escaped from her double braids.

"I've been following *Genuinely_Lila* for years. You're kind of my idol." Skye makes a face. "That sounds weird. I'm not a stalker or something. I just really love your style."

"Thank you. I love yours. Look at that cute top! I'm so jealous."

Skye beams. "I love the dress you wore to that charity gala last summer. The one with the beadwork in the neckline and all the tiers?"

"The only downside with that dress is my hair caught on the beads all night." Lila pulls an exaggerated frown. "Would have been better with an updo."

"I would kill for a dress like that for my graduation party."

"Please stop saying you would kill for fashion," Mitchell deadpans as he hefts Shannon's pack into the van. "It makes me question my parenting."

Lila looks her up and down. "You can have the dress, if you want. We're pretty similarly sized."

Skye doesn't say anything for a minute, just breathes so fast I start to think she might be hyperventilating.

"Do you mean it?" she finally asks.

"Sure. I'd be honored to know it had a good home."

"Can I hug you right now?"

Lila laughs. "Of course."

Everyone else starts piling into the van's three rows of seats. Skye gives Lila a brutal hug before asking for a selfie, too. Lila's smile strains at the edges, but she nods and manages a wide one by the time Skye has her phone out.

The ride into town is full of conversation—the couples

behind me making plans for dinner in Bend, and Skye recounting for Lila all of her favorite posts. I just listen, fascinated. I have social media, but I don't do much with it. Lila's obviously engaged there in a way that encouraged Skye to think of her as a long-distance friend before they ever met in person.

Skye can't stop grinning and waves her hands in the air as she chatters. Lila smiles along, but there's an undercurrent of awkwardness here, too. I've seen her in enough uncomfortable situations over the last few days to recognize the signs. I'm just curious about the reasons.

When we reach Sunshine and Horizon Hikes, Lila gets a reprieve from Skye's enthusiasm while we unload our packs and gather our things. Deena wheels out her purple luggage, as shiny as ever.

"Clean clothes." Lila croons and strokes the bag like she's been reunited with a pet.

"Thought you'd be happy to see that again," Deena says. She looks over her shoulder to where Mitchell and Skye are talking. "I hope you don't feel you have to give Skye a dress in return for this trip. We'll be totally square with the social media we talked about."

"Oh, not at all. I have no plans to wear that dress again. If I don't give it to her, I'll just wind up donating it. It's really no trouble."

Deena still looks skeptical. "If you're sure. After you've had a chance to recover, let's talk about what you have in mind for the posts. Send me a text, and we'll arrange something—I typically alternate trips with our other guide."

"Thank you, I will. Post-shower. And Skye can call me about the dress whenever."

After saying thank you a few more times, our hiking group winds up on the sidewalk for our own goodbyes.

"Are you sure we can't tempt you to join us for a drink in Bend tonight?" Scott asks.

"We'd love to pick your brain a little more about your climbs," Brian adds.

"I appreciate it, but I'll probably just decompress tonight."

Scott glances over my shoulder, where Lila is talking with Shannon and Cindy. "Decompress, huh? Good luck with that."

Their ride share arrives, and the goodbyes become more vigorous before they climb inside and the car pulls away. Lila and I turn to face each other. Her small, genuine smile lights me up.

"I think I owe you a boba tea," she says.

I'm willing myself not to respond with an overeager *Anytime, anywhere,* when Mitchell appears at my side. I motion for Lila to give me a minute. She nods and wanders a few feet down the sidewalk to wait.

"We hope you had a good time with us this trip. I know it's not your usual type of outing, but it's a thrill to have had you with us."

I laugh. "I'm not sure I deserve that, but I had the best time."

In spite of what Mitchell seems to believe, I'm still fully an amateur. I climb because I love it, but nobody's paying attention to what I do. I don't think I would enjoy it as much if they did.

"We mostly get young families, and we love them, but it might be a little light for someone who's not a first-timer. We'd like to offer more adventurous hikes, but we're still working on expanding our crew."

"This was exactly what I needed this time around."

"Glad to hear it. Well, enjoy the rest of your vacation."

I say goodbye and turn to find Lila standing still as a statue not far from me, staring at the car at the curb in front of her. She looks like someone just offered to take her fishing. A man dressed in tan slacks and a white polo gets out of the car and rounds it until they're face to face. He slides his aviator sunglasses off and flashes a wide smile like he thinks someone's taking pictures.

"Josh?" Shock and disgust fill her single syllable.

So. This is the ex-fiancé. Even if she hadn't told me enough to hate this guy on sight, I'd be halfway there already. He oozes arrogance and unearned superiority.

"Lila. I didn't expect to see you as soon as I pulled into town. The stars must be in my favor."

"What are you doing here?"

She doesn't sound happy to see him. I have no right to care either way, but it's still satisfying.

"We always talked about me buying property in town—let's say I'm here on a shopping spree." His gaze slowly drops from her head to her toes and back. Somewhere on the journey, it turns from lascivious to something less appreciative. "You don't look so good, Lilabird. Are you sick?"

Lilabird? I'm ready to grab this guy by his tiny collar and haul him against his car. What kind of pet name is that? There's some small chance he doesn't know about her phobia, but watching him for two minutes has me convinced he specifically chose it because he does.

She smooths out the clothes she's been wearing off and on for days. "I feel great."

He lifts a skeptical eyebrow. "I heard things have been rough for you since you gave up on us, but I didn't think it was this bad."

I'm ready for her to lay into him and shred this guy's pride, but she doesn't say anything. She just stares open-mouthed, like she's at a total loss how to react. She jumped to my defense at the smallest slight back on the trail but can't seem to find the same grit for herself when faced with her ex?

Apparently, her defensive streak has rubbed off on me. What I'm about to do is massively stupid and ill-advised, but the second it comes to mind, my feet start moving.

When I reach her, I slip an arm around her waist and kiss her temple, nuzzling in. She blinks up at me as if I woke her from a daze.

"Hey, princess."

Rhett would be so proud.

FOURTEEN
LILA

I STARE AT GRANT. We're apparently on two very different pages in our flirtationship right now. Not that I mind the contents of his page—I'm a big fan of having his arm around me. It's just that my body's in a little bit of turmoil, considering the big swing from folding in on itself after being confronted with Josh, to bubbling with fizzy excitement when Grant purred the word "princess" in my ear.

Out of the corner of my eye, I catch sight of Josh. He stands there looking increasingly disgruntled, like when he's not recognized right away by the maitre d' at a restaurant and it's suggested he might have to wait for a table.

Grant looks over and notices him. "Hey, man."

It's only two words, but that greeting is the least friendly thing I've heard him say. I finally catch up to the idea this might be more than spontaneous affection. This might be Superman flying in to rescue me.

"Lila, who is this?" Josh's question carries an undercurrent of demand, as though he has a right to know anything about me at all.

"This is Grant, my..." My what, exactly? Stargazing friend?

Snack supplier? Man I've known for all of five days? He squeezes me tighter against him, and my hands automatically go around him.

Dang. He doesn't mess around on ab day.

No, Lila. Focus.

His eyes widen a touch, like he's trying to convey a secret message in the subtle movement. Still, I think I get it.

If I'm wrong, I'll have to move to a whole new country this time.

"He's my boyfriend," I blurt out.

I guess I didn't sell that so well because Josh's mouth curls into a smirk. Someone else gives a very loud gasp, however. I look past Grant's shoulders to see the worst of all possible witnesses: my mother.

Living in Sunshine has its perks, but the odds of running into someone you don't want to see on any given day are exceptionally high.

"Lila." She swoops over to us, eyes darting between the three key players like she's not sure who deserves the more pointed stare. "This is unexpected."

She could mean literally so many things in this moment. My ex-fiancé standing here looking like he's in town for a summer wedding. Grant with his arm slung casually around me as if we do this every day. Me, disheveled and dirty like I just rolled out of the woods. *Oh, wait.*

"Joshua." She gives him a polite nod, but no more than that. Go, Mom.

He appears far more relaxed. "Helena. It's lovely to see you again."

She turns to us. "And this is...?"

"Your mother doesn't know your boyfriend?" Josh says. Can a person pull a muscle in their face from smirking too hard? *One can only hope...*

I fight the urge to wax off his eyebrows, and paste on a big smile for my mother. "Mom, this is Grant. We met on the Horizon Hikes trip. Grant, this is my mom, Helena Parrish."

Nerves skitter through me as her eyes get comically wider. Clearly, she didn't expect me to go into the woods for five days and come back with a significant other. I think we're all in agreement on that one.

I feel weirdly protective of Grant as she looks him over. Given the two choices, it's hard to say who I would expect her to appreciate more. Debonair Josh in his expensive outfit and French cologne? Or rugged Grant who looks like he can split wood with his bare hands?

I got my non-outdoorsy genes from her, so I can't be sure his trail guide chic will win her over. I'll just have to count on the whole *cheated on me* thing to keep Mom's focus where it belongs.

"It's good to meet you, ma'am." He shakes her hand, and I swear she's swooning already.

In a sea of horrible awkwardness, that's one tiny spot of relief.

"Ooh, that accent. Where are you from, Grant?"

"Born and raised in Texas."

"Really?" She looks excessively impressed by that, as though she's always hoped I would snag myself a Texan. Her eyes cut to me, and some of her excitement fades. "Lila, how did you get those holes in your shirt?"

"Marmot. We should probably get going—"

"Wait just a minute. I want to know how all of this started between you two."

Of course she does. Hope and I don't love romance books for nothing. It doesn't matter that we're tired and filthy and standing on the sidewalk on Maple Street for everyone to see. Mom's already got dreams running through her head about the two of us, and she wants to fill in as many details as she can.

"Yes, tell us more about your new *boyfriend*, Lila." Josh doesn't use air quotes, but I hear them.

"I would, but we have to go get Grant checked into his hotel." I pat his stomach and have to force myself not to trace the muscles beneath his shirt. I guess pawing at him isn't only something I do when I'm asleep. *Bad Lila.*

"How about dinner?" Mom says. "My husband and I would love to get to know you, Grant."

I adore her, but a family dinner invite would be totally inappropriate at this stage even if everything with him were totally real. Hope wasn't exaggerating when she said Mom doesn't have a middle setting when it comes to our love lives.

"Grant has dietary restrictions, so..."

"I don't mind accommodating." She looks so happy for us, she'd probably cater to just about anything at this point, including bending over backward for made-up food preferences. One Kosher, gluten-free, vegan, diabetic-friendly menu, coming right up.

"I'll text you." Next month, after Grant is safely back in Texas.

"You're both coming to Hope's engagement party, then?"

I think the creeping feeling moving through me is my bones shriveling up. I just gave myself a faux boyfriend right before my sister's big celebration. Either I drag him with me and field questions about our "relationship" all night, or I fake a breakup in the next week and field questions about *that* all night. This has to be some previously-undiscovered low beneath rock bottom.

Lesser evil, wherefore art thou?

"Yup. Yes. We're definitely doing that."

Mom looks satisfied. I can't make myself check to see how

Grant's handling it. He's been so sweet to me, but it would take a saint to deal with this level of psychosis without a few reservations.

"But now we've really got to run, so…" I tug him along, but he's so big, it's hard to get him moving.

"I didn't catch your last name," Josh says.

"He didn't drop it," I snap. The minute he has Grant's last name, he'll find everything there is to know about him online. Home address, every picture he's ever posted to social media, that outdoors article Mitchell mentioned—Josh loves a good scavenger hunt. I don't want to subject Grant to all of that if I can help it.

Kind of hypocritical, considering I just subjected him to the whole *my boyfriend* declaration. I can't get too self-righteous about wanting to protect the man, but still. Josh wouldn't use any discretion.

Crossing my arm in front of Grant, I shift to his other side so I can steer him away from our audience. I wave goodbye to Mom, but don't bother making eye contact with Josh.

"Good to meet you, Grant," Mom calls.

"You too, ma'am." His accent practically demands a cowboy hat to tip.

We march half a block away before he turns up a side street. We pass a pizza place and a yoga studio, but Grant keeps walking. His arm is still around me—I'm not quite ready to discuss what just happened and lose that warmth.

My roller bag hits an uneven patch of sidewalk and capsizes, so I stop to right it. As soon as I do, Grant takes the handle from me, his duffel bag still over one shoulder. We start walking again, but his arm doesn't return to my waist.

I guess that's my cue.

"I am so sorry about this. I shouldn't have said that back there. It's just…I have no idea why Josh is here, and I wasn't expecting to see him when I'm looking like this." I gesture at my marmot-eaten shirt and dusty leggings. I don't even want to think about the rat's nest that is my hair. "He can be so..."

Manipulative. Dismissive. Condescending. I've got a long list of descriptive words for Josh, and very few of them are good.

"And now my mother is involved in all of this." If I thought birds were my biggest source of nightmares, today is bound to prove that wrong. "She's going to expect us at my sister's engagement party. Everyone's going to know about you by the end of the day. She's a terrible gossip. A sweetheart, but she can't be trusted with information like that."

Grant stops at a huge SUV parked in the lot behind Horizon Hikes. He opens the back hatch and puts his duffel and my bag inside. He's surprisingly chill, considering.

"But don't worry about it. I'll just tell her..." Not the truth. That's far too humiliating. How else could I get him out of this? "We realized we only like each other when we're stuck in the wilderness."

I kind of hurt my own feelings there, but it's a real possibility. We have literally nothing in common. Back in the real world, he might not find me as interesting as he did when I was the only single woman for miles around.

He shuts the car's hatch and leans against it. "Is that what you want to do?"

Let Mom, Josh, and anyone else she happens to tell about my "new boyfriend" believe he dumped me within a week? I'd rather bathe in murky lake water.

"No. I want to show up at my sister's engagement party with a mountain-climbing hottie on my arm so I can have a win for a change."

One side of his mouth tips up. I must have it on my calendar somewhere that this is the day for blurting things without thinking. There's no other explanation.

"Then let's do that."

"You would really pretend to be my boyfriend?" It seems like an awfully big thing to ask of him.

He stares at me for several long seconds, like he's having the same thought. Maybe spelling it out like that is making him reconsider. That would be the sane choice. Fake dating isn't on most people's lists of life goals.

Finally, he flashes a smile. "Yeah. I'll pretend to be your boyfriend."

FIFTEEN

GRANT

RHETT WOULDN'T JUST BE proud of me, he would build a statue in my honor.

Agreeing to pretend to be her boyfriend? I've already started pretending because that's not remotely what I want. We were supposed to come back to town, get that boba tea she'd talked about, and I would set my caution aside to ask her on a date. An *actual* date, not some ruse to save face in front of her mother and her ex.

But maybe this is the better option. We can spend time together and enjoy ourselves—and I'll know where I stand with her from the beginning. Not especially comforting, but I'm not ready to simply walk away. At least like this, I'll know in advance exactly when our cozy little bubble will burst.

It's better than being blindsided.

"Hop in." I gesture at the SUV and climb inside. I plug Moonlight Lodge's address into my phone while Lila gets in on the passenger side. After being closed up in the sun for several days, the rental's new car smell is overpowering.

She starts to dust off her leggings, but stops herself. "I feel bad for the guy who has to detail this car later. My boots are filthy, and I stink."

I back out of the parking space and head down Maple Street. "You smell great. Where do you live?"

"Uh, back there." She tosses a hand behind us. "An apartment on Maple. But it's okay—I can get a ride share from Moonlight Lodge."

"I'll turn around and take you home if you want."

"That's okay. My mom's probably hanging around my door to ambush me with more questions. I don't mind going up to the lodge." She faces me as much as she can. "Unless you don't want me to go with you. I know this is a crazy thing to ask of you. We don't have to—"

"Princess." I side-eye her at a four-way stop. "Relax. I want to."

"Oh. Okay." She settles against the car seat again. "I keep saying okay. I swear I know other words."

I grin at her. "It's okay."

Her laughter doesn't last. "We should probably talk about how this is going to go."

"Going to the lodge?"

"The fake dating."

The concept already sits wrong with me, and it's only been five minutes. "Right. What do you want to talk about?"

"Well, most rom-coms make it kind of transactional—you'll be my date to my sister's engagement party if I'll be your date to the big company event that will get you a promotion, something like that. Except, in this case, both those things are mine."

"This is a common theme in the books you read?" And yet she teases me about the magic and swordsmen in my books.

"Sure. It's one of the biggest trope pillars. It would be juicier if we were enemies to lovers, too, but we didn't really hit those notes." She shakes her head. "Never mind all that. The point is, you don't get anything out of this. What's in it for you?"

Oh, nothing. Just the chance to spend more time with the most enticing woman I've met in years.

"I can't do it because I want to?"

She makes a face like she's weighing that possibility and finds it lacking. "That would feel a lot like pity. And no rom-com heroine worth her salt wants to be pitied."

If she's the rom-com heroine, then this hero doesn't want to be pitied, either. Which, strangely enough, is exactly why this absurd situation holds any appeal for me. If she knew my past, I'd be tempted to think she suggested this pretend relationship to get me back in the dating game. As it stands, she's doing it for herself. I can live with that.

Following my phone's instructions, I take us out of Sunshine proper and back into the forest. We're headed in the opposite direction from where we camped, winding our way up into the foothills. Foothills I intend to explore over the next few weeks.

If she would feel more comfortable keeping this an even exchange, I have a few ideas for her part, after all.

"I have some things I was hoping to do around here on my vacation. Might be nice to have someone with me."

She stares at me until my skull prickles. "What kinds of things?"

"Just a few fun things. Rafting. Biking. Visiting a lake."

She sighs so heavily I'm surprised she doesn't collapse from lack of oxygen.

"It might help with your website and presentation." I sound like my sister-in-law when she's wheedling. The thing is, wheedling works a surprising amount of the time. Even when I think I'm going to hold my ground, Eliza's skilled at getting her way.

"You play dirty."

"Are we enemies to lovers now?"

"Depends on how many outdoorsy things you ask me to do."

"Think of them as add-ons to your hike."

Sarcastic laughter bubbles out of her. "I hate this whole idea, but...more research might help me get that promotion. Ugh. This is the worst. Okay. Fine."

"Great. That's solved. What else?"

Another long pause, but this one's punctuated by a deep breath in. "We should probably talk about how physical we're going to be."

Heat rushes down my spine. I'm all about enthusiastic consent, but this feels more like hammering out a business deal than anything else. It's not how I would have envisioned this conversation going.

"How physical do you want to be?"

I follow a long drive deeper into the woods to a log cabin-style building. A wrought iron arch over the main entrance spells out *Moonlight Lodge.* As secluded as it is, the full parking lot gives away its popularity.

I turn off the engine and face Lila. She's still staring at me, but this isn't the death glare when I proposed my outdoor activities trade. Her eyes hold a spark of heat that lights an answering flame inside my chest. I would pay good money to know the thoughts dancing behind those eyes.

She swallows, and my gaze is on her lips when they part. "Maybe we should figure that out as we go."

Probably for the best, since right now, I'd be tempted to practice absolutely anything she suggested.

Inside the lodge, everything from the massive central fireplace to the stout wooden furniture hits a note of rustic upscale. Even the *rustic* parts are more luxurious than the types of places I usually book for myself.

"It started out as a bed and breakfast, with just this building." Lila gestures around like she's giving me a tour. "But they've been adding cabins to their property over the last few years. You can fish on site, they offer horseback riding, and they have miles of walking trails. It's like camping."

I lift an eyebrow at her.

"With toilets and beds and showers, and no marmots," she adds. "*Better* than camping."

"And here I thought I'd won you over."

She tips her chin up. "Even you aren't that good."

"I'll try not to take that personally."

"I was doing pretty well until the ants."

I laugh. "That was the first day."

"Yup."

At the front desk, a red haired woman finishes her conversation with two guests and sees them on their way before she notices us. She straightens her black plastic glasses and pushes her hair behind her ears. "Lila! I didn't know you were dropping in today."

"I'm just here to help Grant get settled in his cabin. Grant, this is my friend Charlie Callahan. Her family owns the lodge. She's behind all their great ideas these last few years."

Charlie laughs. "You should talk like this to my parents. I could use a raise."

"Charlie, this is Grant Irwin."

"Great to meet you, Grant. How do you two know each other?"

"We met on the Horizon Hikes trip I did."

She doesn't mention our supposed relationship. Does this mean we'll only be pretending when we see her mom and ex-fiancé? Am I supposed to keep my story straight from person to person? I don't know how any of this is supposed to work. Most of the books I read center on adventure quests, not pretend relationships.

"How did that go?" Her gaze drifts over Lila. "Wait, did you just get back today?"

"You can't tell by how ragged I look?"

"Girlfriend, you always look good. I want to hear more about the trip. It will help me make recommendations to guests. But let's get Grant checked in for now." She types around on her computer. "You're in the Archer cabin. That's a beautiful spot."

She slides two keycards and a map of the property toward me. "We're here." She circles the lodge. "The Archer is the farthest out, so you'll take this road and wind your way up. Signs are posted everywhere, so you shouldn't have any trouble finding it. We have fresh-baked cookies in the lobby every afternoon at one. Every evening at five we have a social hour with complimentary cocktails and cocoa. Let us know if there's any activity we can help you arrange."

"Thanks very much." I grab the information she provided, and Lila and I head out.

We don't get far before she groans. "Seriously?"

She slips her hand into mine. I soak her warmth up for about two seconds before I catch on.

Josh walks through the lodge's main entrance. A smooth smile spreads over his face when he recognizes us. "Small world."

"Why are you here?" Lila asks.

"You always talked about this place." His gaze drifts around the lobby. "I wanted to see it for myself."

"Why are you in *my hometown?*"

His easy laughter sounds designed to irritate. "Relax. I told you—I'm shopping."

"For what?"

"I'm looking to acquire a start-up in Bend. I thought my presence might sway them to our terms, so—" He spreads his hands wide. "I'll be in town as long as it takes to seal the deal."

"Lovely."

His smug smile is unaffected by her sarcasm.

"Let me take you two out to dinner tonight. As a sign of good will." He looks to me for the decision, probably because he already knows Lila's answer. "We can talk business or...whatever it is you do."

He sizes me up like he's trying to guess my bank account balance. I don't have a lot of patience for guys who think they know everything about me based on how expensive my watch is. Then again, there was never much hope I would get along with Lila's ex.

"I can't say that I'm interested in that." I squeeze her hand. "Are you ready?"

"More than ready."

Josh moves to the side so we can pass him. "I'll see you around, Lilabird."

Once we're out of earshot, I turn to her. "Can I ask you a question?"

She sighs. "Why did I date him?"

"I wasn't going to be that direct." I choose to believe she saw something beyond his looks and money—mostly because I want her to see more than that in me.

"Okay. What's your question?"

"*Lilabird?*"

She makes a face like she might rather talk about her reasons for dating him. "Your real question is 'Did he know?', right? He knew. I told him I didn't like it, but he said it hurt his feelings that I would think he was trying to make fun of me."

"So, speaking up about a nickname that mocks your fears was you being mean to him? What's the protocol on fake boyfriends getting into fights with real exes in your books?"

"Always hinted but rarely executed." She knocks our clasped hands against her thigh. I think she likes the idea. "That's just how Josh is. He's really good at turning things around on you until he makes you question if maybe *you're* the one in the wrong."

"What else did he turn around on you?" I probably shouldn't ask for details—I'm already tempted to go back into the lodge and make a scene.

"It'd be quicker to tell you the things he didn't make my fault."

The urge to protect her rears up again. Whether it's obnoxious trailheads or insufferable exes, I want to shield her from anyone who would make her feel small. "You know it wasn't your fault, right?"

"You don't even know me, though. It could have been all my fault."

I stop her by the rental car and tilt my chin down until she meets my gaze. There's a hint of sass in her eyes, like she's willing to argue with me for the sake of being contrary. But mostly, I see a woman who can't shake the idea that maybe it *was* all her fault. "I know you well enough, princess."

My relationship with Kelsey felt like following a to-do list—getting married seemed like the obvious conclusion.

Being with Lila feels like two magnets snapping together. It's inevitable. Essential. I'm drawn to her heart-first, all-in.

I don't know much about fake dating, but all I really needed to know was *Lila*.

She grins up at me. "Come on, mountain man. Let's go find your fancy cabin."

BY THE TIME we reach Grant's cabin, we might as well be back in the national forest. The little buildings are set up for maximum privacy—I know we're not alone out here, but I can't see anyone else. I can't decide if that gives more cozy vibes or spooky ones.

I'm tempted to say something snarky about the building's rustic chic, but the impulse fades when I catch Grant's huge smile. He's like a little kid who just got everything he wanted on Christmas morning. His delight is so pure, I want to snap a picture of him and carry it around in my pocket.

I wanted to do that anyway, but he's adorable like this.

"Is that the river?" I ask, as though the constant whooshing sound could be anything else.

"It's close here." He looks up into the canopy of trees overhead. I don't hear him sigh, but I just know he does. He's totally in his element. Like when I'm surrounded by pastel rom-coms or a cheery array of floral dresses.

We step up onto the wide porch while he gets out his keycard. The electronic lock ruins the woodsy aesthetic a bit, to be honest. A hand-carved wooden nameplate over the door reads *The Archer*, but there's something else above it, too.

"What do you think that is?" I peer at it but can't make out what the dots and lines mean.

He glances up. "It's the Sagittarius constellation. The Archer? All the cabins are named after constellations. You didn't notice?"

I legitimately had no idea. "I was thinking Taylor Swift songs," I joke.

"I would have chosen the Paper Rings cabin."

I'm still gasping over the revelation he's a Swiftie when he swings the door open. Okay, now *I'm* in my element. I follow him inside, where a luxurious king-sized bed dominates the room, beckoning me closer to its downy white softness. There's a stone fireplace in one corner with a cozy leather sofa in front of it, and a huge mahogany armoire. One wall holds the kitchen setup, complete with half-size fridge and two-burner stove.

"This is nice." I can't help but run a hand over the fluffy duvet. The bed's waist-high for me. I'd need a step stool to climb into it.

Not that I would need to get into Grant's bed. Just an observation.

He sets his duffel next to the armoire. "You've been in the cabins before, haven't you?"

"Not this one. Look at this wall of windows." I step closer to the sliding glass doors. The river's maybe fifty feet away through the trees. Adirondack chairs are set up on the wide patio, alongside a—

I spin to face him. "You have a hot tub?"

His grin proves he knows how good he has it. "I plan to relax."

"Look at you, roughing it in the woods."

"I never said I'm immune to modern conveniences."

"Is this what your place back in Texas is like? Rustic-fancy?" I can picture him in a setup just like this somewhere.

He winces, but I can't sort out why. "It's secluded like this. I don't spend much time there."

"Why not?"

"My younger brother's townhouse is closer to work, and I stay there a lot. He needs someone looking after him half the time." He unzips his duffel bag. "Do you mind if I take a quick shower?"

"Go for it. We have bathed together before." My laugh gets strangled in my throat. I should just not talk with Grant. We can work out a system of blinks and nods.

I'd probably still find ways to embarrass myself.

He pauses halfway between me and the bathroom door, smiling over my ridiculousness. "Would you like to take one first?"

I duck my head to try to smell my armpit. "I do stink, don't I?"

"I promise you, you don't. It seemed like the gentlemanly thing to offer."

"I can wait until I get home." I've been dreaming about my assortment of shampoos and body washes for days now. Plus, I can't get naked in his cabin immediately after cornering him into being my pretend boyfriend. I have a tiny smidgen of pride. "While you do that, I'm going to indulge in sitting on something other than the ground."

I flop onto the couch. My poor butt is immediately grateful. I bet it's bruised from sitting on so many rocks and logs.

"Fancy. I'll be right out."

He disappears into the bathroom, which, if it's anything like the cabins I've seen, has a generously sized and gorgeously tiled shower. I almost wish I hadn't turned down his offer, but my fiberglass tub and shower combo will get me just as clean. It just won't be quite as relaxing as the rain shower version his probably has.

It takes about three minutes of mindless sitting before the real world catches up with me. The Fourth Fest is in two weeks, and even though I've got everything lined up and double-checked, there's always room for something to go sideways. I grab my phone and take it out of airplane mode.

As careful as I was with it in the woods, it's covered in a fine dust. My poor baby. Can you take a phone in for detailing?

The second my service is restored, my phone starts buzzing with notifications. Emails and voicemails about the festival, comments on my socials both personal and professional, but worst of all—texts.

Mom: I can't wait to hear more about Grant

Mom: Invite him to dinner any time!

Mom: You're going to throw out that rodent-bitten shirt, right?

Hope: Mom says you came back from the hike with a boyfriend?

Hope: ?????

Hope: I need to know what happened in the woods

Hope: Call me immediately

I knew Mom would work fast, but I still thought she might give me a few hours' head start.

Oh, who am I kidding? She probably shimmied right over to my sister's store the minute Grant and I left town.

"Everything okay?"

I startle and almost drop my phone. "That was quick."

"I'm efficient." He walks into my line of sight in front of the couch.

Stare is probably too polite a word for what I do. I *goggle* at him. "You shaved."

He runs a hand over his silky-smooth jaw. "Did you prefer the stubble?"

I'm not sure I could choose which version I like better. The thick stubble added to his rugged appeal, but this clean-shaven version is devastating. Plus, it gives an unhindered view of that dimple. I probably shouldn't be trusted with unlimited access to it.

"You look great both ways."

His boyish smile appears like a sunburst peeking out of the clouds. "Good to know." He sits at the other end of the not-terribly-large couch. "Is anything wrong? You were scowling at your phone just now."

My dimple-addled brain needs a second to catch up. "I was checking my texts. My sister already knows about us. My mom has probably visited half the stores in town by now relaying the news."

If she had a bull horn, she could work twice as fast.

"You expected that, right?"

"Oh, yeah. It's just unsettling how desperate she is to get my sister and me married off."

Panic flickers briefly across his face. His reaction hurts just a little. Which is dumb. This whole thing between us is fake—of course he would freak out at the idea of marrying me. He doesn't even want to date me. The reminder squeezes my stupid little heart.

"Hope's wedding should be enough to keep her busy. She just wants us to be happy."

"You're not happy?"

"I mean romantically happy. You know how moms get, eager for their kids to have love and marriage and babies."

He looks like I'm speaking gibberish. "Not really."

"Your mom isn't like that?"

Is there a mom out there who isn't excited for her kids to have all those things? My experience says no, but maybe things are different in Texas. I doubt it, but maybe.

He lifts a shoulder. "She wants us to be happy, but she's not pushy about the rest of it."

"She wasn't out of her mind with glee when your brother got married?"

"Dean and Eliza eloped, so there wasn't a whole lot to get worked up about. She's happy for them, but it's a normal amount."

"A normal amount of happy?" My mom almost passed out from joy when I told her Josh and I got engaged. She sent me endless links to potential wedding venues, dresses, and hairstyles. She passed on ideas for honeymoon locations, and oh-so casually dropped potential baby names into conversations. "I don't know what that's like."

"It's like this." He pulls his mouth into a closed lip, unenthusiastic smile.

My mom's been happier over getting brunch with me and Hope on a random Saturday. I am weirdly sad for Grant, imagining a lifetime of mid-range smiles.

"My mom's more like this." I slowly drop my mouth open into the biggest, goofiest grin. Eyes wide, I flash jazz hands at either side of my face.

"You're right, that is a lot."

I let my crazy clown smile fade. "You don't have to do this for me."

"I know."

"It's your last chance to back out." I don't know why I keep giving him the option—I don't want him to change his mind. It would be mild to moderately humiliating to face everyone Mom's already gossiped to around town.

Plus, I just want to spend time with him.

Craziest excuse for spending time with a man so far, but it's been that kind of year.

"I'm not backing out. This will be fun."

"Aw." I pat him on the shoulder. "You're cute when you're wildly naive."

SEVENTEEN
LILA

AND JUST LIKE THAT, I feel human again. All it took was a triple shampoo, a deep conditioning, a vigorous scrub with a loofah, a sheet mask, and slathering myself with my favorite lotion.

Bliss.

Grant dropped me off outside my building after we arranged to meet up for my beloved boba tea tomorrow. It's strange not to have him somewhere close by. I'm having proximity withdrawals, as if that's a thing.

The other thing that's not a thing? After being out in the fresh mountain air for a week, my apartment doesn't smell as great as I used to think it did. It's nothing gross like the mildewy communal hallway, it's just...indoor air. I never thought I would miss the smell of the woods.

My all-brick studio sits above a block of businesses on Maple Street. I get it for a steal, mostly because it's woefully out of date and more or less unappealing in every way. But it's super convenient to shops, and the exact same apartment would go for four times as much in Seattle, so really, who's the winner here?

My phone buzzes as though it's saying *Not you.* It's barely let up since I turned it back on.

> Hope: When can I expect details?

> Hope: Don't make me come find you

> Hope: I know where you live

I guess I'd better get this over with.

> Lila: On my way down

It takes me about five minutes to walk to my sister's gift shop, The Painted Daisy. I still haven't decided whether I'm going to let her in on what's really going on between Grant and me when I walk through the door.

The truth is a pretty sad scenario: asking a guy I barely know to pretend to date me so I could have a fleeting win against my ex-fiancé. But I'm not sure I can spin the make-believe story much better: I got a fresh new boyfriend within a week of my sister's engagement party. Both versions reek of desperation.

Inside, I'm comforted by smells I don't mind at all—a variety of lavender and citrus soaps and lotions, and about six different kinds of pies from the bakery next door. At least my brain hasn't been altered to dislike *every* indoor smell.

I focus on Hope beaming at me by the back counter so I don't get sidetracked by a pair of cozy slippers or the latest set of handcrafted earrings she got in. Spending money here indiscriminately is one of my worst habits at the moment, and I'm trying to rein it in.

Most of the time.

Nobody's in the small shop, which seems like a crime, considering all of the wonderful handmade goodies in here. But it does mean whatever interrogation she has in store for me will be private.

She's got her hands spread wide when I reach the counter. "So? Is it true? Or did Mom see you with a man and go overboard?"

"Ha. That would be so wild, wouldn't it?" Is it a step up or down from what actually happened?

"Totally on-brand for her, though. So which is it?"

"Mom did see me with a man," I admit. "Two, actually."

"Grant Somebody and...?"

"Josh is in town."

That earns a scowl. He's the villain of many of our conversations. "Wait. Mom caught you with your ex *and* the new guy?"

I'm a little surprised she left that part out, but I can see how she would have been too excited about my new boyfriend to mention my old one.

"Yup. It was weird."

"Did she make it even weirder?"

"Naturally. She invited Grant to family dinner within thirty seconds of meeting him."

"Classic. We'll come back around to Josh. Tell me everything about the new guy, please."

"He's..." I don't know where to start telling her about Grant. His unfailing kindness about my cluelessness on the trail? His easygoing nature that made me feel like no matter how bad the situation, things were going to be okay? His low-key flirtation? His patience? That freaking dimple?

Hope sighs, but it's not her usual sound of exasperation with me. More like...a romantic sigh. "You're really smitten with this guy."

"What? I didn't even say anything."

"That's the point." She grins like she just figured out all my secrets. "You're speechless over him."

"Are we talking about Lila's new man?"

Wren Krause pops in from the pass-through that leads to their family's bakery next door. The easy access is a great feature for shoppers, but less so for anyone wanting to tell their sister something and keep it just between them. *Ahem.*

"You already told Wren?" We're all friends, but I'm still disappointed she couldn't wait half a day to confirm or deny Mom's stories.

Of course, I haven't told Hope anything, and I've done nothing but confirm, confirm, confirm.

"Your mom told our mom when she grabbed a pie about an hour ago." Wren's older sister Tess appears behind her. "She used the word 'adonis' to describe him, so it's fair to say our curiosity has been piqued."

I peer behind the blond sisters into the bakery. Normally, there's a line running all the way back to the door over there. Now? Zip. "Does every business on Maple Street shut down at this part of the afternoon to share gossip?"

"Hey, we have gossip to trade back." Wren bobs her eyebrows, tilting her head toward Tess. "If you give us valuable enough info."

Tess narrows her eyes on her sister, and I almost expect her to clamp a hand over her mouth. "There's no *we* here."

"That's right, it's all you."

Tess is the sunniest of sunshines, but I think a little steam comes off of her.

"How are you settling into your new apartment?" I ask. She moved out of the family home she shared with her mom and sister, and into a place with just her and her five-year-old son about a week before my trip. She's been excited about the change, but nervous how he would adjust to it. I was so busy finalizing everything for the Fourth Fest, I didn't have a chance to ask for an update before I left.

Also, it's a great time for a deflection.

The smuggest smile plays over Wren's face. "It all goes together."

I look from one sister to the other. "The news and the apartment?"

Wren nods slowly, but Tess rolls her eyes.

"I'm so lost."

Two women walk into The Painted Daisy and start *oohing* and *ahhing* over the pretty contents on the shelves. Excellent. I didn't even have to deflect again.

"Let's meet at Delish after we close up." Hope isn't suggesting. It's more of a command.

"I don't know…" My hesitation is based squarely on the fact that I'm bound to tell these women everything if we have zero interruptions. I'm just not completely sure yet which *version* of everything I'm going to tell them.

"Come on, you must be starved after eating camp meals for so many days."

My stomach chooses that moment to remind me that yes, in fact, I am famished. "Okay. But only because I need food."

Wren and Tess agree to the meet up, too, and start to slip back over to their side of the pass-through.

"Wait." I take a few steps after them. "Does August like the new place?"

Tess's son is the sweetest little guy ever. He treats everyone he meets like his new best friend, and he's got a little-kid way of speaking that makes everything he says cuter than cute. He's well out of the baby zone, but he tends to bring on a case of baby fever whenever I spend time with him.

Her smile loses the strain it held just a minute ago when Wren was goading her. "He loves it. It's got a big yard, and he spends time almost every day playing with our neighbor's dog."

My heart acts up just imagining him romping with a dog. "I love that for him."

"Don't skip out on us," Hope says when I move back onto her side of the wide doorway.

"I won't. You had me at Delish."

"You had a good time though, right?" she prompts.

The trip flashes through my mind like a horror movie montage: the ants, the marmot holes, the camp toilet, the threat of leeches. But a true highlight reel springs up right after: swimming in the lake, the mountain views, gazing at the stars with Grant.

Everything with Grant.

"Yeah," I say softly.

She grins wide. "I knew it."

———

It's probably not good for my stomach to go from the tasty but sensible meals Mitchell made on the trail to a massive hamburger and fries, but the heart wants what it wants. Next to me, Hope taps out a text to Griffin. I'm not trying to spy, but his answering *Have fun! Love you* is hard to miss.

Also, apparently, a bacon emoji? I don't understand these two.

We snagged a booth at Delish along with Wren and Tess, but like most locals, we don't bother opening the menus. They change it up seasonally, but you'll hear about their latest offering before you ever see it listed anywhere. I don't love small town gossip, but when it comes to letting me know fresh strawberry milkshakes are back in season? Bring on the rumor mill.

Amy Ellison wanders over to take our orders looking at us like we're her favorite customers. "It's been a while since we've seen all of you in here together. Is there a special occasion?"

"Girls night," Wren answers.

"Oh." She makes a face like she knows we're here to tell secrets. Probably because she and her wife Jodi have served us burgers and shakes since we were in our teens. If we asked her to, she'd sit down and join in the gossip. Amy and Jodi are Sunshine's honorary cool aunts, and we love them for it.

She takes our orders but pauses next to Tess. "Is everything going all right over at the duplex? Ian's not giving you a hard time, is he? My nephew's been prickly lately, but if he's extending that to you, I'll talk to him."

Pink washes over Tess's cheeks as soon as Amy mentions Ian. Curious. I'm starting to understand the intertwining gossip Wren teased earlier.

"He was a little prickly at the beginning, but I think we're getting along now." Tess smiles sweetly, but oh, she does not want to talk about this. She's wearing a customer service smile that doesn't go all the way down. "Thank you again for renting us the apartment."

Amy waves off her thanks. "It's our pleasure to have you there. I'll go get your orders in."

As soon as she walks away, the rest of us lean toward Tess.

"I feel like we need to hear more about your neighbor," Hope says.

"The guy with the dog?" I ask.

"The *hot* guy with the dog." In case her naughty tone wasn't enough, Wren bobs her eyebrows.

Tess raises both hands. "I just stopped thinking of him as a growly hermit two days ago."

"Her exact words were 'plundering Viking.'" Wren's little sister sing-song voice is as good as Hope's.

Tess's glare could melt metal. "We've known each other for two weeks. Could we please not jump straight into the deep end here?"

"Okay, but he did come into the bakery the other day, and sparks were flying all over the place."

"Loads of people come into the bakery." Tess's defense feels like a borderline confession even to me.

"Yeah, but nobody else who looks at you like you're the only thing he wants in the whole store."

Tess does a quick scan of the diner, probably checking for her neighbor. It is a small town, after all. "Even if he does—and I'm not saying he does!—I haven't been on a date since before August came along. I don't know how to do any of this anymore. I don't know what he expects, or what I'm willing to give."

That reminder tones down our teasing. She doesn't bring it up a lot, but Tess hasn't had an easy time as a single mom. I'm nervous enough to think about dating again after a six month break—Tess is looking at ending a six *year* break.

"If he's the right man for you, he'll be understanding about all of that." I don't know where I'm getting this advice, but I have to believe it's true. "He'll want you just as you are right now. And if he can't be patient while you sort things out, then he's not the guy. But someone else will be."

Tess's cautious expression lifts. "Thank you."

Hope takes a sip of water. "Wow. Out in the woods for a week, and she comes back a guru."

I jab my elbow into her side. "Why did I agree to come to dinner with you?"

"Starvation."

"Okay." Wren aims double-barreled finger guns at me. "It's your turn. You went into the woods single and came out with a boyfriend who looks like a Greek god. How does one recreate that? If one were to go into the woods looking for a Greek god?"

"First, Grant looks like a normal man."

She drops her chin into her hand. "Funny. That is *exactly* what Tess said about Ian."

I lock eyes with Tess. Her "I'm sorry" smile isn't all that comforting.

"And Ian's a total smoke show." Wren's only too happy to drop that bomb.

"Second," I say, carrying on, despite her detour. "Boyfriend's kind of a strong word after only a few days together. Isn't it?"

I need an answer here, people.

"I would run with it," Hope says. "Mom was about to invite that single pediatric dentist to the engagement party to keep you company. If you walk it back to friendship, she might change her mind and dump him on you anyway."

"Does she realize I could have a good time at your party without a date?"

"Obviously not. When she said you had a boyfriend, I thought you were just trying to get her off your back. But she said she saw him, so he can't be made up."

My laugh comes out a little too high-pitched. "How sad would that be? Pretending to have a boyfriend just to save face at your engagement party."

So pathetically sad.

Jodi brings out platters of burgers and fries, and Amy delivers our shakes before they leave us to it. I take my first bite of burger, and all my hike-shriveled cells cheer in celebration.

"Mmm," I groan. "Real food."

Wren wipes her mouth after a particularly big bite of fries. "Okay, but you haven't said anything about the adonis yet, except that he's not an adonis, which I'm not buying for a second."

How to explain? I can't tell them none of it's real, not now. After Josh's cheating, losing everything in Seattle, and scrambling to get by here in Sunshine, I need *something* to feel like a win. Being with Grant, even just for a little while? That's the biggest win around.

I think through our five days together, and land on the part I know my friends will find most impressive.

"He read to me at night in his tent."

The booth fills with swoony, romantic sounds.

"That's all I need to know," Wren says. "He's a keeper."

The thing is, I'm starting to wish he could be.

EIGHTEEN
GRANT

IN A STRANGE CASE of déjà vu, I see Lila before she sees me. She's strolling up the sidewalk, peering into shop windows she passes, oblivious to me standing outside Perk Me Up. I don't know much about fashion off of a mountainside, but her shorts and top combo looks effortlessly stylish but still entirely casual. She could be getting on a sailboat in Italy or boarding a private jet in Aspen. Or preparing to introduce a virtual stranger to boba tea.

A virtual stranger she's claimed as her pretend boyfriend.

Yeah, it still sits weird. Too many qualifiers in there.

When her eyes hit mine, her grin sparkles. My stomach dips in return. I don't want to lose whatever it is that makes her shine like that.

She beelines over to me, adding a little skip to her step. "Am I late?"

"Right on time."

"Good. I'm usually late to things, but I wanted to be on time for you." She wrinkles her nose, as though I wouldn't appreciate that bit of information. "To show you the magic of boba tea, I mean."

"Of course."

I open the door and trail her inside the coffee shop. A fresh, almost spicy scent drifts along with her. It's delicious just like her—like a crisp summer day—but I can't place it.

At the counter, she orders two boba teas from the young barista. I pay for them while the two talk, but Lila catches it.

"I was supposed to treat you."

"Not this time." It's unlikely I'll let her pay next time either, but she'll figure that out eventually.

We stand at the counter while the barista prepares the drinks. Lila watches her progress so eagerly, she might as well be making grabby hands and saying, "Gimme."

"Not to oversell it, but this is going to be your all-time favorite drink."

There's that sparkle in her smile again. I'm lost for it. If this is all it takes, I'll drink boba tea with her every day.

"Better than water fresh from a mountain spring?" I tease.

"You won't even have to filter giardia out of it."

"I'm curious about the blobs in the bottom of the cups."

Her sparkle dims a touch, but she nudges me with her shoulder. "Blobs. That's the boba. They're tapioca pearls."

How did I not know that? I'd seen pictures of them, but had I ever heard what they're made of? My stomach turns an unfortunate direction.

She nudges me again, leaving our shoulders touching. "What's that face for?"

"My grandad used to eat tapioca pudding. It was his favorite dessert." I shudder against her, thinking of the bland, gloppy dish. "I'm not a fan."

"It's not like tapioca pudding. They don't taste like very much, really, they just add chewy goodness to the drink."

"A chewy drink." Maybe I should have thought this boba tea date through a little more.

She slips her hand around my biceps. "Stop with the gross face. You're going to like it."

"I feel like there's an 'or else' in there."

Her smile is all wickedness. "How perfect is this? We're already finishing each other's sentences."

I'm in good shape, but this flirtatious side of her just might give me a heart attack.

The barista presents us with our drinks, and Lila releases me to claim hers. I take mine, examining it. It's half tapioca. I have one very specific reservation about drinking it.

"Looks like fish eggs."

"Says the man who swims with leeches," she scolds before grabbing a table.

"I never eat the leeches."

Lila's already sipping at her straw when I sit down across from her. Eyes closed, triumphant smile on her lips, she savors the drink. I have never been so jealous of an inanimate object.

She opens her eyes. "So good."

I take a drink of mine. The milk tea is pretty good— I'm more of a coffee drinker, but I like the flavor. Then I get one of the tapioca blobs in my mouth. It's a little disconcerting, but she's right. It's got the barest hint of sweetness as I chew. Nothing at all like granddad's gloppy pudding.

She leans forward, hands braced on the white formica table. "So? What's the verdict?"

"Not bad."

Her eager expression falls into an unimpressed glare. "I think you mean it's incredible."

I take another sip. "Passable."

"A party for your tastebuds."

"Tolerable, I suppose."

She sits back. Eyes narrowing to slits, she's frozen in place as she stares. Five whole seconds tick by. "Did you just quote *Pride and Prejudice*? Or was that completely by accident?"

My smile might be as wicked as hers.

She slaps the table. "That's a yes. I can't believe it. I've never met a man who's read *Pride and Prejudice*."

"You've been meeting the wrong men."

"That's a fact." She leans closer to jab a finger into my arm. "But you said it's 'tolerable.' That means you're secretly intrigued. By the end of the week, you're going to be all in for this fair drink with the tapioca pearls and fine eyes."

"I don't want to think about eyes when I'm chewing these things."

"You're a fan now, and I won't hear anything else." She takes another happy sip of her drink. "What did you do last night after you dropped me off? Soak in your fancy hot tub?"

"I did. I turned all the lights off and looked up at the stars from the comfort of the jacuzzi." I decide not to mention the opossum that wandered past in the dark. That might ruin any chance of her joining me there, and a man's got to have a dream.

"Oh. That actually sounds nice."

"You're always welcome." Probably shouldn't admit just how welcome.

"Don't offer because I *will* take you up on it."

"That's why I offered."

"Okay. It might help my stiff muscles. Is it normal to be this sore after a hike?" She stretches her neck from side to side, and I have to stop myself from staring at all that beautiful skin.

"Of course. You're not used to carrying so much. It makes sense you'd be sore."

"Are you sore?"

"Why do you think I got in the hot tub?"

"It's bad that I'm happy you're sore too, right?"

I laugh. "Just a little."

She doesn't seem all that concerned.

"That's not the only thing I did last night. I also scrolled through *Genuinely_Lila*."

Her smile disappears, and her eyes drop from mine. Not the response I expected from someone whose account reaches so many thousands of followers.

"And?"

"You're a great photographer." That, at least, gets her to look at me again. "You've got a good eye for details."

"It's a useful skill to have in marketing."

"No doubt. Rhett does all that for us, and he's not nearly as talented as you are." He doesn't manage to breathe life into his subjects the way she does, either. Our accounts might do a little better if he tried.

She looks like she can't decide whether to accept the compliment or deny it. "You don't find it...insipid? Inane?"

Something tells me she didn't land on those words by accident. I'm not a violent guy, but it'd be for the best if we don't run across her old friend Josh anytime soon. Everything I've heard about him makes me want to land a punch.

"I won't pretend it's all relevant to me, but it doesn't need to be. It's clearly important to you, and that gives it value right there."

She shakes her head. "I call shenanigans. It's valuable because I like it? Feels like a line."

I set my drink aside. "Princess, I have logged ungodly numbers of hours in World of Warcraft. I booked a trip to New Zealand entirely around visiting Lord of the Rings movie locations. I built a lightsaber from scratch. So, yeah. I think if something is important to you, it has value."

A smile slowly works its way across her face. "Does the lightsaber work?"

"It lights up, but I have to make the *zzshm zzshm* sounds myself."

She laughs at the way I flick my imaginary lightsaber around. "You are such a glorious nerd. I love it. I want to see the lightsaber some day."

Lila visiting me in Texas? Nothing sounds better. "Absolutely."

She shakes her drink, redistributing ice and tapioca pearls. "I started *Genuinely_Lila* a few years ago to try to make friends, if you can believe it. I wanted to connect with people who like the same things I do—cute dresses, cheery motivational quotes, pretty places around the city."

"You're still posting about Seattle." Nothing on her account indicates she lives in Oregon, let alone Sunshine. It's all cityscapes and botanical gardens and coffee shops hundreds of miles away from here.

She straightens in her seat. "Yeah. I'm not sure my followers are very interested in Sunshine."

"You could give it a try. There's a lot of good photography opportunities here."

I can't tell if she's going for a smile or a grimace.

"They're two very different places."

"Sure, but you've got endless natural beauty. Classic brick storefronts. And think of all the local shops you could feature."

"Grant, no. It won't work."

"Why not?"

She casts around for an answer. "There's no overlap between people who like big cities and people who live in small towns."

"That doesn't seem true. Don't you think they would want to see the real you?"

"Real?" She draws back as if the word might bite her. "Like how my life fell apart all around me? You think I should share *that* with my followers? They don't want to hear about that. Nobody wants to hear about that."

"Lila, if you give people a chance—"

"*No.* If I start posting Sunshine's buildings and parks and all their cute little shops, I promise you I will *bleed* followers. I've seen it happen to other creators when they try similar shifts. I just—" She splays her hands, begging me to understand. "I can't lose the last scrap of success I have left, okay? Once that's gone, I've got nothing. I'm not ready for that."

Her belief she really has nothing else hits a sore spot in my heart. I take her hands in mine. Comfort I don't deserve wells inside me when she holds on. "I'm sorry, princess. I shouldn't have pushed. I know what it's like to hold tight to the last pieces of normalcy in your life."

Her deep sigh loosens her shoulders. "No, I'm sorry. I got worked up over nothing."

She tries for a fake smile, and I hate that she feels she has to pretend. With me, for me, any of it.

"It's not nothing. Your account is a big deal—you have every right to handle it however you want. It's not my place to tell you what to do."

How many times have Rhett and Dean told me I push too hard? Once. Twice. A thousand.

"I still find it mildly horrifying that you saw all that stuff."

"Don't be. I liked seeing another side of you."

We still have our hands clasped on the table between us. I can't tell if she's forgotten that point or if she's indulging in it the same way I am. I want to run my thumbs over her wrists, but if I do, it might wake her out of this spell we're under.

"Was it better or worse than the side of me in the woods covered in black ants?"

"Princess, I like all your sides."

We stay like that several moments, staring into each other's eyes. It takes serious effort not to lean forward and kiss her right here in the coffee shop. I've half-convinced myself she would welcome it when she pulls her hands from mine.

"Do you want me to give you a tour of Sunshine?"

I grin. "Sounds perfect."

I have no room to talk when it comes to Lila's social media. My easy-going attitude right now is anything but real.

NINETEEN

LILA

"I LIKE ALL YOUR SIDES."

It's sad that my fake boyfriend is the first man to say something like that to me, isn't it? Even when we were at our best, Josh always had little criticisms. Helpful suggestions for how I could change myself to be a better girlfriend or a better employee. I wanted to make him happy, and he didn't shy away from telling me exactly how I could. Perfect match, right?

The reality was, I was constantly scrambling, trying to keep up with his ever-changing expectations.

But Grant and his "I like you just as you are" line? I don't know what to do with it. Well...I *want* to dive in and swim around in it until I get all pruney from the unbounded acceptance. But I *should* put up "Swim at Your Own Risk" signs to remind myself how much heartache waits for me in those waters.

I can't get attached to my fake boyfriend like a leech in the shallows. Even though that's exactly what I want to do—I want to glom on and hold tight until he shakes me off when he goes back to Texas.

Like right now—it's taking a crazy amount of willpower not

to attach myself to his arm while we stroll downtown Sunshine. I point out businesses and shops, giving morsels of town history along with a dozen glowing recommendations for anything that might be on his shopping list.

I'm probably going on too much, but I can't help it—I'm excited to show off our little town. I haven't had a true visitor here before. It feels like a taste of what's to come with my future job.

Hopefully my future job.

"That one across the street with the red storefront and the canary yellow door? That's my sister's gift shop."

Even from here, I can see she's got a few customers inside. I love it.

"That's a must-visit, I'm guessing?"

"It's one of a kind. She's an artist. She paints vibrant, cozy scenes." Her bright orange and red dahlia painting helps keep the gloom away in my apartment. "She sells all handmade items, most of it from local artists. That store is the biggest threat to my paycheck each month."

"I should stop in and get gifts for my mom and sister-in-law sometime. Maybe you'd help me pick out a few things?"

"I would love it. I already have so many ideas." Somewhere in my purse, my phone buzzes. It's done that at least ten times since I left my apartment to meet him. "Uh, speaking of moms."

Not the best transition, but this was never going to feel perfectly natural.

"My mother would really like to confirm you're coming to Hope's engagement party this weekend. There's no pressure, of course. You don't have to do it—"

"I want to."

"Oh. Okay. Great." He's surprisingly chill about the whole fake dating thing. Me? I'm a tangle of frizzy nerve-endings. "I hope you're prepared to act like a smitten boyfriend."

"I'll be ready."

We slow down in front of the old, empty department store. It's a sad gap in an otherwise busy street, but Mom hasn't found a business willing to lease such a big space. Like my apartment, the exterior has a vintage feel, but the inside needs some love.

He tilts his head toward the forgotten building. "You brought me on the scenic route."

"It was beautiful a few months ago. Hope filled the front window with toys and lights for her Christmas festival."

"Are you doing something like that for the Fourth of July?"

"Obviously. Even though I'm kind of mad I didn't come up with it first. It'll be all flag-themed merchandise from local stores, with some lights above it to give a hint of fireworks." I stand right in front of the window and gesture around like I'm painting the scene for him. "I set aside a couple of the flag buntings for the backdrop too. Outside, I'll put some helium balloons up for as long as they last."

"You'll make Captain America proud."

"Your eyes will be dazzled by the star-spangled goodness." I spin to face him. "It's a little free advertising for local businesses, and if we're really lucky, we'll find someone to lease the building."

"It's a great plan. I can't wait to see your vision become reality."

"I hope I live up to my own hype."

"I don't see how I could be disappointed."

I could bask in this man's praise like a happy little kitten in a sunbeam. "Grant Irwin, you're a charmer."

He flashes a boyish smile. "When I want to be."

He's got my insides pirouetting around, and he's barely said anything. Either he's just got that much charisma or I'm starved for approval. Maybe both.

Over his shoulder, I spot Josh across the street. My content cat smile freezes in place.

"How ready are you to turn up the charm?" I whisper.

He leans closer. "Just say the word."

"That's good because Josh is watching us." I keep the happy smile pasted on as if we're still flirting away.

Grant tenses like someone just zapped him with static electricity. He puts a little more distance between us as if to stop it from happening again. Not the response I was going for. I grab his hand and lace my fingers in his, tugging him closer.

"I'm sure he'll realize he's being a creep and move on in a minute." Actually, I'm not sure of that at all. Josh has proven he's got a flawed opinion of what constitutes bad behavior, especially when it comes to his own.

Grant clears his throat and goes right on staring at me. The boyish smile is gone, replaced by mild panic. He looks like he's been set in the cockpit of a gliding airplane and somebody told him he has to land the plane. Clueless, basically.

The hint of uncertainty in this capable man would probably be a lot more attractive if my pride weren't riding on him snapping out of it in the next three seconds.

"What do you want me to do?"

"I don't know...pretend to flirt with me." He was doing it before. Why is it making his brain shut down now?

"Hey...baby."

My fake happiness disappears. "Not baby."

I never liked that nickname, but after seeing it in Josh's *whoops* text to the other woman, the nickname makes my stomach crawl.

He only looks more confused. "Darling girl."

"That's worse," I hiss through a pretend smile. "How are you so bad at this? It was your idea!"

"Was it?"

Josh is still standing across the street, maxing out the amount of time you can casually watch a couple having a private moment before it turns into stalking. I need to sell this. If he figures out Grant isn't interested in me, everyone I knew in Seattle will hear about my pathetic show.

It shouldn't matter. I don't care what they think. Except... after the crummy year I've had, it *does* matter. I need to salvage something.

"Just...act natural. Pretend you like me."

A crease forms between Grant's eyebrows. "I like you."

"Romantically." I give him another smile as though Josh is counting them, and when he reaches a set amount, he'll be on his way. "Pretend I'm your dream girl."

Something flickers in Grant's eyes. Whatever it is, it flips the switch. He moves closer until he's in my space. I back up a step, hitting the department store's window. He places one hand on the glass and leans in.

He smells good. Something minty and herbal lingers on him, and I'm tempted to take a deep sniff just so I can memorize the exact make up of his soap.

"You are my dream girl. I like everything about you." He dips his head nearer until we're breathing the same air. "Your laugh. Your ambition. Your dedication. Your heart."

Heat spreads through my body from my toes to my scalp. My blood is molten, my organs singed to a crisp, and he hasn't even touched me. A tiny part of my brain recognizes the danger in giving myself over to this moment, but I don't move. I'm not sure I can.

I am Icarus, flying higher and higher.

Grant shifts his hand to my neck, splaying his fingers lightly across my skin from my collar bone to my jaw. His thumb skates up my chin to press ever so softly to my lower lip. "I can't stop thinking about your mouth. I want to..."

He draws even closer, his eyes on the fiery spot where he's touching my lip. His breath ghosts over my mouth. My eyes drift shut, and I tilt my chin, ready for him to put me out of my misery and kiss me already.

Seconds pass. I...might not be breathing.

"Was that enough charm for you?" he says softly.

My eyes fly open. He still hovers millimeters from my face. His eyes have lost their sultry fire, replaced now with something I can't read. He moves his thumb from my mouth, letting it slide along my cheek. I'm sure to any outside observer—say, somebody standing across the street being nosy—it looked like we kissed.

Turns out, he's so good at this, it almost *felt* like we kissed, too.

I am Icarus, crashing to the ground.

I straighten in his grasp, and he lowers his hand. It takes me a few seconds to compose myself. Outwardly, anyway. Inside, I'm a needy, disappointed mess. I run my suddenly clammy hands along my shorts and lick my lips. His eyes follow the movement, but instead of shifting closer again, he puts a little more distance between us. It's barely anything, but I feel it like a hundred paper cuts.

You wanted a fake boyfriend? Congrats, you got one.

My smile is a sham, but that fits. "That was the exact right amount of charm."

He smiles, too, but it reminds me of the mid-happy smile he demonstrated yesterday. It isn't nearly enough. It might not even be real.

"Is he still around?"

"I don't know." I don't want to look. The idea that one of the sexiest moments of my life was all for the sake of my ex sets something slimy loose in my stomach.

Grant's just-barely-there smile falls. "Was that too much? We never talked about our limits."

"No." I croak it more than say it. I swallow because I'm super chill like that, and try again. "No. That was fine."

Fine. Sure. That neck caress and lip touch will be forever ingrained in my memory. But it's fine.

He tilts his head, no doubt running silent scans on my mental state. He's been pretty dang perceptive so far—I really don't need him digging around under my skin right now. All the evidence in there is labeled *Incriminating*.

"You make an excellent fake boyfriend." My voice isn't usually this squeaky, is it? "A very believable forgery."

His mouth twists just a touch. His lips have no right to be that full. With that mouth, if he did kiss me it would be transcendent. Unforgettable.

Focus, Lila.

"And thank you, too." I exhale a tiny laugh to prove how unaffected I am by all of this. "I know we weren't expecting the fake boyfriend stuff to kick in just yet."

"Don't thank me. It actually makes things easier for me."

"What things?"

His genuine smile peeks out. "I found a place to take us whitewater rafting."

TWENTY
GRANT

IN THE LAST SEVENTY-TWO HOURS, I've gone on two day hikes, explored more of the national forest, and seen phenomenal views of the nearby mountains and lakes. I've soaked up the quiet in my cabin and gazed at stars from the comfort of my hot tub. But I haven't looked forward to anything as much as rafting with Lila.

Seeing her like this makes the wait worth it.

She's decked out in an athletic tee, quick-dry shorts, and sneakers, with a bright orange personal flotation device over the top. Her dark hair is pulled back into twin braids, she's awash in eucalyptus oil again, and she's glaring at me just a little.

"You bought this?" she says low. "You paid actual money for it?"

"They didn't have much selection."

We arrived at the rafting offices before she realized she'd left her hat at home. She refused to take my perfectly acceptable Longhorns hat from me, so I found something for her in the gift shop.

Let's just say it doesn't match her aesthetic.

"'I pee in rivers!'" She looks past me to make sure no one

else waiting for our trip heard her. Seems unnecessary, since two other guys are wearing the same hat.

That probably wouldn't comfort her.

"I don't want your scalp to get burned. Here." I take mine off and set it on her head. I'll assume her hesitation was more about stealing my hat than an aversion to the Longhorns. "I'll wear this one."

I pull the "I pee in rivers" hat low over my forehead and flash her a grin. "Good?"

She rolls her eyes, but she can't hold in her giggles. "You're ridiculous. You need to set that on fire as soon as the trip is over."

"No way. This is a souvenir now." Rhett will be jealous.

She shakes her head at my taste in clothes, but she's still smiling so I have no problem wearing the tacky hat.

The Wildwater Rafters offices are on about an acre of wooded land. Rafts are stacked on trailers, and guests wind their way from the main building to the shuttle vans in the parking lot. Our safety presentation will start soon, and then we'll take a thirty minute ride to where we'll put in on the river.

"I still don't think I'm up for this much responsibility." She hefts the plastic oar we selected for her. "Doesn't seem safe."

"I wouldn't put you on a river where you would be in danger." They have trips that cover class IV and V rapids, but this one will barely hit class III. We could probably handle it in an inner tube—which I would never suggest.

Actually...taking a few hours to raft a slow section of the river, just the two of us? Sounds pretty good to me. I'm not sure which scenario would make her more uncomfortable, though.

She twists her mouth to the side. "We don't define *danger* the same way."

"Princess, the age range is four and up. You're going to be

fine." I get a light smack on the arm for my sass. She looks a little more relaxed, though. Kids run around all over the place, and exactly none of them are taking their responsibilities with the oars seriously. She has no chance of being the weakest link on this trip.

"A rogue wave might wash me overboard." She plays coy like she knows she's grasping.

"I would hold onto you."

It's been hard to think about much else since our show for her ex. My hands on her, pulling her close. Her sweet and spicy perfume drifting around us. How her eyes had fluttered shut in anticipation. I should have kissed her until she forgot the guy ever existed. But I hadn't wanted our first kiss to be in front of him, and I'd held back.

Makes no sense, considering he's the only reason we're pretending. Well...*she's* pretending. I'm not doing anything I wouldn't have already done.

"I don't know." Her eyes drift across my chest and down my arms. "I'm not sure you could hold me tight enough."

Is that an invitation? Let me RSVP.

I grab her around the waist and haul her into my arms until we're eye to eye. She shrieks with laughter but wraps her arms around my shoulders. Our PFDs put a bulky layer of padding between us, but I like the feel of her in my arms. She feels like she belongs right here.

"I can handle you."

One of her hands moves over the hair at the nape of my neck. Heat spreads outward across my skin like my own personal supernova, searing everything in its path. That small touch is too much and not nearly enough.

"You did say you like a challenge," she says softly.

Her weight is no issue, but I don't think she's talking about that. Does she think *she's* a challenge? Too much for me to deal with? Too much, full stop? I've got a strong suspicion who gave her that idea.

"You're not a challenge, princess. You're a privilege."

Her full smile is like the sun rising over a mountain peak. We go on staring at each other as though the rest of the people out here don't exist. It's just Lila and me.

I've heard this theory that if you stare into someone's eyes long enough, you'll fall in love with them. I might be proving it true. I want to crush her against me like a wild man. I want to kiss her face, her mouth, her neck. I want to keep her in my arms like this forever.

It would make both of our jobs more difficult, but I'm willing to give it a try.

"Ten-minute warning for the eleven o'clock group!" One of the guides peeks his head out of the main office door just long enough to snap us out of our moment.

Pink washes over Lila's cheeks as she tracks the space behind me. If we're having anything like the same thought, she's remembering we're not the only two people on the planet.

Slowly, I lower her to the ground. We put a little space between us—but only a little.

"So do you have river certifications, too?" she says too casually.

Casual. Here's where my fake boyfriend acting skills finally come into play.

"Nah. That's my brother Rhett. He's a whitewater rafting fiend. He'd be a guide on a river right now if he didn't have responsibilities at our family's stores."

"Just like you would have been a mountain guide."

"Something like that."

She watches me too closely, no doubt drawing all sorts of harrowing conclusions.

"It's our family business. We always knew we would work

there eventually." One day, I'll most likely take over for our parents at the helm of operations. It doesn't feel like that fact would help my case when she seems to think I gave up my dreams for the family business.

I barely even think about it anymore.

"Yeah, but what about doing what makes you happy?"

"That's what vacations like this are for." Not that I want the reminder that that's all this is. Some downtime where I get to pretend we're together before I have to go back to reality. Hold Lila close for a little while before I let her go.

"I used to think that way, but after spending years at a company that didn't appreciate me, I've realized I'd rather create a life I don't need to take a vacation from."

"That's the tourism job for you?"

"Yeah. If I get it. I spent years trying to maintain the cool-guy image of a tech firm. Everything was all about their bottom line, how smart they are, and making what they do vaguely admirable. Working for Sunshine, I'll be boosting everyone's businesses and helping a whole community. I'll be doing the social media and event planning I enjoy, and also doing something *good*. I haven't had that in a long time."

She could want this promotion for entirely superficial reasons, and I wouldn't blame her for it. But her earnest desire to build up her hometown and make a difference is like seeing a piece of her golden heart shining out just below the surface. I love that glimpse.

I want all the glimpses.

"I hope you get it."

"Me, too." She narrows her eyes on me, her x-ray vision peering into my head. "Do you like your job?"

It's a genuine question, and it deserves a genuine answer.

"Working for Irwin Outdoors is all I've ever known." Aside from when I was away at college, I've had a job there in some form or another for twenty years. I've never considered working anywhere else. Even if a different opportunity sought me out, I don't think much could compel me to take it. It's too ingrained in who I am. "But I like working with people, and talking up the gear in our stores. I don't mind the routine of monthly reports and sales numbers. And I like being in charge."

Her eyebrows tick up, and I swear her eyes turn a darker brown in the dappled sunlight shining through the trees. "I didn't see that coming."

"Being in control has a certain appeal." I refuse to let that train of thought take hold, or I'll derail this entire conversation. "I admit there's a...sameness to the job lately, but I'm not unhappy in my work."

For a split second, she looks almost disappointed, but that quickly flickers into a bright smile. "Good. If you were, I would have a thing or two to say to your parents."

"I don't doubt it."

Behind us, other rafters start filing into the offices for the safety presentation. Our ten minutes are just about up.

"Are you ready to do this?" I ask her.

"Not in the slightest."

———

I wish I could take pictures of Lila just like this—screaming her head off as we go over every stretch of tumbling water like she's on the best rollercoaster ride of her life. Grinning at me in the spaces in between, when the river's almost peaceful. Completely at ease.

I wasn't sure she would be. Chances were high her screams would be sincere. But she's enjoying herself even more than I'd hoped, and it's a beautiful thing to see.

I'm not nearly as relaxed. Our conversation rolls through my mind in the quiet moments, gnawing at something tender I haven't looked at in years. I would expect Dean to be the one to have an existential crisis on a whitewater rafting trip, but it turns out that's me.

I'm not unhappy. The more I repeat it, the more off it sounds, like a guitar string slowly going out of tune until it's unrecognizable. I enjoy my job. I like working with my family. I know all of my responsibilities inside and out.

And yet...

I took a month-long sabbatical and can't adequately explain why I needed it. I spend most of my time at Rhett's apartment because my own house is haunted by the ghost of my mistakes. Dean and Eliza's joy makes me so deeply envious, sometimes I can't handle being around them. I'm somehow in a fake relationship with the one woman in years who makes me want to try for a real one again.

I'm not unhappy...but I don't know exactly what I am. I'm not sure if I'm living the life I want or the life I think I'm supposed to have.

The last time I thought I knew, I was dead wrong.

I used to go into the mountains for clarity. Right now, maybe I need a little chaos.

"Check out the osprey!" Our guide in the rear of the raft points to the bird in flight thirty feet or so past Lila's shoulder. It slowly flaps its wings, seemingly content to join our party.

She clutches her oar to her chest and leans to the center of the boat. "No, thank you."

The guide laughs. "They've got a big wingspan, but they're small birds. Only about three pounds."

"And they'll claw your eyes out."

The little girl riding in the front of the boat with her mom whips her head around to face Lila. "What?"

Her small face contorts with fear, and I suspect Lila's nightmares are about to spread to a new home.

Lila sits up straighter and grins wide. "I said, you have to keep an eye out. Because...they're so cool to see."

The girl grins back and looks at the bird as it climbs higher. "Yeah, they are."

Lila meets my eyes and cringes adorably. I can only nod at her as affection rushes over me like I'm standing in the middle of this raging river. Maybe the life I want is right here, after all.

TWENTY-ONE

LILA

GRANT IS SO IRRESISTIBLY cute when he's gloating. I never thought those words could fit together, but I never met anyone like Grant before. He's not even gloating about himself, it's about me. He's just so pleased I had a good time on the river—like my happiness is a prize, and he's standing on the winner's block.

I admit, I had a lot of fun out there, despite getting too close to yet another bird of prey. The little rapids we paddled over were exhilarating, but I never felt anything other than safe. Although, I'm pretty sure most of that was because I had Grant right beside me.

The only thing that could possibly mar the memory is the "I pee in rivers" hat my mountain man wore the whole time. I will just block that part out when I reminisce.

Also? It's a good thing I wore a bathing suit beneath my clothes. Anything still dry after the rapids wound up drenched during the water fight. On one calm stretch of river, the four boats in our group faced off. Apparently, there's an art to splashing someone with a paddle, and the people on the other teams had crazy talent. Grant and I changed into dry clothes when we got back to the rafting offices, but I can't shake the chill.

"Can we turn on the heat?" We're probably halfway back to town, and it's pushing eighty-five out, but I'm shivering in his roomy SUV.

Grant's gaze drifts over me. "Are you cold? Here." He stretches his right arm behind him to grab something off the back seat and lays it over me. Then, he turns on the heater and directs the dash vents my way.

I worm into the gray hoodie he gave me and slide the zipper straight to the top. It's soft and cozy like he's worn it for years, and his minty-herbal scent wraps around me as if I'm cuddled in his arms. Why are men's hoodies so much better than women's? I'd like to trade my drafty apartment for this hoodie and live in it forever, please and thank you.

"That's the good stuff," I say, snuggling deeper into the fleece.

His gaze hits me again. "No arguments here."

How does he manage to go from cute to smoldering in point-five seconds? I look like I spent the day battling Poseidon, and he still makes me feel like the most gorgeous woman in the room. Car. Wherever. It's one of his many irresistible qualities, and warms me up even better than his hoodie that I'm already plotting to steal.

"Would this be an acceptable time to take you up on your offer to share your hot tub?" Not that I've been longing for a dip since I first saw it or anything.

"With you shivering like that? You'd better."

"Ooh, it's almost five. Will you stop at the lodge so I can get a hot cocoa first?"

"Of course. Will you stay for dinner? I was just going to make pasta and an Alfredo sauce, but I have plenty."

I grin at him as I slowly pull his hood up over my head. "That's my favorite."

"Mine, too."

When we finally roll into the lobby, I'm delighted to discover that one of the urns for the cocoa packets is full of warm milk instead of water. The cocoa cart is loaded up with a variety of high-end mixes to choose from, a caramel syrup dispenser, and sturdy glass canisters holding marshmallows, sprinkles, wafer cookies, and toffee bits.

The cart next to it holds glass carafes full of a fuchsia-bright drink and short stacks of cocktail glasses. The carafes are labeled *Madras*, with a little canister of lime slices next to them. Looks yummy, but I'm not in the mood for an alcoholic drink tonight.

I've made enough sketchy choices lately. No need to add tipsiness into the mix.

Grant stands right next to me, his arm against mine, while I carefully pour ingredients into my paper cup like a mad scientist working out a new concoction. A couple of hotel guests sit in the lobby chatting over their drinks, but with no one in line behind me, I have time to indulge in all the goodies. I love me some hot cocoa.

"My teeth hurt just watching you make that," he says in a low voice.

I glare up at him. "You don't have a sweet tooth, do you?"

The snacks he brought on the hike should be answer enough. *Sugar? What's that?* He didn't really like the boba tea, either, although that might have had more to do with thinking the tapioca pearls looked like fish eggs.

Ever so slowly, he raises one hand and lightly trails his knuckles along my jawline. "I like some sweet things."

This must be how people spontaneously combust. Grant Irwin says something sexy and barely touches them and—poof!

Inferno from the inside out. Can he see the flames in my eyes? Does he have any idea what he's doing to me?

I'm trying to come up with a flirty response when I hear Josh's laughter behind me. Those delicious flames wink out, replaced with shards of ice. Did Grant see him first? Is that why he went full seduction just now? I'm not sure I want to know.

We turn to face him. He's in chinos and a white dress shirt, hair immaculate, shoes shiny. Probably just waltzed in from trying to buy that company in Bend out from under the owners for less than it's worth. His wide smile tempts me to see what his crisp shirt would look like covered in hot chocolate stains.

I resist, only because someone would have to mop up the floor afterward. Revenge sounds sweet, but not at my friend Charlie's expense.

"Lilabird, your taste in fashion has changed since you came back to Oregon."

Grant's hoodie is so big, it covers my shorts. I look like I'm standing here in a sweatshirt, sneakers, and nothing else. After the splash contest, there's no way my primer held onto my makeup the way it should. I probably have raccoon eyes to rival a deranged clown.

His gaze skates over my body like an unwanted touch. "You'd be so much prettier if you tried a little harder."

Grant steps between Josh and me so fast I barely register him moving. "Don't talk to her like that."

He's calm and collected, but his voice is the equivalent of putting up his dukes. This man is *not* messing around. In this moment, I don't care about perceived gender roles and damsels in distress. I like Grant stepping up. A lot.

I peek around his shoulder to see Josh's fake smile widen. Like right before a snake reveals its fangs. "Do you know who I am?"

It's one of his favorite questions, and a last resort when he isn't getting his way. Eventually, the person in question realizes that he's from one of the wealthiest families in Seattle and owns a multi-million dollar tech firm. I've seen it play out dozens of times, and people always back down once they figure out he's "somebody."

This time around, though? Grant takes a step closer to him.

"Yeah, I know who you are. You're the jerk insulting my girlfriend. Don't ever do it again."

Maybe *this* will be what causes all of my organs to burst into flame. Grant Irwin calling me his girlfriend. I'm a toasty marshmallow melting to goo.

He turns back to me. The hardness in his expression transforms into tenderness. "Is your cocoa how you want it?"

I fight the urge to laugh—after casually growling at my former fiancé, he's thinking about my hot chocolate? "I'm good."

He nods, takes my hand, and leads me out of the lodge without another glance in Josh's direction. He storms across the parking lot, clutching my hand tightly like he needs to be sure of me next to him. When we reach his SUV, he opens the passenger door and gently takes my paper cup to tuck the cocoa safely into the center console.

He straightens and stares down at me as if he's expecting a reprimand. "I'm sorry, but I couldn't stand there and let that guy—"

Nope. No way will I allow him to apologize for a single part of that interaction. I reach up until I've got one hand on his shoulder, the other on the back of his neck, and pull him to me. In the split second before I get him where I want him, understanding dawns, and his eyes darken.

Our mouths meet, merge, fuse. I am bonded to Grant, and I have no intention of letting him go. His hands trace over my back and draw me into him, removing the last hint of space between us.

His lips are firm and decisive as he quickly takes control of the kiss. He tilts my face to one side, gently maneuvering me to open up to him. He pauses the barest moment, like he's giving me room to resist or pull away. I love his concern for my comfort, but I don't want to stop.

I scrape my nails against his scalp as our tongues slide together. He groans against my mouth, a needy, insistent sound. There's something intoxicating about making this easy-going man lose his cool over me. I want more.

He flexes his fingers against my back, massaging in small strokes until they rest on my hips. The kiss turns slow and languid, more like a hundredth kiss than our first. Like we have endless time ahead of us to kiss and caress and cuddle.

A teeny tiny thought whispers through my kiss-fogged brain that we don't have endless time. I can't keep him. He's going home in a few weeks, and I'm fighting for my promotion here in Sunshine. This month together is all we get.

But now is not the time for sad thoughts. I shut out the reminder and focus on him. His firm shoulders beneath my hands. His insane warmth that makes me wonder why I ever thought I needed an outside source of heat. His afternoon stubble scratching my mouth in the best way.

Finally, our kisses gentle, both of us easing away until we're staring at each other. It's not late enough for sunset, but this might as well be the golden hour. He looks more handsome than ever in the late afternoon light. My rugged, sweet mountain man.

I think I just unlocked a new core memory, and I won't mind at all if this one turns up in my dreams.

TWENTY-TWO

LILA

I HADN'T CONSIDERED JUST how awkward it would be to hang out in Grant's hot tub after he gave me the best kiss of my life. For the record, it's super awkward. Mostly because I want to splash over to his side and go in for another round.

Impulse control has never been my favorite.

We soak in the warm water and fiddle with the tub's jets and most definitely do not mention the kiss. Not mentioning it has to be equally as awkward as mentioning it would be, though, right? The silence raises too many questions. Does he regret it? Did we take our faking too far? Was it fake for him? Is it remotely possible his feelings are just as tangled up as mine are?

But I don't bring up the kiss. I opt for something less confusing.

"What is World of Warcraft?"

His eyes snap to mine and it takes him a second to process that. Maybe he was thinking about kisses and questions, too. "What do you want to know? I can tell you way too much about it."

I sink deeper into the water until my chin dips beneath the surface. The delicious heat has chased away the last of the lingering chill from the river. "Is it a fighting game? A quest game? One of those where you create characters and pretend to be a wizard?"

I've never played anything like that, but I'm at least aware enough to have some concept. An extremely vague concept, but it counts. I mostly play games on my phone where I move a jewel to make rows of three shapes or colors. Easy to learn, easy to get addicted.

"Yes to all. Except I usually play as a paladin."

"What's that?"

He shrugs. "They do a few things, but usually I'm the strongest one you send in first. The one who stands on the front lines and takes hits to protect the rest of the team."

"That makes sense for you." I like imagining him as some kind of pixelated protector taking out bad guys to keep his group safe. Just like he kept me safe on the trail. Looking out for other people comes naturally to him. Maybe it's the big brother in him.

"Don't read too much into it."

"Oh, it's already done. You like being the one who charges in and puts himself in harm's way before trouble can reach your team. You're the dependable one everyone else relies on."

I suspect he's the same with his family and his job. Responsibility and protectiveness run deep.

"It's just a game." His little mouth twitch confirms more than he probably realizes. That's his modesty shining through—which completely proves my point.

I extend my legs to poke his knees with my toes. "A game you've poured a ton of time into. One might say your personality has seeped into the character you play."

"One might say." He grabs my feet and pulls them into his lap. My legs are just long enough to reach without having to stretch through the water too obviously. His hands clasp my soles, his thumbs gently rubbing into the arches. "Sometimes I play the rogue, too."

Ooh, yeah, he does. Who isn't into a good guy with a spicy streak? "Are those the ones who give the tastiest bits of their snacks to hapless wanderers, and share their tents with shivering women whenever needed?"

Wait. No. I should not be thinking about sharing the tent right now. Definitely should not speak of it. Sharing a hot tub is difficult enough without pouring gasoline over all of these flames. Plus, the foot rub is not optimal for maintaining non-flammable thoughts.

Between that and the mischief shining in his eyes, my insides are nothing but mush. I grip the molded plastic edge of my seat, ready to push myself firmly back onto my own side... or launch myself straight into his arms. I haven't decided which.

"That's the paladin," he says, delicately massaging each of my toes. "The rogue would pickpocket you."

"I'm safe. I don't have any doubloons."

"Coppers."

"Yeah, yeah." I haven't had a foot massage in ages, and I'm already a little loopy from this double-barreled version. "I feel like a rogue would steal a kiss."

Is that a hint or a cry for help? I have no idea.

"He would go after the most valuable thing you have."

Grant's hands on my feet don't stop moving, but I freeze. The warm water laps at me and I sway like a buoy as his response screams through my head in flashing red neon. I don't want to misinterpret him, but I have literally so many ways to take that, and all of them feel wrong.

"I might have a penny in my pocket after all." My attempt at a joke sounds flat and sad, even with the breezy smile I stick on.

He squeezes my feet and releases them. My balance shifts,

and I slowly tilt toward him, almost meeting in the middle of the hot tub.

His rakish grin starts my stomach on a mini rollercoaster ride. "The rogue would want to win your heart, princess."

———

I'm not even a little bit shocked that Grant's a good cook. A guy doesn't have this many layers of responsibility baked into his personality and wind up useless in the kitchen. He lets me help in small ways, but mostly, I watch him work.

"You're good with a knife," I say as he chops up parsley for garnish. "But I knew that already from watching you whittle."

He grins over the cutting board. "I'm trying to impress you with my strongest skills."

Such a liar. If that were true, he would go in for a repeat of that parking lot kiss we're not discussing.

Or thinking about. Because how awkward would that be, right?

So awkward.

"Tell me how the engagement party is going to go. I don't think I've been to one."

I snap myself out of musing over what it would be like to kiss him hello every time I see him. "Your brother didn't have one?"

"They eloped."

"Oh yeah. That didn't make people mad?" Specifically, their parents. Mine would lose their minds if Hope or I tried that. They want us happy, but they want to witness the happiness.

"No?" He makes a face like it's a strange question.

Men are so wild.

"Right. Well, engagement parties might be more common when your mom is over the top."

"I suspect that's why Eliza chose to elope."

Smart woman. My mom never got the chance to plan a party for me. Josh and I were supposed to have a long engagement—plenty of time to organize the perfect wedding, the ideal reception, the dream honeymoon. We thought a year or two at least. Now, I feel like our willingness to put off our future together should have been a sign. Hope and Griffin would get married tomorrow if they could be sure everyone they love most could be with them to see it.

A year ago, I would have advised her to slow down and make sure every last detail is exactly right. Now, I envy her certainty that Griffin's the right man for her more than any idealized wedding scenario.

Grant sets aside the parsley and wipes off his hands. "I should tell you, I don't have nice clothes with me. If it's very over the top, I'll need to find something better than casual pants and a button down."

"You'll look great in anything."

He lifts one skeptical eyebrow, but his mouth curls with the beginning of a smirk.

"Not these athletic shorts, obviously." I'm a huge fan of the way they hug his amazing booty, but I don't want to share that view. "Pants would be best."

"I can swing pants. Anything else I should know?"

"Hope and Griffin are super chill about it, but I think they're giving Mom a little responsibility now so she doesn't go crazy with the main event." I wish them the best of luck with that. It'll be like reining in a tween at the makeup counter with her mom's credit card. "It's really just a casual party so my mom can say, 'Hey everyone, at least one of my daughters is getting married.'"

Grr. I need to learn to shut my mouth when I'm ahead. I would have been better off rhapsodizing about his butt in those athletic shorts.

He looks up from the creamy sauce he's stirring. "Will this be uncomfortable for you?"

"No. *No.* It's fine. No." If I say no enough, maybe one of us will believe it.

He goes on watching me. Being around someone this perceptive is comforting and annoying at the same time. Sometimes I need him to *not* see what I'm feeling for a change.

"Maybe a little? Not because I still want that." No universe exists in which I would ever take Josh back. "Just the weirdness of everybody knowing I *was* engaged, and now I'm not. It's kind of putting my failures on display, you know?"

All of our friends and family know by now, but that doesn't mean they won't have questions. I can only hope they'll be too dazzled by my sister and her fiancé to ask any of them.

"I know." The intensity in his gaze is like an electric shock rippling across my skin. "You wonder if everyone's trying to figure out what you did to deserve it. How much of the break up was your fault. If there's something wrong with you."

I draw in a breath. He just sucker punched my heart right on its livid bruise. Completely by accident, I'm sure, but I wasn't ready for the ache those words pull to the surface.

"Exactly." My voice is a tiny little whisper.

He shuts off the burner and moves the sauce off of the heat before he steps toward me. My skin feels too tight, like my body's pressed beneath a microscope glass and I can't get free. Is he asking himself the same questions? What did I do wrong with Josh? Did I deserve to be dumped? Was his cheating my fault?

"Lila." Grant's oh-so soft in his soothing. He reaches up to tuck a loose strand of hair behind my ear, his fingertips barely touching me. Then, his arms come around my shoulders and he pulls me against him.

I sink into his embrace, my cheek on his chest, one hand gripping his side. Goodness, this man is warm. And so, so sweet. I am *not* going to cry—I won't keep spilling tears over how unwanted and unloveable Josh's betrayal made me feel. But Grant's hold calms that too-tight sensation until I can relax in my own skin again.

He tips his chin down to rest against the top of my head. "There's nothing wrong with you, princess. You deserve so much better than anything that guy could ever give you."

I nod my head, not trusting myself to speak and not ask if I deserve *him*. This isn't about that. Grant's not trying to hit on me. He just wants to make me feel better. He's looking out for me without expecting anything in return.

It's like being away for a long time and finally falling asleep in your own bed. That overwhelming sense of belonging—of being safe and comfortable and *home*.

"Anyone who's met that guy knows it was never about you."

He's so certain, yet so very wrong. "One of my friends told me guys don't cheat if the woman they're with treats them right."

One of many supposed friends who dropped out of my life the minute Josh did. I hate that her words still stick in my head like a noxious smoke I can't clear from a room. But the questions linger. Was it me? Was I not attentive enough? Did I spend too much time at work? Did he stop finding me attractive? Could I have avoided it?

Grant growls—legitimately growls—the low, angry sound rumbling against my ear as he hugs me tighter. "Anyone *decent* would know it was never about you."

I know it's not as simple as all that, but I love his fervent defense of me. I could have used a friend like him last year.

I could use one now. Only, I'm not sure I could be just friends with Grant. Not when I already want so much more.

"I'm glad I found out he was cheating." It's easy to tell him things cocooned here in his arms, where I don't have to look into his eyes or see his reaction. "It gave me a solid enough reason to leave. His criticism was a hairline fracture that kept spreading, but I convinced myself I could live with it. Maybe I even deserved it. But the cheating was a clean break I couldn't ignore."

"Lila." He runs his hands over my back, soothing and grounding me. "You're making it hard for me not to go to every cabin out here until I find him and do something I will regret. He never deserved you."

His unasked question hovers over us. What did you see in him? Grant's too polite to be that mean, but he's got to be wondering.

"Josh didn't always treat me this way. In my defense, he can be quite charming when he wants to be."

Grant gently pushes me back until we're face to face. He trails his fingers into my hair, cupping the sides of my head, moving his thumbs over my temples. "He hides it well."

I laugh, but the sound dies out. He's still caressing me. Still looking into my eyes like it would be impossible for him to look at anything else. Still making my stomach swoop and dip in anticipation.

Just when I think he's about to lean in, he releases me. "Let's eat."

Yup. Yes. That's exactly what I was anticipating, too. The pasta. Obviously. Not another kiss. The comfort food can be enough for me.

His cabin has a tiny dining table, but we have just enough room for both of our plates. He serves pasta for us and brings slices of the bread he'd warmed in the oven, then pulls a bottle from the fridge and holds it up.

"Wine? I opened it yesterday. It's a good riesling."

"Yes, please." Only one glass, I promise myself. More, and I'm pretty well guaranteed to crank up the awkwardness on this evening to eleven. I need to keep it in a solid seven range. Confiding about Josh pushed the limits, but I think I can bring the average back down.

He pours us glasses and sits across from me. Once we're settled, I take my first bite of pasta. As I suspected, it's bliss.

"This came straight from Alfredo sauce heaven," I say behind a hand.

"Thank you. I've been experimenting with the recipe."

"You can stop tinkering. It's perfect."

His soft smile is almost enough to distract me from the pasta. *Almost*—I only have so much willpower. If I'm not going to get lost in his sizzling kisses, I will just have to indulge in a food coma.

"I'll need to recreate it the next time Eliza enlists me to make dinner."

I give him a curious look. It's all I can manage with my face stuffed full of fettuccini.

"She's trying to make Irwin family dinners happen," he explains.

"It's not going well?" I say as soon as I'm sure pasta won't go flying out of my mouth.

"Oh, it's going. Eliza tends to get her way. Every other week, we have a standing invitation to their house for Tuesday dinner. Rhett is pretty much guaranteed to show up for the free food, and I join them most of the time."

He's leaving out a pretty big chunk of the family in those dinners. "And your parents?"

"They don't join us very often." He pauses. "I think they've shown up twice."

I can't gauge how he feels about that. Usually, he's pretty open, but right now he's careful with his words. "Is there some kind of animosity between you? Or your sister-in-law and them?"

"There's no animosity. They just have other things to do."

"So...they just don't show up?"

His smile is an exact copy of his mid-happy version. "Their usual reasoning is that we see each other in the office every day as it is."

My mom is in my business twenty-four-seven, but it would still hurt if she never joined Hope and me for dinner because she'd already seen me around town. "That's something you say to your coworkers, not your kids."

His eyes light, and I would almost think he's impressed by my little outburst if I didn't realize immediately just how rude a thing that was to say about his parents.

"I'm sorry, I shouldn't have said that. I just can't wrap my head around parents who aren't involved in their kids' lives."

I want to understand, but I don't know what to ask. Every question in my head feels like an accusation. Like *How can your parents not want to spend time with you?* Or *How can they expect you to make lifelong commitments to your family business but not do the same when it comes to your personal lives?* Or the real stunner *Is this why you feel so responsible for everyone? Because nobody is looking out for* you?

"I see that look. You're ready to fight them on my behalf."

I straighten, and try to get the bloodthirsty expression off my face. "It's going around."

"I like that look. But there's no need to hunt down my parents to give them a piece of your mind."

I make a sour face. "I'm still thinking about it."

"They love us, no matter how it sounds. Once they opened their store, the business came first."

"That doesn't sound as good as you think it does," I whisper. "You and your brothers needed people there for you."

My parents run their own businesses, too, but I always knew I could count on them for anything. I can't imagine feeling like their work success was more important.

"My brothers had me. And we were never neglected. We stayed with our Grandma Gloria and Grandpa Connor whenever our parents were overwhelmed with keeping the business afloat. We tore through their huge yard and big old house like little devils. They knew how to keep us in line."

I don't think he realizes how much more tenderness he shows when he talks about his grandparents than when he talks about his mom and dad. "Are your grandparents still with you?"

"We lost Grandpa several years ago, but Grandma still gets up to trouble. She moved into a retirement community a couple of years back, and Dean bought her house. He and Eliza have made it their home." He splays a hand toward me. "Which is why Eliza is doing the family dinner thing."

"Yeah, but your *parents*..."

He shrugs, but I'm not sure he's as indifferent as he's making out to be. "They keep busy."

I open my mouth to respond that they shouldn't be too busy for *family*, but his quick smile makes me hold my tongue. It's a good thing he finds my indignation amusing because I have plenty of it after hearing about this.

I get up to serve him seconds just to show him he can be taken care of too, even in some small way. Well, that, and to keep him from staring into my angry face while I internally explode. My mom meddles too much, but at least I can justify it by how much she loves Hope and me. Not bothering to see your kids outside of work is hard to explain away as an excess of affection. But I can't very well go on a rant about his parents.

I set his refilled plate in front of him, and he looks up at me.

"Thank you." His beaming smile melts a little bit of my anger. "You would make an excellent paladin, by the way. Very strong defender."

I laugh and drop into my seat. "Are they the best dressed?"

"Oh, yeah. Armor like you wouldn't believe."

"Can you have more than one paladin on a team?"

"Sure."

"Then maybe we should team up and take on the bad guys together."

Even if it's only make-believe.

And even if it's only temporary.

TWENTY-THREE

GRANT

I WALK my bright orange mountain bike through Get in Gear's doors, hot, sweaty, and still breathing too hard. I might have overdone it on the trails.

The guy behind the counter looks over his shoulder. He's putting the chain back on a road bicycle that's upside down on a stand. "Good ride?"

When I picked up the bike first thing this morning, another employee gave me a few options for the day's trip. I chose the longest—out of ego or punishment, I'm not sure. But not even a grueling ride through pine trees with stops to take in gorgeous views could keep my mind off of Lila.

When she pulled me to her and kissed me, it rewired my brain. I can't get her out of my head. To be totally honest, I'm not even trying. For years, I've been careful. Minimal dating, and never with anyone I could have feelings for. Meaningless first dates where nobody walked away wanting more. Enough to say I'm trying without ever having to actually try.

Enough to be sure that what happened with Kelsey never happens again.

And now? I spent all day wondering what Lila's wearing and whose ear she's chatting off and how many hours until I see her again. I miss her, and we've only been apart a day.

But I don't think this guy with the tattoo sleeves down both arms wants to hear about how a whirlwind of a woman brought me to my knees.

"Great ride," I answer. "It was a bit more than I bargained for, though."

It's been a while since I biked on terrain that uneven and unpredictable. I think I jostled my spine out of alignment, and I probably have bruises in places I'd rather not name.

His beard twitches with a hint of a smile. "The ones that push you are the best rides. Which one did you do?"

"Garrett Trail." Half a dozen biking paths start within a fifteen-minute ride of the bike shop, everything from paved loops for the family to the bone rattler I opted to try. "It's unbelievable what you've got right outside your front door."

No disrespect to my hometown, but I have to drive thirty miles to Georgetown to get a similar experience.

"We're in mountain biking heaven out here."

"Do you have a recommendation for something similar to Garrett but, let's say, a step down in technical difficulty?" I wouldn't mind getting out there again before I leave, but I don't need to go home with a slipped disc.

"Sure." He pulls a laminated map to the counter between us and indicates different trail names. "You've got a few options, depending on how much time you have to burn. My favorite all-day—"

A clanging behind me makes both of us turn. A blond woman barges through the shop door, practically knocking the bell off its hook. She stalks past the rows of bicycles and over to the counter, glaring like she's about to tear the guy apart.

She crosses her arms over her purple apron. "Your truck is in my spot again, Callahan."

He just blinks at her. "Is it?"

"You know darn well it is."

He pulls his hand over his beard as if he's contemplating this. "The alley spaces aren't assigned, are they?"

I don't know the man, but his innocent act could use some work. Then again, it's probably meant to be obviously fake.

"That's the one that's closest to the bakery's back door. The one I park in every day when I open like I have since I was sixteen. And yet, whenever I come in *after* you're here, where do I find your truck?"

"In an unassigned space that's convenient to my business's back door?"

She looks like she's trying to mentally melt his face off. "You're doing it on purpose."

"I am. It's my favorite spot."

"I asked you nicely."

He snorts. "When?"

She purses her mouth into a frown. "I've been here longer than you."

"Do you want to point me to the part in the lease agreement where it says seniority guarantees premium alley parking?"

"I'll point you to exactly where you can go, you big—"

"I'd love to keep chatting with you Krause, but I'm with a customer."

She turns to me like she hadn't registered I've been standing right here the whole time. Dropping her arms, her murderous gaze softens.

"I apologize," she says, suddenly sugary sweet. "That was rude of me to interrupt."

I brush off her apology. "It's not a problem."

"If you come in next door, I'll give you a free hand pie to make it up to you."

The bike shop owner's eyes narrow on her, but otherwise, he doesn't move.

I feel like I'm on a tightrope strung between the two, and one wrong step will spell disaster. "Thank you, but it's not necessary."

She turns back to him and lifts an eyebrow in a silent challenge. "Callahan."

"Krause. Always good to see you."

She spins on her heel and leaves the store, bells on the door jingling behind her.

Once she's gone, the man's shoulders relax. "Sorry about that. We, ah...aren't on the friendliest terms."

"No need to explain." I won't mention that the last couple I saw snipe at each other like that are married now. "Callahan—you wouldn't be related to Charlie Callahan over at Moonlight Lodge?"

The flint that had been in his eyes when the woman was in here disappears. "That's my sister. She and my folks run the place. Are you staying there?"

"For a couple more weeks. It's an impressive location." I don't want to leave, but that's not entirely due to my comfortable accommodations.

"It is. My grandparents started it, and my parents built it up. Now Charlie's turning it luxury." He wipes his greasy hands on a rag and extends one to me. "I'm Shepherd."

"Grant. Good to meet you." I nod at the array of bikes around us. "Is this place yours?"

"In all its glory." He spreads his hands wide. "The high-end resort life wasn't for me. I'm better with tires and gears any day."

"I understand that." If my folks' business had leaned a

different way, I don't know if I would be as invested as I am. "I'm surprised there aren't more bike rental shops in town, considering all the trails."

"I'll enjoy my monopoly while it lasts. I've been pushing for expanding the trails even more. If that means competition, I'll take it."

A couple with two small children walk through the shop's doors. The boy and girl immediately run to the kids' bikes, and Shepherd's attention shifts their way.

"I'll leave you to it."

"Glad to meet you," he says. "If you rent a bike again, let me know the type of trail you're looking for, and I'll point you in the right direction."

"Will do." I still want to get Lila on a ride, but we'd be better off on paved paths and cruiser bikes. Get in Gear has a wide selection of bicycles though, so that shouldn't be a problem. I start to head out.

"And hey, Grant?"

I turn back to him. "Yeah?"

"Take Krause up on her offer of that free hand pie. Blackbird's next door has the best pies you'll ever eat."

———

I can't get comfortable. I ate dinner, soaked in the hot tub, and tried to read *Walden*, but nothing helped. I even flipped through television channels. And I thought I wanted a month of this?

Normally, I don't mind my own company, but tonight, I'm crawling out of my skin. It's not the quiet that bothers me—it's that *she's* not here.

I can't do this. I can't get used to someone I'm going to have to give up in a couple more weeks. I can't miss her when she's only across town. Soon enough, she'll be across the country, and what will I do then?

I legitimately need to know.

Two minutes later, I pick up my phone.

Grant: How did party planning go?

I lay out on the king-sized bed in my T-shirt and shorts. Night seeps through the cabin, leaving everything but the halo of light around the bedside lamp in shadow. I can't imagine it's too late for her, but as the minutes tick by, I start to second guess.

Finally, my phone buzzes in my hand.

Lila: We're all set for tomorrow!

Lila: Sorry, I was in the shower when your text came through

I refuse to let my thoughts go *there*. It was bad enough sharing a hot tub. If I think about sharing a shower, I'll go crazy.

Lila: Are you ready to make goo-goo eyes at me for my family?

Grant: I've been practicing goo-goo eyes all day

Lila: How was the bike ride?

Grant: Brutal. Know a good chiropractor in town?

Lila: Of course. But maybe you should take it easy on your old bones

Grant: Old? OLD?

Lila: I said what I said

I send her a couple of the better pictures I took on the trail, including a selfie with one of the mountains peeking out from behind me. I get a string of fire emojis in return.

Lila: That's the best one

Grant: Just wait til we get you out there

I won't even see the views.

Lila: It's been a while since I rode a bike

Grant: Years?

Lila: Decades

Lila: Maybe we could do a tandem bike

Lila: You can do all the pedaling, and I'll lounge
in style

Grant: I'd be into that

At this point, I'd do pretty much anything in tandem with her.

Grant: Did you know the bike shop owner is
trying to expand some of the biking trails?
Might be something there you can use in your
presentation

Lila: Really? I'll talk to Shepherd this week

Hmm. Probably shouldn't have told my princess to visit the tattoooed, bearded guy.

> Lila: You've ruined my sleep lately, you know
> that?

Maybe we're more in sync than I thought. My sleep's been absolutely wrecked by dreams about her. About *us*. I never thought I had that great of an imagination before, but it's been working overtime lately.

> Grant: I could say the same about you

> Lila: ???

> Lila: I keep thinking about where we left off in
> your book

I have to read that three times before my brain catches up. Right. She's not talking about *those* kinds of dreams.

> Lila: What did you mean?

> Grant: That's what I meant, too. Gotta know
> what happens next in the book. It's an
> addictive story

Well, this has been fun. I sound like an idiot. I guess she thinks so, too, because it takes a while for her response to come through.

> Lila: Or maybe I just like the sound of your
> voice

Ooh la la. I hit the call button before I overthink it.

She answers on a laugh. "Did you want to talk about the

addictive story?"

"Not really," I admit. "I wanted to hear your voice, too."

"What did you mean when you said you could say the same about me ruining your sleep?"

"I think you already know."

Her breath comes out on a soft sigh. "Yeah. I think I do."

We breathe *in tandem* for a minute, because apparently that's what happens after two people admit they miss hearing each other talk—they have no idea what to say.

"What would help you sleep?"

"Not hearing more of your book," she says. "Everyone has funny names, and they drop you straight into the story like you know what's going on. It's confusing nonsense. I mean, what even happens after the main character got kidnapped by those thieves? Hmm? What?"

"You want me to keep reading?"

"Yes, please."

In a flash, I get up and grab my e-reader from the couch and cozy up on the bed again. It'd be better if she were here listening in person, but if I think too much about that, I won't be able to focus on the book.

Not that that's much of a concern. I read to her for an hour, but I couldn't tell you what happens in the scenes. My voice is a soft caress, as though I'm telling her something else entirely in every word.

I missed you today.

I would read to you every night if you asked me.

It's way too soon to fall for you, but I don't want this to stop.

She yawns as though she's ready to cuddle into her pillow. "Thank you, Grant."

I thought I had it bad before? Hearing her say my name in those sleepy, content tones is a drug. I'm immediately hooked.

"You're welcome, princess."

We hang up, and I lay flat out on the bed in the darkness. I won't be the same man when I go home to Texas. I don't know if I would want to be. Whether she knows it or not, she's marking on me in permanent ink, tattooing herself on my soul.

TWENTY-FOUR

GRANT

I STARE at the pair of non-cargo hiking pants and a plain blue button-down shirt I've laid out on my bed. They're not grungy, but they could be a whole lot better. Finding a nicer outfit somewhere in town had seemed unnecessary until this very minute. Lila will certainly be dressed to impress. I'll look like a chump standing next to her at her sister's party.

To be fair, there was never much chance of anything else.

I don't know if I should put the clothes on or not, so I do something I never thought I would: I text a woman a picture of my outfit to get her approval.

Her reply comes in right away.

Lila: You're going to put them on, right?

Grant: Very funny

Naturally, that gets my thoughts spinning toward all the things we could do without fancy party clothes on. Doesn't take much incentive lately.

Grant: I can still find something else if you want

I have a couple of hours before I'm supposed to meet her at her place. I might be able to come up with a nicer shirt if I need to.

Lila: I guarantee you the groom-to-be won't wear anything fancier

Lila: Hope will be lucky if he's not wearing flannel

Grant: Sounds like my kind of guy

Lila: You two are going to be BFFs

Lila: You'll talk about expert outdoorsman stuff all night

Grant: Never. I'll be right by your side all night

Lila: Promises, promises

Lila: See you soon

Another text comes in after hers.

Moonlight Lodge: Grant Irwin has received a package. Please come to the front desk to claim it.

A package sent to me on vacation? The first thing that comes to mind is that Dean forwarded a printout of the monthly sales report just to be a stickler. Unlikely, but in the realm of possibility.

I walk the half mile or so of dirt trail to the lodge. It's peaceful out here, winding through the pines. Off to the west, a mountain peak looms, and the river serenades me the whole way. I'm not one of those people who gets the urge to move to every place they vacation, but it's hard not to want to stick around a while in Sunshine.

At the front desk, an older woman talks with a couple who are holding fishing poles and gear. Gray strands streak through her red hair, and I have a strong suspicion this is Charlie and Shepherd's mother. When she finishes up doling out advice about the best locations on their property to fly fish, she comes closer to me.

She offers a warm smile that I know is her customer service duty, but I still find it comforting. "What can I do for you?"

"I'm Grant Irwin in the Archer cabin. I received a message that you have a package for me."

"We do. Let me go get it."

She disappears through a door behind the counter. I'm still trying to figure out who would send me a package to Oregon when someone interrupts my thoughts.

"Irwin? Of the Eastlake Irwins?"

I look to my right to see Josh leaning an elbow on the front desk counter wearing a lazy smile. His expressions run the whole gamut from *smug* to *smirk*. Every single one just begs to be wiped off by someone's fist.

"No." I turn back to wait for Mrs. Callahan to return. This guy isn't worth getting worked up over. Even if the memory of the things he said to Lila's face the other day make me want to teach him a lesson in manners.

"Hey, no hard feelings, all right?" he says. "I hope you'll be able to make Lila happy. It isn't an easy job."

His laughter has my hands balling into fists.

"She's beautiful, but high maintenance." He just doesn't know when to quit.

"Was she? Or did you just not want to put in the effort?"

"Oh, I put in the effort. It was never enough for her. I just hope she doesn't leave you at the altar like she did me." He taps the counter twice. "Good luck."

He walks away, leaving me with my chest caving in.

———

I pace my small cabin, the package I'd gone to retrieve unopened on the bed. My brain is a tangle of Josh's smarmy warning on repeat, my stomach an ever-tightening knot. Lila wouldn't have done that. Couldn't have.

Would she?

The man is a slimeball through and through. She's admitted it took him cheating before she finally got the courage to leave. I just have no idea the timeline there. Surely she wouldn't have waited until their wedding day to call things off.

Some women do, though.

I want to hike, bike, run—anything to escape this ache hollowing me out.

She never described their breakup as leaving him at the altar. But would she? Would anyone willingly admit to doing something like that? She has a hard time admitting tough truths to people. I don't think she would lie about it, but would she simply avoid telling me?

I sit down hard on the bed. I've done exactly that—I haven't told her about my past, either. I can't be upset with her for potentially glossing over the truth when I haven't done any better.

Next to the package, my clothes still wait on the bed, ready for me to put them on and meet up with Lila. I drag my fingers through my hair, raking them over my scalp. I'm supposed to pretend to be her boyfriend in two hours. Put on a big show for her family and friends.

So far, I haven't had to act in this fake dating scenario, but tonight, I just might.

I rip open the package that led to all of this. There's no note, but it doesn't need one.

It's a bright red T-shirt with bold script that says *Do the Stupid Thing*.

Maybe I am.

———

Twenty minutes later, I stand outside Lila's apartment door. I texted asking if I could come by early, and she'd agreed. But now that I'm here, I don't know if I'm ready for this conversation. I don't want whatever we say to ruin what we have.

But I know well enough that *not* talking doesn't solve anything.

Ready or not, I knock.

She pulls the door open, and I physically cannot draw in a breath for several seconds while I stare like my last two brain cells have fainted dead away.

Lila's stunning. A soft, floral dress flows around her like a pink and orange cloud. Her hair is slightly curled, and a hint of makeup accentuates her cheeks and eyes. I want to stand here for a day to drink in the sight of her. I want to bend down and kiss her glossy lips. I breathe deep, and that sweet but spicy scent I'd caught on her before fills my lungs.

"You look magnificent," I finally say. Because even though my stomach feels like a credit card stuck halfway through a paper shredder, I can't say anything else.

Her smile is both a shot of adrenaline to my heart and a punch straight to my gut.

"Thank you. Come on in. It's kind of..." She waves me inside. "Well, it is what it is, and it's not great."

Her apartment is a brick-walled studio with high windows facing Maple Street. She's got a small outdated kitchenette, a cozy gray sofa, and several bookshelves. Her bed is plush with pillows and a hunter green throw blanket.

The insane thought that her blanket exactly matches the color of Irwin Outdoors' employee vests rattles through my brain. Is that kismet or some kind of cosmic torture?

"Look at you." She shuts the door behind her and moves to face me. "See? Your outfit options turned out great."

I run my hands over my shirt as if I can iron it with their clamminess. "Yeah. Thanks."

A little crease mars her forehead. "Is everything okay?"

Yes. Everything except I'm having severe déjà vu from my worst nightmare.

"Not entirely. I need to talk with you."

She sobers instantly. Maybe she has a collection of dreads of her own. "Okay. Do you want to sit down?"

We move to the sofa, where I'm entirely too close to her, but I can't very well get back up and loom over her while I stand.

"Do you remember our conversation when we were stargazing in the woods?"

Pink washes over her cheeks. "Yes. We talked about our breakups."

"We did. But I wasn't entirely honest with you about mine."

She goes stiff, and I can tell I'm messing this up already. I need to just dive into the deep end.

"The relationship that blindsided me? We were engaged, too. But she didn't end things until the day of the wedding."

"Oh, Grant." Lila wraps a hand around mine. "I'm so sorry."

I don't talk about this. Mostly, because everyone in Magnolia Ridge already knows. There's nothing for me to explain. Even with my brothers, it's not a thing we discuss.

They lived through it with me, they know the ins and outs. It's hard to know where to start.

"Kelsey and I had friends in common and similar interests. It'd seemed...natural that we would wind up together. But both of us were just ignoring the truth." In a word, I'd been Rhett's favorite thing: stupid. Avoiding arguments doesn't mean a relationship is working. And feeling like you *should* be with someone isn't the same as having a bone deep *need* to. "I'd bought us a house, everything was ready...and then Kelsey never showed up to the church."

I can't even remember how I felt getting ready that day. Joy? Anticipation? It's all been blurred out by the sick, sinking sensation when one of the bridesmaids took me aside to break the news.

Lila wraps an arm around my shoulders, her hand on mine tightening almost painfully. It's oddly comforting.

"Grant. I had no idea."

"I don't like bringing it up." People in Magnolia Ridge have *blessed my heart* so many times, I should be invincible.

She rubs her hand over my back. "Did she ever apologize to you?"

"Not quite. Eventually, she got in touch. Admitted she realized she wasn't in love with me and couldn't go through with it." The worst part might have been when she told me I wasn't really in love with her, either. It'd felt like a parting shot, but now I know she was right.

"Grant. That was so wrong of her. You deserve better than that." She gets quiet. "Is that why you don't like your house? Because it was for the two of you?"

"It reminds me of my mistakes."

"They weren't your mistakes. They were hers."

I'd like to indulge that belief, but I shake my head. "We both screwed up. She could have had better timing, but we're better off this way."

"She should have been honest with you, face to face, and dealt with the fallout. That's a horribly selfish thing to do."

I flip my hand over to hold hers tight. "Thank you."

"I'm sorry this Kelsey treated you that way. She's unbearably stupid for letting you go."

I try to hide my smile. She's so certain in her defense of me. "Josh was stupid to ever think to cheat on you."

And stupid to toss out that lie about her leaving him at the altar. Whatever he does with apps and software, his greatest skillset seems to be manipulation.

"We were both with absolute buffoons," she says. "We need to make better choices in the future."

"No question."

"Can I hug you?"

"Please."

She ducks under my arm and cuddles into me. I hold her tight, banishing every last regret about Kelsey. If things had gone down any other way, I wouldn't be here holding Lila in my arms. And nothing's worth losing that.

Our breathing slows until our lungs move in time, matching each other's pace. I run a hand along her bare shoulder, marveling at her soft skin. Really, it's her big, soft heart I'm in awe of. I don't know if I'll be able to let her go when my time here ends.

I do love a challenge, but giving Lila up might be the hardest one I've faced yet.

Eventually, she pulls back, keeping her arms lightly around me. "I need to say something."

I brace myself. "Okay."

"You deserve to be top priority in someone's life."

I swallow hard, but I can't look away from her brown eyes blazing into mine.

"I'm mad at your parents for not putting you and your brothers first in their lives when you needed them most. And I'm furious with that woman who walked away without a word and left you to pick up the pieces."

My sweet, soft-hearted paladin, ready to take out my enemies for me. One of her hands takes hold of mine again.

"You, Grant Irwin, should be someone's whole world."

More clearly than ever, I want that someone to be her.

TWENTY-FIVE

LILA

"THIS IS GOING TO BE FINE." I nod as though I'm in total agreement with myself, which I absolutely am not. "And if you decide it's all too much, just say the secret code word, and we'll leave."

Grant and I stand in front of the wooden fence that leads into my parents' backyard, his hand clutched in mine. Classic rock music drifts around us, and cars line the block. I know what I'll find when we open the gate because I helped Hope set it all up yesterday, but I'm still buzzing like a nervous bee.

Grant has zero reason to do this for me. There's no quid pro quo the way my rom-coms tell me fake dating is supposed to go. He could back out right this second, and I wouldn't blame him.

There are a *lot* of people out there.

And even though Mom asked me approximately ten thousand questions about him yesterday, I know for a fact she hasn't had her fill of Grant yet. Tonight, she'll be able to go straight to the source.

"What's the code word?" he asks.

My heart lurches that he even wants to know. "Um...how

about 'marmot?' You say that, and I'll know you're done, and we can go."

"What if I want to tell the story about the marmot?"

"Ugh, they'll probably want to hear that. Maybe 'bite-valve?' Will that work?"

"Your code words are fascinating."

"I want it to be easy for you to remember. Escape pods should be simple to operate."

"I don't need an escape pod, Lila. I'm here for you."

I can't help but smile up at him. He's just so *good*. He's kind and generous and so stinking handsome, I don't think my stomach has stopped doing backflips since the first time I saw him.

And here he is, sweetly offering to walk into the lion's den wearing a meat suit and calling, *Here, kitty kitty.*

"Okay, well...let's get weird."

I push the gate open, and we walk the paver path into the back yard. It's my mom's pride and joy, an oasis of native plants and evergreen trees. One corner holds a fire pit, already blazing, and another boasts three cozy outdoor sofas around a little table, currently bearing an ice chest full of drinks. It won't be dark out for a while yet, but Hope and I strung lights overhead, which Mom says will remain a permanent fixture.

Also? The yard is stuffed with people. Family and friends spread out over the space, mingling by the hors-d'oeuvres table on the patio and spilling out over the lawn. The couple of the moment are plastered to each other in the lounge area, surrounded by congratulating guests. It's festive, cheery, casual fun—exactly what Hope wanted. And yet, I still don't want to join in.

So much of my life feels like a lie, I can't tell if it's fitting or just really, really horrible that I created a fake boyfriend partially for this event. And is it better or worse that I don't want a single bit of him to be fake?

Grant squeezes my hand. "You okay, princess?"

I don't have a chance to respond. Mom's seen us. She shouts, "Lila!" like she's Marianne Dashwood spotting Willoughby across a crowded ballroom. Everyone turns to gawk. Any hopes of playing this cool just disintegrated in the fires of her glaring enthusiasm.

She rushes over, snagging my dad away from where he's talking with Griffin's brother. Her gauzy pale green dress and half up-do makes her look like a goddess on her way to bless us with fertility.

Which she would absolutely do if it occurred to her.

Dad, of course, is effortlessly handsome in the way older men get to be—looking dapper *because* of his wrinkles and salt and pepper hair, not in spite of them. Personality-wise, he's the perfect complement for Mom: calm and cool, where she's excitable and eager. Kind of like Griffin is for Hope.

I refuse to entertain all the lunatic thoughts that bounce around in my head about whether or not Grant could be that for me.

"We're so pleased you could make it tonight." Mom extends a hand to him. "This is my husband Paul. Paul, honey, this is Grant Irwin."

His name rolls off her tongue like she's been practicing it. She's probably written our names side by side, too, just to see how they look.

"Nice to meet you, Grant." The two shake hands. "Although, I have to admit I'm a little fuzzy on how you two met. Do I have it right that you don't live around here?"

I didn't expect my sweet father to go straight for my jugular like that.

"That's true. I live in Magnolia Ridge, Texas, a small town north of Austin."

"Lila's always talked about visiting Texas," Mom cuts in.

"I'm not sure I've ever said that." Not that I wouldn't, but she's making it sound like it's my life-long dream.

Her eyes widen in a comically warning look.

"So you're just here for..." Dad prompts.

"Vacation," Grant finishes. "I'm staying in the Moonlight Lodge for a few weeks."

Dad nods, but the fact that he doesn't seem to have more to say deflates my spirits a bit. He's obviously sizing Grant up, and I want to jump in to defend him. I'm just not sure from what.

Hope and Griffin join us, and another set of introductions go around. As I suspected, Griffin and Grant—which, by the way, is going to make every interaction they have one big tongue-twister—are dressed pretty similarly. Hope's coral A-line dress is understated but classy.

It's their giant twin smiles that let everyone know they're the guests of honor.

"Congratulations," Grant tells them. "I wish you every happiness."

"Thank you." Griffin pulls Hope snug against him. "I've got it."

She glows like a sunbeam. I've never seen her as happy as she's been these last six months. Between her thriving business, her increasingly popular artwork, and finding the love of her life, she's had a pretty awesome year.

I lean closer against Grant. I'm doing fine. Or I will be. Soon enough.

"So you two met on that hike Lila did?" Griffin looks like he's battling laughter. "I'm trying to imagine how that went."

"I had a lot of fun, thank you very much." I turn my nose up at my soon-to-be brother-in-law. He's honestly the best, but he doesn't need to turn his teasing against me this early in the night.

He arches one eyebrow. Really, they're all leveling me similar looks.

"Okay, it wasn't the time of my life," I say. "But I finished it. I didn't ask to be airlifted out or rescued by the National Guard."

Hope beams her smile my way. "I'm proud of you. You weren't sure you could do it, but you did it anyway."

I'll take the praise. I don't want to get sidetracked tonight talking about the hike, but it *wasn't* easy.

"Tell us, Grant," Mom says. "What drew you to Lila?"

Hope hisses, "Mom," but otherwise, our little circle goes completely silent. I'm surprised nobody asks to turn down the music so they don't miss a word of Grant's answer.

I still. We didn't discuss any of this in our hasty *Let's pretend fake dating will be easy* conversations. We should have prepared a cover story, or an alibi, or a deadly allergy Grant could fake right this minute.

He releases my hand and slips his arm around my waist, grounding me. "I don't think it was any one thing. I was enchanted from the first moment I saw her. She's gorgeous, obviously, but she has this bright, shining enthusiasm that's impossible to ignore. Like she's made of light."

Mom sighs. Frankly, I do, too.

"And she has a huge heart." Grant keeps praising me like he's gunning for a raise down at the fake boyfriend factory. "The real question is, how could I have met her and not been drawn to her?"

I maybe stare at him too obviously, but what else can I do? That might be the most romantic thing I've ever heard. If I watch him long enough, something in his expression is bound to confirm whether that's fake or real. An eyebrow twitch or a smirk. Anything. But he just gazes back at me, looking for all the world like he truly means it.

He leans down and kisses my temple to cap it off. I don't know if he's trying to really sell it, or if he just wants to make my knees go weak. It's working either way. Kudos to him.

Mom's eyes are suspiciously watery. "That's the sweetest thing. We're so glad you two found each other."

"And Lila?" Dad says. "What interested you in him?"

His voice holds an edge I don't remember hearing before. Josh's cheating and the little he knows of the rest of his behavior has ticked up his protectiveness a notch. Until right now, he hasn't had anywhere to direct it.

"Well..." It's only just this minute that I realize what a horribly intrusive question that is. Putting someone on the spot and asking why they fell for their partner? That's got to go against some kind of party etiquette, doesn't it? "He was always really...kind to me."

That answer lands like a balloon slowly losing air and making a rude sound as it falls to the floor. Their eyes on me are like feelers searching for a better response.

I risk a sideways glance at Grant. His tiny, fake smile makes me want to kick myself. He was honest—or as honest as a real boyfriend would be. He fully immersed himself in the character. I can do the same. And I won't even have to make anything up.

"We all know I was never going to be amazing in the wilderness," I start in. "And I wasn't, right from the beginning. I was tired and slow and completely unprepared. But Grant didn't care how long it took me to get over a rise or complain when I stopped to retie my shoes twenty times a day just to catch my breath. He was patient with me and always made sure I was taken care of."

I hug him a bit closer even though I can't look up at him right now. "He never spoke badly of me or anyone else, and he never lost his positive attitude. I knew right away he was nice, but I learned he was *good*, too. And...yeah. I've never met anyone quite like him before."

They're all still watching me, but every last one of them has the same sort of smile on their face—the way you look when a little kid has told a story that revealed a lot more personal information than you were expecting to hear.

"And he saved me from several vicious birds," I throw in. "So he's pretty much my own personal superhero."

"Lila," Mom scolds. "Did you have a ribbon in your hair again?"

"*No.* There's just an alarming number of birds in the wild."

Griffin turns to Hope. "I'm missing something here."

I hold a hand out to stop her. "Please don't tell him right now. As a good hostess, it's your duty to not embarrass your guests." I take my case straight to her fiancé. "Grant loves the outdoorsy stuff even more than you, Griffin. You guys should discuss that."

"Lila." Mom apparently wants me to stay on topic.

"If you need suggestions for anything, let me know." Griffin doesn't seem to mind the subject change. Apparently, he has an impressive arsenal of scenic spots and favorite outdoor activities he's shared with Hope. From all she's said, most of them involve making out in the woods.

Which...actually wouldn't be so bad, now that I think about it. Maybe he should give Grant some location ideas.

Grant tips him the classic guy chin nod. "I will, thank you."

"Hope said your family owns a sporting goods store?" Mom

says. As if she hasn't been eating up every crumb I've been willing to give her.

"Outdoor stores," I correct. "There are thirteen locations across Texas. And they sell more hiking and camping-related gear than team sports stuff."

One side of Grant's mouth tilts up. "Have you been researching new activities to try?"

"I looked at the website once or twice for strictly informational purposes only." And then pored over the *About Us* page where there's a picture of the whole Irwin family. Fresh air apparently grows gorgeous babies because all three brothers are straight fire.

"Does that type of work involve a lot of travel?"

Mom's extra hopeful and not at all subtle question is a little dagger straight to my heart. It's a question I've been dying to ask, but haven't had the guts. So far, we haven't talked about what happens after his weeks here are over. We're just...enjoying the middle part, even though the end is unknown.

I don't even realize I've gone achingly stiff until Grant's hand moves over my lower back, soothing me out of it.

"It doesn't usually," he answers. "But I have other reasons to travel."

Kinda wish it were an hour or two later so it would be too dark to see how flaming red my cheeks must be right now.

"Lila!"

I'm rescued from further embarrassment by one of my favorite people. Tess's son, August, zooms at me through the crowds scattered in the yard. I hoist him up into my arms. He gives the best hugs. He fully commits with his head on my shoulder and his arms around my neck.

"Don't you look nice tonight?" He's wearing khakis and a plaid short sleeve dress shirt like a little businessman. His messy pale blond hair ruins the look, but I love it.

"Mama said if I dress up I can have cake. And I always want cake."

"Didn't your mama make the cake?" Tess's desserts are sinfully decadent. If she weren't so impossibly sweet herself, I might think she sold her soul to the devil to come up with the recipes.

"It's for Hope and that guy." He twists in my arms to point at Griffin.

The adults all laugh, the question of whether or not Grant will ever return to Sunshine forgotten. Or in my case, pushed aside to agonize over another time.

Griffin shakes his head, but his grin proves he's not too disappointed. "We're still not on a first name basis, huh? That hurts, little man."

"Don't take it too hard." Tess pops up next to Hope, with Wren behind her. "Names aren't his strong suit."

"I know Ian." August seems to feel the need to prove his mom wrong. "And Dutch."

I eye Tess. "Do you now?"

She shakes her head the tiniest fraction. "It's because he sees our neighbor every day."

There's more going on there, but this is a terrible time to question her about it. For her, anyway. For me, it would be a fantastic diversion.

"Well, try to remember this guy's name. This is my friend, Grant. Grant, this is my buddy August."

Grant reaches over to shake his little hand. August's suddenly serious, completing the businessman look.

"Nice to meet you, August."

"I saw you over at Shepherd's." Wren says it like an accusation. "I should have known you were the adonis."

Mom titters as though she wasn't the one who got that nickname going. I clear my throat, hoping that will activate a time machine to blip us backward thirty seconds.

"I'm Wren. This is my sister Tess. We've been dying to meet Lila's boyfriend."

August leans closer to Grant. "Are you going to marry Lila like that guy's going to marry Hope?"

And that's why every event should be child-free.

TWENTY-SIX
GRANT

IT TURNS out there's something to be said for engagement parties. Or maybe I just enjoy any place I'm given the freedom to wander around holding Lila against me.

We mingle through the yard, and she introduces me to her friends and neighbors. It's obvious she's liked and admired. Everyone has something to say about the part she played in the last Christmas festival or their high expectations for the upcoming Fourth Fest. She's asked for her opinion on everything from current fashion trends, to cozy bedroom paint colors, to where to buy earrings like hers. And every time, she finds a way to direct them to a shop in town like she's already Sunshine's tourism director.

She's energetic and open, but it's her smile that gets me. She's not stingy with it. After the slight awkwardness with her parents, she relaxes into the evening. She's full of laughter and heart, and she's the brightest star in the night.

Clearly, I'm ready for someone else to ask what drew me to her.

When we've made our rounds and evening casts long shadows through the yard, she leads us over to the fire pit.

August dances around the crackling flames holding a marshmallow on a stick that hovers just over the fire. Lila and I sit on one of the outdoor sofas, and her sister and friends take up the others next to Tess.

"Is another marshmallow going to be too much for his blood sugar?" Wren asks her sister.

"I'm toasting it for that guy." August throws a hand toward where Griffin cuddles Hope.

Griffin groans, but Hope consoles him with a pat on his chest.

August stops his jig. "I mean *Griffin*. I'm toasting this one especially for you."

I'm very much enjoying the way his l-sounds are more like extra ys. *Especiayee.*

"He's the toastmaster general tonight." Tess smiles at her son from across the raised metal fire pit. "How many is that?"

"Eight. But—oops."

The marshmallow's engulfed in flames. He blows it out, grinning away.

"But some caught fire," he finishes.

"I like a toasty marshmallow." Griffin has a graham cracker and a piece of chocolate ready. "Bring it here, buddy."

They work together to slide the molten marshmallow onto the little stack.

"Perfect!" Griffin offers him a hand, which he slaps. "What's my name?"

"Griffin!"

"Atta boy."

August yawns massively but holds up his toasting stick. "Who wants one?"

"I think it's time for us to go, honey. We've got to get you to bed." Tess helps direct him to put the s'mores supplies away and encourages him to wish us all goodnight.

He goes around the group offering goodbyes. Lila gets another huge hug. Then, he turns to me. "Goodnight, guy!"

Griffin nods, wiping melted chocolate from his mouth. "The torch has been passed."

Tess and August wave one last time and make their way to the side gate to disappear into the night.

Wren sits with her ankles tucked up under her nibbling on a loose graham cracker. "You throw a good party."

"Five stars on Yelp," Hope says.

Lila melts against me a little more. "Thanks. I think it turned out pretty great."

"Isn't that part of what you used to do? Didn't you throw big parties for those—" Wren snaps her fingers several times like she's trying to find the right word. "What do you call them? *Jerks* at your old job?"

"They did like to celebrate themselves."

Hope laughs. "You sent me the copy that went with one of their last app rollouts that was just so..."

Lila lifts a hand. "You don't have to finish that thought. I'm familiar with my work."

"Dad says people like that are in love with their own genius."

"Sounds like Josh was the worst of them all." Wren stops cold and looks over at us. "Uh, sorry."

"Don't be sorry for my sake," I say. "I agree with you."

"But dang, you've made great changes all around." Wren uses the last of the graham cracker to salute Lila. Just in case there was any confusion about her meaning, she tosses a wink in, too.

Lila makes a soft, almost purring sound. "I sure have."

I've had a lot of memorable moments in my life, but this one sparkles like it's something more.

Conversation moves between the others as a Journey ballad

serenades us. Lila shivers, and goosebumps break out on her arm beneath my fingers.

"Are you cold?" I say softly.

"I should have brought a wrap, but I didn't think about it. Mom probably has something inside I can borrow."

"I could keep you warm." The offer is out in a flash, my deepest wants rising up to seize their opportunity as though I haven't had my arm around her all evening.

Her gaze drops from my eyes to my mouth. She swallows. Every little movement of her throat requires study. The pulse in her neck. The shift at the hollow of her throat. How can such a common action have such overpowering appeal?

"Okay." Her response is more breath than sound.

She shifts, and I slide her onto my lap, wrapping my upper body around her. My arms cage her in, hands slipping down her bare arms before crossing at her waist. Her head is right next to mine, my mouth at her ear. "Good?"

"Mm hmm."

In the firelight, her face glows pink. We breathe in time, a duet I wouldn't mind sharing again someplace more private. Her perfume is soft, nearly gone this late in the evening. I slip her hair to one side and drop my nose to where her shoulder meets her neck and breathe deep.

The scent affects me on a cellular level, everything inside me claiming *Mine.*

She shivers again, but no goosebumps appear.

"What is your perfume?" I wrap my wandering hand back around her before it can trace the length of her neck or dance down her spine.

"It's, um...tomato."

"Tomato?" The scent is fresh and clean but zesty, too. I wouldn't have called it as tomato, but that fits.

She nods, turning a touch to try to face me. "It's from a

place that sells unusual scents like grass or laundry or dirt. You might like that one."

"I like yours. Why did you choose it?"

"Because I didn't want a perfume everyone else is wearing. I wanted something that belonged to just me."

She certainly has. I'm going to go home with this scent imprinted on my synapses. I could walk into a room thirty years from now and smell that perfume, and I'll come straight back to tonight. *Lila.*

"Do you fly fish, Grant?"

Griffin's deep voice shakes me out of my Lila-perfume haze. "Yeah. A little bit."

"I know a few good spots, if you've got time while you're in town."

"He knows all the good spots." Hope's got him wrapped up tight in her arms. "He's teaching me how, too. I mostly just cast and don't catch anything, but we could make a whole day of it if you want, Lila."

She turns to Wren. "You can come, too, if you want—"

Wren waves her off. "That's not necessary. I don't eat anything with scales."

Lila burrows deeper against me. "I fished on the trip. I don't really need to again."

"Did you have any luck?" Hope asks.

"Yes and no. Yes, I caught one. No...the subsequent fish-related trauma scarred me for life."

"Did they make you gut it?" Griffin's a little too gleeful in his questioning. Hope smacks his chest.

Lila turns almost green again. I run a hand along her arm to soothe her. "I'll catch and release. How about that, princess?"

"No fish murder?"

I nod like it's a done deal. "No fish murder."

She sighs against me. "Thank you."

"Man," Griffin says. "Calling it *fish murder* kind of sucks the fun out of it."

———

When we head inside to say our goodbyes, nearly everyone else has left for the evening. We find Lila's parents in the kitchen washing dishes.

"We're going to go," Lila tells them.

Her mom rushes over. "Before you do, I wanted to invite you to sit with us during the parade at the Fourth Fest, Grant. Lila will be running around in the morning, making sure everything goes smoothly, and I hate the idea of you all alone during the festivities."

The offer is flattering and weirdly comforting. "Thank you. I'd like that."

"We'll have chairs and snacks. You just bring yourself. Lila can tell you where to find us. Or give me your number, and I'll text you a map."

"Do not give her your number," Lila says. "You don't need to see the family group chat craziness yet."

My chest swells with that one small word. I can live with *yet*.

"Grant, do you golf?" Mr. Parrish asks.

"I have, but not for a long time."

He beckons me to follow him. "Come see my new clubs."

The others groan. I'm guessing the new clubs have been a favorite point of pride. I follow him into the garage, where he leads me to a navy blue stand bag kitted out with shiny golf clubs.

"That's a nice set." I know enough about the sport to guess he dropped a considerable amount of money on those clubs.

Feels a bit like a test. Will I be impressed? Too impressed? Will I try to outdo him?

"They're not why I asked you out here."

Oh. A trap, then.

"Why are we out here, sir?"

"I don't like you seeing my daughter as some temporary vacation fun."

Mr. Parrish's voice is hard, his arms crossed tight over his chest. A sinking sensation of guilt without cause courses through my stomach. He'd been friendly enough during the party, but he's got the protective father stance down now.

"I know she's a grown woman, and she wouldn't appreciate me speaking up for her like this. But I didn't speak up for her the last time around, and that was a mistake."

It's not a threat so much as a rebuke of himself, and I respect the hell out of him for it. I've wondered just how much her ex kept his true personality under wraps while they were together. It sounds like he made an effort but never managed a complete job of it.

I want to defend myself, and not just to avoid whatever repercussions I might have coming if I don't. "She's not just temporary fun. Meeting her was unexpected, yes, but I'm not treating it lightly."

Although, if he had any notion about the *fake* part of our deal, I don't think he would be very understanding.

"I'm not sure how much you know, but her last boyfriend was a real piece of work," he says.

"I've met him."

"Then you understand why I worry."

"I do. But I have only good intentions when it comes to Lila. I care for her very much. The last thing I want to do is take advantage of her or hurt her."

I won't be that guy. I won't indulge in all the things I want with her under the guise of playing pretend. I need to be sure that however this plays out, she doesn't regret anything when I go home. If that means playing the role of fake boyfriend a little less whole-heartedly than I have been, I'll do it. She's been through enough already with someone who only took from her, I won't risk doing the same thing.

His eyes narrow on me so long my skin crawls in anticipation of him using those fancy new golf clubs on my skull. But finally, he relents and eases up on his stare-down.

"She's got a big heart. It's been trampled by someone who couldn't see it for the gift it was. If you're smart, you won't do the same."

I've only known her a few weeks, but I understand how precious a gift her heart would be. If I had the chance—a *real* chance—to win it, I would never let her go.

"No, sir."

He nods. "Good."

I take a step toward the garage door.

He lays a hand out to stop me. "Where are you going? I still have to show you the clubs."

TWENTY-SEVEN

LILA

TONIGHT WENT BETTER than I expected. I never thought I would praise my Mom's subtlety, but she could have been a whole lot more direct with her pushy questions for Grant and me. Luckily, she had Griffin and Hope to coo over all night, so she still got her fill of dreaming up romantic weddings for somebody.

The drive home, though, doesn't feel like the same success. The air in the car sticks and catches, and Grant's lingering silence forms a hard little ball of worry in my stomach.

Really, an engagement party is a terrible choice of date for this early in a relationship, no matter how faux. It's a lot of pressure on a guy. Like going on a first date on February thirteenth.

"Was that too much?" I finally ask when he parks in front of my building. "Did my mom scare you off?"

He glances my way. It's hard to tell in the dim light of his SUV, but he seems surprised by the question.

"No, your mom didn't scare me off."

"Oh. Well, that's good." But without that, I'm stumped to explain his silence.

We get out of the car, and I let us into the building so he can walk me up to my door. I hope he doesn't notice the musty old-building smell somebody keeps trying to cover with lemon-scented air freshener. My fingers are crossed someone will buy out the owners and update the apartments, but if they did, it would probably triple my rent. Kind of a catch-22.

It's late. I should *not* invite Grant in. But after snuggling up to him all evening and sitting in his comfy lap for so long, I can't think about much more than extending the night just a little. Maybe another kiss? One last cuddle?

I can be strong. I can give him a hug and say goodnight and leave it at that. I absolutely can.

"Do you want to come in?"

I see my mistake right away—his smile has too much apology in it. My stomach twists. Yeah, okay. Maybe I should have tried harder to resist the urge to ask him in.

"I shouldn't," he says.

I need to just let it go, say goodnight, and move on. But I can't do that any more than I could have resisted asking him to come inside my apartment.

"Is everything okay? I thought you were having a good time tonight, but now I feel like maybe I messed up."

As often as I told myself I would run at the first sign a guy was criticizing me again, right now, I just want to make things right. I'm not even sure the mistake is mine.

"You didn't do anything wrong, Lila."

"Then what happened?" But an answer comes to me. I should have thought of it before I ever brought him to the party, but I was too focused on myself. "Did it remind you of Kelsey?"

His eyebrows practically knit together in confusion. "Kelsey?"

"Everyone congratulating Hope and Griffin, talking about

the wedding..." I run a hand over his arm, hoping to find some way to comfort him. "It was thoughtless of me to take you there right after you told me about what happened with her. I'm so sorry. I should have been more careful with you."

"Careful with me?" He looks to the ceiling, shaking his head, but finally drops his gaze. His eyes lock on mine like a thunderbolt. "I didn't think about her for one minute, princess. Not one."

"Then why—"

"Because I'm the one who should be more careful. I don't want any confusion."

"About what?"

"About us." He pauses a beat, watching me. Telegraphing everything he's not saying.

My stomach is a bowling ball plummeting through the floor to crash into the pharmacy downstairs in a cloud of dust. I've reminded myself he's only my fake boyfriend over and over again this week, and it pinches every time. But it's so much worse when he mentions it. Like a slap you never saw coming but maybe you deserve.

It *is* pretend. Also...none of it is. But we never agreed to more. Letting actual emotions get tangled up is all on me.

He's right to point out that the romantic part of our relationship is just for show. Between spending so much time together and our soft little confidences and reading together at night, I'd started to think... Well, *started* is the wrong word. I'm waist-deep in those thoughts and sinking farther by the minute. But his reminder grabs me by the armpits and lifts me out of that muck onto solid ground.

Solid, realistic, sensible ground.

"Right," I say. "Us. Yes. There's no confusion here. We are pals only. Best buds. We have mutually friendzoned each other."

He narrows his eyes like my agreement went too far. Or not far enough. How am I supposed to tell what he's feeling anymore? I can't. I shouldn't even try.

"Lila—"

"I need to get to bed anyway. It's been a long day." I fake a huge yawn until a real one kicks in and nearly unhinges my jaw.

He frowns, but I definitely don't want to hear more about how he doesn't want me to be *confused*. I didn't think I was until he said that. Now I am *all* confusion.

I sat in his lap half the night. He kissed my face. He smelled my neck. Which seems to be a common thing for him, but still. He was the perfect boyfriend in front of my family and friends. I *know* it's all fake. I do.

So why is his clarification making me this muddled?

I can't let it. I need to get back on that fake boyfriend train and ride it until—wait. No. Terrible metaphor.

"You'll tell me if you have more outdoorsy things you want to do, right?" I am so cheerful it hurts. Mostly in my sad, confused little heart.

His mouth twitches like he's debating his options. I shouldn't be internally begging him to say yes. Haven't I learned anything? Seems like the lesson doesn't want to take.

"How about a bike ride this week?" he offers.

It's a crumb, but I'm only too happy to snatch it up. *No lessons learned here. I am unteachable!*

"The electric kind?"

"They might have some, if you want."

I sigh dramatically. "Fine. I'll pedal."

"I didn't know pedaling was such a burden." He smiles, and even if it's not the huge one that makes my chest go light and fluttery, it's something. He nods at the door. "I'll wait for you to go in."

Right. No going inside with me, no goodnight kiss. Just a

reminder I'm getting things confused and the promise of an outdoor activity I haven't done in at least fifteen years.

Go, me.

TWENTY-EIGHT

GRANT

I HAVE NEVER STARED at a text message so hard in my life. I'm not even trying to decipher an emoji code—the message is loud and clear. It just so happens that I hate the message.

> Lila: Would it be too much to ask my fake boyfriend to come help me set up decorations in the department store window? I have tiny arms that can't reach

She included one all-important word in that sentence. Probably because I'm the idiot who brought it up over the weekend. Now she's drawing a line in the sand to prove there's no confusion over what I am to her.

I haven't seen her in two days. Haven't spoken to her in the morning or read to her at night. She's sent the occasional text to check in on my plans around town, but she hasn't indulged in long exchanges. The result is, I miss her more each hour, my mistake when I dropped her off clanging louder in my mind until it throws me off balance.

Seems like it's time to start wearing the shirt Rhett sent.

She sends a bunch of heart emojis I don't read into, along with the address, but I know the place she means. Five minutes later, I'm in my rental, slowly winding between the wooded cabins. I pass the lot for the main lodge, and a guy in a suit catches my eye. Josh. If I never see him again, I'll be a happy man.

I'm not entirely sure his business deal is the real reason he's here. Not that I want to think about his motives much, but it's fair to say I don't trust him. Worse, I don't entirely trust myself. If he makes one more snarky comment to Lila, I'll be throwing punches.

When I roll up to the empty department store, the front doors are propped open and jarring rock music drifts out onto the sidewalk. The front window is still papered over, but shadows move just behind it. My heart kicks up in time with the thrumming song.

Stepping over the threshold, I peer inside. Lila's wrist-deep in American flag decor, arranging patriotic plates and napkins next to teddy bears holding tiny flags. The window space is awash in red, white, and blue, everything from wood block firecrackers to patchwork pillows to gnome-like Uncle Sams.

At least, I assume they're Uncle Sams. They could be painfully American Gandalf dolls, for all I know.

"I feel like I should salute the window."

Lila jumps, knocking a stubby Uncle Sam onto the floor. When her gaze hits mine, her fear dissolves into a little scowl. "You could have said something!"

"I did. Sorry, princess, I didn't mean to frighten you."

"I wasn't *scared*." She rights the gnome, patting his head. "I get into a zone when I'm working, and you startled me out of it."

"It looks good."

"Yeah? It's overkill up close, but that will really make it pop from the street."

I move closer, but not nearly as much as I want to. Her pale teal one-piece shorts outfit—Is it a jumper? Romper? I don't know the right name—reveals toned legs I shouldn't eye the way I am. My fingers ache to run through her hair, and I bet her tomato perfume swirls around her like an airborne drug. Basically, I'm a mess, and if I get any nearer to her, I'll prove it.

She smiles too bright as silence worms in between us. Silence I put there. It's clear she's still thinking about that conversation. She has a loud face—she couldn't conceal all the emotions coursing through her if she tried.

I don't want her to try.

"Now." I saunter closer because I must love punishment. "What did you need these arms for?"

I flex a bicep and slap it with my other hand like some kind of gym bro. Her eyes go wide, her mouth does the same, then laughter spills out of her.

"Don't flex them!" she scolds. "We only have so much room in here."

There's the princess I've missed.

"What are you wearing?" She checks out Rhett's shirt with a little laugh. "That would go great with your new hat."

"I knew I forgot something."

She unspools string lights and directs me how to hang them over the window scene. I climb the ladder she brought and get to work. It's a slow process, but it isn't strictly a two-person job. Nor is any part of the work outside of her reach, despite her shorter arms.

If my smile is smug, I'm only human.

"How long has this building been empty?" I ask.

She shrugs. "A couple of years. Mom had it deep-cleaned at the start of the new year, though."

"That would explain the freshly-sanitized smell." It's a little overpowering, probably from being shut up all the time. "What was it before?"

"Henderson's was an old-school department store. They had a little bit of everything, but they couldn't compete with the big box stores in Bend. Mom's the realtor, and she's tried to draw in a new business, but it's a tough sell."

"It's a big space. What would you want to take over?"

She sighs. "Sephora."

I laugh. "That would be convenient."

"But seriously, a bookstore in Sunshine would be amazing. Or a toy store. We don't have a dedicated home decor store, either."

"Or an outdoor store." I'm on vacation, but I still noticed. I had to shop at one of the national chains in Bend yesterday. I'm surprised my dad didn't sense it through the Force and call to scold me.

"Yeah, but are those really all that necessary?"

I can see the mischief shining in her eyes from up here.

"They're vital, princess."

She gives me more slack on the string lights. "Honestly, it's probably going to wind up becoming another thrift store one of these days."

"Will finding a new tenant be part of your tourism job?"

"Not directly, but that won't stop me from trying. We have a few empty spaces in town I'd love to help fill."

"Maybe you'll get your makeup store, after all."

"That's always the dream."

After I get the string lights secured, she has me hang spangly tinsel puffs that look like fireworks. Then, metal stars at varied heights to make a backdrop. She's right—it's a lot crammed into one space, but she made it work.

I climb down from the ladder, and she shifts two dividers

covered with a huge flag bunting behind the display to block the view of the rest of the store.

"Can I ask you a question?"

She stills. "Sure."

"What is this music?"

She laughs and grabs her phone, the source of the questionable sounds. "You don't like Four Arm Burn?"

She shimmies her hips, and—okay. The music isn't so bad if it gets her to dance like that.

"It sounds like teenagers playing out-of-tune instruments in somebody's garage."

She turns down the music and sadly, stops dancing. "I think it is. You remember Skye? Mitchell and Deena's daughter? She raved about the band when she picked up that dress I gave her. I wanted to give them a try. In the spirit of supporting local music."

"You're even more dedicated than I thought."

She flashes an indignant look. "Some of their songs are enjoyable."

I stare her down. "We've been listening for almost an hour, and I wouldn't call any of those songs enjoyable."

"It probably helps if you're dating one of the guys in the band."

"Yeah, well, you're spoken for, so you're free to turn that racket off at any time."

She holds my gaze for several long seconds. This might be where I get the pointy end of her defensive stick. Not for the teenage warbling coming from her phone, but in defense of herself. I can't remind her this is all pretend and then claim her as my own.

Why did I ever do that first part?

Oh, right. The threat of imminent bodily harm from her father via shiny new Callaway golf clubs. Also: Huge, unwieldy fear that this is all too much. Too soon, too big, too vulnerable. Distance seemed the wiser choice, but I haven't done so well with two days of it. I don't want more.

Finally, her mouth tips up. "You sound like an old man."

I release the breath I've been holding. "That music makes me feel like an old man."

"Maybe it should. You're more than twice their age."

I put my hand over my heart. "Salt in the wound, princess."

We go out front to admire her work. The window is an explosion of flag-themed merchandise, but that feels just right for the Fourth of July.

"Festive," I say.

"I like it. Glittering and full of charm."

"Just like you."

Her mouth takes on a skeptical slant, but her eyes light up when she looks past me. "Hi!"

At this point, I almost expect to find Josh behind me, but I don't think she would greet him with that much warmth. I turn to see two older women almost on top of us on the sidewalk. They both have gray hair, a slight stoop to their shoulders, and sly smiles.

"Lila!" one says. "How nice to see you."

"We won't keep you long," the other says, eyeing me. "We can see you're busy."

Lila slips an arm around my waist without hesitation. "Ada and Isabel, this is my much older boyfriend Grant."

The two women *tsk* and laugh over her teasing. I glare down at her, but she's wholly unrepentant, lightly digging her fingers into my side like she's searching for ticklish spots.

"He doesn't look much older to me." Ada lifts her eyebrows scandalously.

"Behave." Her friend rolls her eyes as if she's used to these antics.

"What can I do for you?" Lila asks.

"We just wanted to let you know we're pushing for you to get that tourism job."

"I only wonder why they haven't given it to you already," Isabel adds. "You're the perfect fit."

Lila's fingers on my side go still. "I didn't realize people knew about that."

Ada flicks a hand. "Oh, everybody knows. Think of what you'll do for our little town with your talents."

"You'll really put us on the map." Isabel beams in her confidence.

"Well. You know. There's an applicant pool." Lila's laugh is so thin, it might break apart. "But I've got my fingers crossed."

"We all do, honey."

"I can't imagine what you have to worry about. With your talents, I'm sure they'll offer it to you." Ada checks her watch. "But we can't stay to chat. We're meeting our book group at Delish for dinner."

That catches Lila's attention. "What kinds of books does your group read?"

"Mysteries," Ada says, at the same time Isabel answers, "Histories."

Ada clears her throat. "Historical mysteries."

Her friend steers her along the sidewalk, but waves her fingers at me. "Nice to meet you, much older Grant!"

Once they're a block away, Lila turns to me. "They're definitely reading romances, right?"

"That would be my guess."

She starts to slip away from me.

"Hey." I take her hand before she can put more distance between us. "Why does it bother you that they know about this job?"

She scrunches her nose. "It doesn't bother me."

"Princess." Like I said—everything's right there in her eyes.

She sucks in a breath, squeezing my fingers. "It's a lot of pressure. Some people have high expectations for me. They think I'm...*successful*."

"You think you're not?"

"Mountain man, I have a part-time job and spend the rest of my days composing social media posts. When I was in Seattle, I had an executive suite. Here, I'm working out of my kitchen and Perk Me Up."

"Yeah, but were you happier in the executive suite?"

Her lips part and close again like she's fighting her answer. "No, I wasn't happier. But if I don't get this job, everyone's going to know about it. It's a lot to face."

"I understand. Would it make you feel more confident in the job if you added another outdoorsy outing to your presentation?"

She groans and tugs at my hand, trying not to smile. "Why are you like this?"

"What can I say? I'm a mountain man."

"I regret calling you that."

"You do not."

She shakes her head at me, but doesn't pull away.

"We can rent bikes and do a short loop on a paved path. I've already scoped it out. You'll do great."

"I have time Thursday afternoon, but everything else is booked so I can get ready for the festival Saturday."

"Thursday it is."

"I can't look at you." Her laughter sets off sparklers in my chest. "Gloating is unattractive."

"I'm not gloating. I'm eager."

She looks down at our intertwined fingers. "That's *too* attractive."

"I'll take the upgrade."

Lila finally loses her battle, and her brilliant smile shines out. The full force of it hits me like a lightning bolt. I am a superhero charging up my powers on her sheer joy. All this light streaking through me brings clarity to one important point: if this woman breaks my heart one day, these moments with her will be worth the heartache.

"Do you want to get dinner?"

Her smile loses some of its luster. "I can't. I have to meet with the crew in charge of the live music pavilion. We're having a pizza party while we run through all the details."

"No problem."

"My schedule really is packed these next few days."

"All the more reason to look forward to Thursday." She's working hard on this festival. I'm not going to give her grief over it.

She tilts her head, gazing up at me. "But...maybe I can call you tonight and find out what happens next to that wizard and his friend?"

There's that lightning strike again. They say it doesn't hit twice, but this joy humming through me feels pretty permanent when I'm with her.

"Deal."

TWENTY-NINE

LILA

FOR SOMEONE who hasn't been on a bike for half her life, I'm doing pretty well. Sure, I was a little wobbly there at the beginning, and I've kept my hands far away from the gear shifters because I don't trust them not to make the chain fall off, but I'm doing it. I'm riding a bike, in nature, on a lovely summer day. Feels pretty good.

It'd feel a whole lot better if little kids stopped passing me on the trail. Seriously, there are so many kids out here today. In a way, it's reassuring. How hard can it be? Six-year-olds do it. But also, getting lapped by a first grader feels like something I should tell my therapist.

Grant, of course, rides with me as though my five miles per hour is a perfectly acceptable speed. He never complains, never gets snippy or asks me to pick up the pace. He's always right here with an encouraging smile.

Honestly? It's starting to drive me up the wall. I love how calm he is most of the time, but right now, I can't take this much mellowness. Nothing ever gets to him. Nothing ever rattles him. Not even me.

Maybe that's what bugs me the most. We can snuggle,

confide in each other, and have the greatest kiss since people first tried shoving their mouths together, and he's completely unbothered. Meanwhile, my feelings for him are like a cluttered junk drawer—everything's in there. I miss him every day we're not together. I can't sleep without hearing his voice. My heart does cartwheels every time I see him. I have no idea what I am to him, and he's just happy to be here.

I thought I could handle living off his crumbs, but I want more. I think I want everything.

Another family passes us by, and I heave a sigh. "That one had training wheels."

Cute pink bike, though. Streamers dance in the breeze behind the handles, and she's got a baby doll in a seat on the back. Her hot pink helmet says, *Eat my dust*.

I want to be her when I grow up.

"Want to snag that bench up ahead?" Grant asks.

I don't even look. The answer is yes.

I bring my bike to a stop and lean it against the wood and metal bench. Stretching my legs, I pull off my helmet and shake out my shoulders. It's a pretty place to stop. The river bends around this little piece of land, a shimmering ribbon in a sea of green pine trees.

Naturally, I pull out my phone to get some more pictures for my presentation.

"It's a great spot for a selfie."

I turn to face Grant. Admiring his handsomeness is *not* the point here. "I know what you're trying to do."

He still thinks shifting my content is the right way to go. Photos of my new location, my new hang-outs, my unadulterated face—he's convinced my followers will want it all.

He just grins. "Am I that transparent?"

"About this? Yes." About what exactly is going on with our little fakery? That's a big no.

I move closer to the riverbank. I don't think sitting on the hard bench will do my poor rear any favors right now.

"Your followers are there because they want to know about you, right?"

My laugh is a little too harsh for this pristine wilderness. "You don't spend a lot of time on social media, do you?"

He draws up short. "I have it."

"That's not the same thing. Let me give you a crash course. *Some* people follow me because they want to know more about me. Others hate-follow. They just want to find reasons for their mean comments."

"You mentioned some rude responses."

"Sometimes it's because I'm sharing a shot of my boba tea and my brand-new manicure instead of something deep and political. Sometimes it's because I featured a food truck they don't think is any good. And sometimes it's just because of me. It doesn't matter what filters I use to blur out my imperfections or how I conceal my flaws, somebody finds them." I kick at a tuft of grass. "I've grown smarter, though. I've customized my comment filters to block words like vapid, ugly, wasteful, and ignorant. Plus all the usual insulting names."

They still don't catch everything, but they've helped my mental health immensely.

His eyebrows pull down, and he leans forward like he's ready to fist fight the internet for me. "You didn't say it was that bad."

"It's not a fun conversation. The point is, I'm not ready to deal with people's responses to all of this right now. My move? The small town I'm living in?" I gesture at my face. "My best bet is to pretend I love the great outdoors, get this promotion, and then...I'll let future-Lila figure out the rest."

I just don't expect it to be in the near future.

"I understand you've got a lot going on, but I hate that you feel like you have to fake your way through your life."

Wow. He found my sore spot and then threw all his weight against it. Most of my life right now is fake, including my favorite part. *Him.*

"Yeah, well, we're probably not the best people to be having a conversation about what's real and what's fake."

He goes completely still. For several beats, I can't hear anything beyond the softly splashing river and the whirring of bikes as they pass. I've never liked quiet ambient sounds, so I keep talking.

"I know I asked for this, but you're *really* good at being my fake boyfriend." I kissed him days ago. *Days.* We haven't spoken of it. Sure haven't repeated it. So...what now? "I'm all messed up, and you're completely unaffected."

"You have no idea."

His low voice is not so much a threat as a promise. That prospect stirs a flame to life inside me. I see the mistake ahead of me like a red light I can't stop myself from plowing through.

"Then show me." I wish I could be the sultry ingénue in this moment, but my voice is too soft. Too crowded out by fear that he won't do what I'm asking. "Show me something real."

His sweet, cinnamon roll persona falls away as quickly as Superman throwing off his cape. He stalks toward me like a predator closing in on its prey. My body turns liquid, but I don't think of running. I want to be caught.

His hands sift into my hair to cradle my head as he claims my mouth. No hesitation, no questioning pause—only lips, tongues, and a silent but enthusiastic *yes*.

He kisses me like he intends to unravel me completely. Every touch spirals outward until my skin hums from it. I can't do much more than cling to his shoulders while he rewrites my concept of what a good kiss is.

I might not know exactly what we are to each other or what happens when our few weeks together are over, but I know with complete certainty that nothing about this kiss is fake. Henry Cavill doesn't kiss his co-stars like *this*.

One of Grant's hands slips down to the nape of my neck, holding me steady. It's a good thing, because without it I would absolutely crumple. He doesn't kiss me like I'm the only woman in the universe—which sounds good enough. He kisses me like out of all the billions of women in the world, *I'm* the one he wants.

Like he's marking me as his own.

His mouth goes exploring down one side of my neck, lightly nipping at the top of my shoulder before retracing the journey. He kisses behind my ear, sets his teeth against my ear lobe enough to make me shiver, and across my jaw to take his rightful place at my mouth again.

I trace my hands over his arms and scratch my fingernails over his scalp. He groans at my touch, and I smile against his mouth. Maybe he's not the only one doing some claiming today.

Our kiss softens into something less fierce, almost painfully sweet. He's still proving something to me, but the message is gentler. Not just desire, but tenderness. Affection. My heart fills up with it, overflowing like a rushing river.

A kid riding by makes a loud "Woo!" sound, interrupting us. *Thank you for your service, volunteer kissing police.* We draw apart, and I suddenly remember just how many families are out on the trails today. How many kids got an eyeful of us? We kept it PG-13, but barely.

Grant doesn't let me go far. Paying no attention to our potential audience, he tips his forehead down to meet mine. "Make no mistake, princess. You affect me on a molecular level. If I seem calm, it's only because it's taking all my focus not to pull you into my arms to kiss you again."

Hello, cinnamon roll with extra spice.

"You don't have to focus all *that* hard."

"Then I'll scale it back." He grins down at me, and leans in for another quick kiss to my mouth. "You are perfect exactly as you are. No filters. Just you."

I kiss him again before I do something stupid like cry.

THIRTY

LILA

WHY DOES the universe hate me? The Fourth Fest is the most important event of my summer, a day for me to show off my event planning talents and prove Sunshine can trust me with the tourism position. It's my day to shine. Instead, all I want to do is curl up on the sidewalk and moan.

Other than that, it's going great.

When I came downtown early this morning to run our final checks for the parade, I thought the oppressive heat was just an uncharacteristically brutal July fourth. I chalked my tumbling stomach up to nerves. I didn't have much explanation for how badly my skin ached, but I ignored it as much as I could.

When I finally noticed I was the only one sweating through their clothes, I started to catch on that it wasn't just a hot summer morning. The call is coming from inside the house. Something always goes wrong on event day. I've just never been the obstacle before.

It doesn't matter. I have to get through this. Tonight, after the fireworks are over and I collapse into bed, I can let myself be sick. Until then, I've got to power through.

Like a boss, my internal cheerleader says. She's too tired to lift her pom-poms, but it's the thought that counts.

It's fine. Everything's going to be fine. It'd be cool if the street would stop spinning, but as long as it doesn't interfere with the parade floats, I can live with it.

I have a small group of volunteers helping me coordinate the parade participants and make sure everyone's lined up and heading out on time. The lead-up to the official route is a rattling chaos of marching bands, classic cars, emergency vehicles, and floats created by various local organizations, but I barely see them. It's taking everything I have to stay standing upright.

I managed to snag a patch of shade for my supervisory duties. So. Technically still a win. My head throbs and my skin hurts and my mouth is Sahara dry. But getting a drink of water at one of the hydration stations feels like a dangerous game to play with my stomach. I close my eyes and pray for a miraculous healing.

The blessing will come. Any second now.

Any. Second.

When the last firetruck heads onto the parade route, I take a minute to sag against the closest building. Brick is not the most comfortable material to rest on, but it's this or the curb. I promised Grant I would meet him after the parade, but getting to him feels like Frodo tasked with taking the ring to Mordor.

Grant would like that little simile.

I need time to recover, but every minute that goes by amplifies one of my symptoms. The day isn't over just because the parade is. I've got to check in on the market vendors and make sure everything's going smoothly at the music pavilion. Get in touch with volunteers and sponsors. Greet people with a smile. Not to mention I planned to oversee the fireworks tonight. I've got to suck it up.

Unfortunately, I have lost all ability to suck.

Or something. My brain isn't functioning right.

"What a parade, Lila."

I straighten and flash a huge "I'm not sick at all" smile. Mayor Martinez has found my sulking spot. "Did it look good out there?"

Back here, it was a lot of practice baton-twirling and exhaust fumes, but everyone lined up on Sunshine's downtown streets surely had a different experience.

"Might be the best I've ever seen. Easily twice the size of last year's. You and your sister have brought new life to Sunshine's events calendar." He looks me over, and his enthusiasm fades. "Are you feeling all right?"

"I just got overheated in the sun. Thank you." Obviously I'm not going to tell him that my internal organs are liquefying as we speak. That would be unprofessional.

"After seeing what you've done with the parade, I can't wait to find out what you have in store for us in your tourism presentation next week."

"I think it will wow you." Oh please, let it wow him.

His warm, fatherly smile shines out. "I fully expect it to."

He really is the nicest, but I cannot keep up this chat. It's taking too much effort to stay upright. I can't carry on a conversation, too. I wave him along the street. "You should check out the live music. It's a bluegrass band playing first."

Mostly, I need him to walk away so I can slump against this nice, cool brick building again.

"I'll do that. See you next week, Lila."

He steps off the sidewalk to greet some of the other volunteers. Disaster averted.

For the moment.

I swallow hard and start my trek toward the intersection where my family planned to meet. If my thoughts were a little more coherent this morning, I would be concerned about Grant spending the whole parade with my parents. Mom probably fished for information the full hour. If he's lucky, Hope stuck him next to Griffin.

Actually, the most likely scenario is Mom set her camp chair between the two of them and dug around in everyone's love lives to the tune of "Stars and Stripes Forever."

Walking the two blocks to the little patch of grass on Larch Street was a terrible idea. I should have flagged down the motorcycle-riding clown with the dog in a sidecar and asked for a ride.

Ugh. I've got to be out of it if I'm thinking about hitching a ride with a clown.

Finally, I spot a bunch of heads I recognize: Mom and Dad, Hope and Griffin, and Grant. Another sign of how out of it I am? The way my heart dances to see him with the people I love best, like he belongs right there with them.

As though I love him, too.

He turns and sees me, and he instantly *knows*. Not about the stupid thoughts in my delirious head, thank goodness. But his brow furrows, and he frowns my way like he can tell at a distance something's off. Might not take intuition, though. I'm walking like I've got glass in my shoes.

He jogs over to me. "Princess?"

I smile up at him. "How was the parade?"

"Impressive. You did a phenomenal job putting everything together." He tilts his head down trying to reach my eye level. "Are you okay?"

I raise my hand to wave off his concern, but it feels like I'm moving through jello. Air should not have this much resistance. "I'm great."

He slants his mouth at me as if that's all it takes to get me to confess my sins. Like I'm going to immediately cave. Like I'll just do whatever he wants—

"I think I'm coming down with something," I say softly.

He lays a hand on my forehead. I close my eyes and lean into it as if that's normal. His palm is nice and cool. I could stay here a while.

He drops his hand. "You're burning up. Let's get you home."

I snap my eyes open, wishing for the hand of comfort back. "I can't leave yet. I have to make sure everything's going smoothly with the market vendors and check on the live music over at the..."

My mind totally blanks. I blink into the crowds, searching for the right word. Finding nothing, I improvise. "The live music place."

Nailed it.

His small smile hits me straight in the heart. He really should watch it—I'm not prepared to withstand him today. If I look at his dimple, I'll pass right out.

"I can hear it from here. Things are going just fine over at the live music place."

My family joins us, camp chairs slung over their shoulders as they prepare to head out. Mom takes one look at me and frowns.

Okay, maybe I'm not hiding my sickness as well as I thought.

"Lila honey, what's the matter?"

"I'm just feeling a little off. I'm okay."

"She's going home," Grant says.

I glare at him. My admiration for his *in charge* side comes and goes. Right now, it's gone. "Not until I check on the rest of the festival events. I have a job to do."

"I can help." Hope steps up looking just as worried as the rest of them. "What do you need me to do?"

"I don't need anything. I can do it." It will take approximately three hours to walk the single city block to the festival, but I can do it.

"Lila, please."

My sister doesn't fight fair. If she turned around and argued with me on this, I would just dig in and refuse to back down. But using her soft and gentle voice? I want to sag in defeat.

"You helped me with my festival. Let me help you with yours."

Okay. I kind of do sag in defeat. At this point, everything should be fine. Nobody's texted me with an emergency. So far, mine is the only setback for the day. Fingers crossed it stays that way.

"If you would just check in with Sonja. She's handling the musical acts. I texted her this morning, but I wanted to see it for myself."

"We'll go right now." She nods at Griffin, who didn't need the encouragement to join her. "I'll take some video for you. How about that?"

"Thank you." It's a whisper. I'm stupidly emotional.

Because I care so much about live music. Obviously.

"Now you need to get home and get to bed, young lady." Mom manages to soothe and scold like I'm a little kid. It's honestly kind of nice.

"I just want to see the market." I've seen it before, but today, it's *mine*.

"Then I'll help her get home," Grant adds.

"Thank you so much." Mom sounds like he just offered to give me a kidney.

"Take care of her." Dad nods at him as though this is a solemn duty. But Grant nods back like he's making a promise.

Okay, then. I'll let him be in charge for a little while.

Grant scoops an arm around my waist, and we slowly start walking toward town square. Every step is a tiny torture. Truly, this was a terrible idea. I can just recuperate right here in the gutter, can't I? That's about as far as I want to walk surrounded by excitable crowds. I can't bear having this many people see me so out of it, but the need to make sure I've done a good job over-rules my tattered pride.

"When did this start?" he asks softly.

"This morning." Probably don't need to add that it's getting worse.

I make it as far as the street bordering town square. Inside, colorful awnings cover market booths, and crowds swarm the stall aisles. Kids run around waving flags and dragging balloons behind them. It's noisy, happy, festive fun. Exactly the way I'd hoped it would be.

I just wanted to have some of the festive fun, too.

I spot the refrigerated red Blackbird's cart where Tess and Wren are selling hand pies. Next to them, August does a complicated dance featuring glow sticks that aren't providing much glow in the bright sun.

I point him out. "August's having a good time."

A man with red hair pulled into a knot at the back of his head and a trim beard walks up to the cart. He wears a T-shirt and athletic shorts that reveal a prosthetic leg. He's grinning at August, but it takes a second for Tess to finish up with a customer and turn to him. She's obviously surprised, but even from here, I can tell she's happy to see him.

True, she's usually happy to see everyone, but this feels like a different sort of happy.

"Oh," Grant says. "I didn't know Ian Vaughn lived in Sunshine now."

"Who's Ian Vaughn?" I watch like a creep as Tess, August, and the man who must be their neighbor, Ian, walk together through the crowd, leaving Wren at the bakery cart grinning like a Cheshire Cat.

"A famous climber. He got injured two years ago, and then sort of fell off the face of the earth."

Grant goes on about this climber guy, but the wind shifts, blowing smells from the food trucks over to us. The strong odor of hot dogs and barbecued meats makes my stomach clench. Maybe things are worse than I thought.

"We need to go," I say, interrupting him.

"Bad?" he asks, already helping me move away from the festival.

"Very."

We make slow time up the block toward my apartment. I'm as patriotic as the next girl, but I just want this day to be over already. Unfortunately, it's got yet another fun surprise up its sleeve.

Josh, of course. He looks put together as always, fashionable and handsome and cold. He slows in the middle of the sidewalk, not caring that people have to shift to walk around him. They're beneath his notice, so their inconvenience doesn't matter.

Why? Why did I ever fall for him? Was I really so caught up in his looks and the status symbol of being with Seattle's golden boy tech guru? There was more, once. In the beginning, he wielded charisma and confidence like a master. He drew me into his circle, and I was only too happy to be there. But after his flattery turned to criticisms, it became impossible to keep up with his expectations. And now that I've seen through him, he has nothing but contempt for me.

My stomach churns harder as he strolls the last few feet to us.

"I was hoping to run into you two." He wears false friendliness so easily it's disgusting. "I've been thinking about buying interest in a retail business. Diversify a little. Know of anything I could dabble in?"

It's his way of letting us know he's researched Grant's

family business. He's probably dug through every scrap of information available to the public, looking for something to exploit. Grant doesn't take the bait, so Josh keeps going.

"It would have to be publicly traded to be worth my time. Anything else is just a hobby business." He grins as though he's offered us valuable advice instead of a direct insult. "Right, Irwin?"

Maybe it's the fever affecting my brain or maybe I am just completely done with Josh Brandt, but he found my limit and pushed me over.

"You can stop the games. We don't care what you dabble in. You're a conceited, thoughtless jerk who isn't worth Grant's time. And you lost the right to *my* time when you cheated on me." I stand as straight as I can when I would really rather double over. "You are beneath us."

That speech would feel a whole lot more satisfying if my stomach wasn't capsizing.

His sleek smile slips. "Lilabird—"

I lurch a step closer to him. "Never call me that again. I've always hated that nickname. If you call me that again, I'll...I'll..."

It's too late. I don't have time to run, turn, or even move. My stomach heaves, and I throw up right on his shoes.

It's disgusting, and I have to be an absolute wreck to do something so humiliating in broad daylight on a public street, but I couldn't stop if I tried. The crowd parts around us, but there's nothing I can do about it now.

Two very telling things happen at the same time: Josh dances back several paces to try to escape the splash zone, and Grant holds onto my arm and rubs my back making sympathetic sounds.

He is an angel in human form. A human angel, cinnamon roll, mountain man.

"These are Tom Ford, Lila!" Josh doesn't shout, but his low-level seething is hostile enough. "Calf leather! You idiot! They're ruined."

Grant straightens, still holding me upright. "If you say one more word to her, more than just your shoes will get ruined today."

Okay. *Deadly* human angel, cinnamon roll, mountain man.

Josh's mouth twists like he's trying to figure out how a fist fight would affect his company's stock price. Or maybe he's trying to figure out how losing the fight would affect his face. Eventually, he skirts past us, straightening his shirt and muttering about his shoes.

My stomach picks that moment to make a truly terrible sound. Fair to say, my digestive system has thrown me under the bus and then backed over me today. Maybe it's retaliation for all the trail rations I had on the hike.

"Okay, that's it, princess." Grant's voice is sweet and soft again. "Let's go."

I don't resist. "I need to call somebody to clean that up."

It's right on the sidewalk and everything. People move around it, watching me like they expect another show. Whatever good opinion people in Sunshine had of me, I just vomited all over it.

"Text them if you need to, but we're getting you home."

I wish I'd stayed there in the first place.

———

The day and night are a miserable blur of feverish chills and frantic vomiting. I try to dissociate. It's not me puking my guts out while Grant holds my hair. It's not me stripping down to a tank top and shorts because I'm so terribly hot. It's not me lying on the cool bathroom tile while Grant strokes my back and puts wet washcloths on my forehead.

He stays through it all.

It's horrifically mortifying.

It's incredibly comforting.

———

I wake up in my bed, daylight poking at my eyelids. I've got that too-aware sense of clamminess that lets me know my fever broke. I'm still too hot, but that might be because I'm cuddling something warm. No, wait.

Someone.

I crack an eye open, and it takes a minute to register that my hand is wrapped around Grant's bare thigh. He's sitting up next to me in my bed—fully dressed in shorts and a shirt, FYI—but I've got a death grip on his leg just above his knee. Why is my number one goal in sleep, *cling to Grant?*

Oh. Well. I guess I know the answer to that. *Because he's deliciously cuddly.*

I tilt my head to peer up at him. He's smiling over one of my paperbacks. This man is reading one of my rom-coms. If I had any strength, seeing him like this would whisk it all away.

Eventually, his eyes catch mine, and he sets the book aside. He gently brushes hair from my face, delicately trailing his fingers over my skin. "How are you feeling?"

"Less like a goblin. You're reading one of my books."

"The vampire cat is an interesting take."

"He's one of my favorites."

His fingers smooth over my hair, and he smiles at me as though he didn't watch me empty my stomach all night. "What do you need?"

"I need to know how long I've been accosting you like this." I extend my fingers...and curl them around his thigh again. I will claim medical immunity.

"Not long. Next?"

"I'm sorry you missed the fireworks. They were supposed to be really fantastic." All part of the Fourth Fest Extravaganza I tried to provide and utterly failed to witness.

"I'm not sorry. What else?"

Hmm. Not food—that feels too optimistic. Not more cuddles—sleep-Lila apparently gorged on them.

"Maybe a shower." I'm still sticky from sweat, and I probably smell like a sewer.

"I'll help you." He hops out of bed, coming around to hover and help me sit up.

I'm still a little woozy, but my stomach doesn't lurch at the change of position. That counts as a good sign. He slips an arm around my waist and slowly helps me to the bathroom, stopping on the way so I can grab a clean change of clothes. He arranges me on the closed toilet seat while he starts the shower as though we do this every day. When the temperature's just right, he kneels in front of me.

"If you have trouble standing on your own, I'll help you shower."

I stare at him until an actual hint of pink hits his cheeks. He just might be the sweetest, most wonderful man in the world. Universe, even. Not even Krypton makes them like him.

"Platonically," he adds.

"Are we? Platonic?" This isn't the smoothest time for defining our relationship, but he's the one who cracked that door open.

"No. But I can be a gentleman in a medical emergency."

"You're always a gentleman, but I think I've got it."

He nods once, leans forward to kiss my forehead, and stands. "Call me if you need me."

He closes me up in the bathroom, and I think I might

swoon. Sure, it might be from severe dehydration, but most of it's him.

I take a quick shower, and if I don't totally feel like myself when I finish, I'm at least clean. I open the door and lean against the jamb. Grant's at my side before I can even tell him I'm ready.

"I've got you." He helps me pad across the floor, watching me for any signs of distress. I climb into bed, pulling the sheet over my legs. "Do you feel up for some water?"

I nod, and he crosses the room to my kitchenette. He grabs a glass and fills it from my filter in the fridge. It's the tiniest of gestures, but it feels just right. Like he belongs here with me.

When he returns, I only take a few sips. I don't want to upset the precarious balance my stomach's got going on. I snuggle back down in the sheets. Grant stands by the bed, and I can feel his wheels spinning from here.

I reach out to take hold of his fingers. "Will you stay a little longer?"

"Sure." He rounds the bed to get in next to me. He lays down on top of the sheets and soothes one hand over my back. I've never felt so taken care of before. Like I'm the most important person in his whole world.

I'm practically asleep again already. "Did I really throw up on Josh's shoes?"

The memory's too vivid to be my imagination, but it doesn't feel real.

"A surprising bit of revenge, princess."

My eyes are closed, but I hear the smile in his voice. I love that smile.

I think maybe I love all of him. His gentleness and kindness. His ability to absolutely kick butt anywhere outdoors. The way he defends me and believes in me and encourages me to believe in myself.

"Thank you for taking care of me," I whisper into the sheets.

His answer comes back soft and low. "It is my genuine pleasure."

I love Grant's heart. It was taken for granted in the past, but I would cherish it. I would always know what a gift it is to be able to love him and be loved by him.

And I would never, ever puke on his shoes.

THIRTY-ONE

GRANT

"ARE you sure you're up for this?" I ask.

Lila squeezes my fingers. "I'm always up for shopping."

The stomach bug kept her home for three days. I cooked for her when she could handle solid food, read to her when she got tired, and made myself scarce when she drew herself a bath to refresh.

But now, she seems to have her energy back. Her color's better, too, and her eyes have lost the dark circles that marred them when the fever raged. I suggested she get some fresh air, and she opted for this outing—walking down to her sister's store to help me buy gifts for my mom and Eliza.

I'm not an avid shopper, but I don't think there's much she could suggest we do that I would turn down.

"Tell me about your mom," she says. "What kinds of things does she like? What's her style?"

I've never given my mom's style a second's thought. Does that make me a bad son or an average one? "Pretty relaxed. She mostly wears clothes she gets from our vendors. Outdoorsy chic is a thing."

Lila snorts, but it's true. Our bigger stores carry some pretty nice dresses, all designed to be lightweight and breathable.

"She likes an expensive perfume Dad buys her every year. She's well organized."

I'm a little embarrassed I can't be more articulate about what she likes.

"So...some nice things, but mostly casual?"

"Sounds about right."

"And Eliza?"

I laugh. "Eliza rotates through bright hair colors, and she tends to match her outfit to the color of the month. She runs her own handmade soap business, so she likes to do things her way. She's surprisingly pushy for a tiny woman, and Dean is absolutely gone for her."

"As he should be. She sounds awesome."

We stop in front of a red storefront with a bright yellow door. Lila puts her hand on the knob and raises her eyebrows at me.

"Prepare yourself for the razzle-dazzle."

She pulls the door open, and I step inside. And...okay, she's not wrong.

The small store is a riot of color and texture, filled with everything from tiny jewelry pieces, to bulky ceramic mugs, to huge paintings. It's a lot to take in, but it feels cozy, too. Maybe that's just the size, but it's more likely the people in it.

"Hey, you guys." Hope rounds the back counter to greet us. "All better?"

Lila lifts a fist into the air. "Unstoppable."

"Perfect timing. We're trying to pull together a lake day. Maybe Thursday? Your town council thing is Friday, right?"

"Yeah. I could do Thursday." She looks up at me. "What do you think? You said you wanted to do something on a lake."

"I thought you weren't outdoorsy," I tease. "Now I find out you do *lake days?*"

"For me, lake day means sitting in the sand getting a tan. Don't get your hopes up."

Watching Lila suntanning is the very thing I would hope for.

"Whatever the plan is, Thursday works," I tell her.

"Great." Hope beams. "Griffin's in, and so are Wren, Tess, and August."

"Is Ian joining the fun, too?" Lila asks. "We saw them together at the festival."

Being looped into Lila's *we* makes my chest go warm.

Hope grimaces and shoots a glance over her shoulder. "Tess decided she's not ready to try for something more with him," she says softly. "Wren wants to throw this together as a fun distraction for her and August."

I'm missing pieces here, but it isn't hard to connect the dots.

"So," Hope says in her regular voice, throwing off the air of gossip, "we're going to go have a great afternoon. The more, the merrier, if you guys want to come."

"We're in," I tell her. Even if all Lila does is lay around in her swimsuit. Which I'm not going to think about while we're standing with her sister.

"But right now, I'm here to be Grant's personal shopper." She slips away from me to inspect a nearby jewelry rack.

"Ooh, exciting." Hope straightens a bag that was out of place and returns to her seat behind the counter. "Let me know if you have any questions."

Lila makes a slow pass through the store, touching every-thing. I can't stop staring at her hands. She picks things up and carefully maneuvers them one by one. I knew she was tactile, but this slow and methodical assessment does something to me.

It's not just her delicate hands caressing practically everything in the store. It's the confidence behind it—she knows quality when she sees it.

A very small, very stupid, very insistent voice in my head says she's seen quality in me, too. That whisper cracks something open in my chest. Fear, doubt, and insecurities I've held onto for too many years spill out—but so does an overwhelming hope. Hope for her. Myself. *Us*. Hope I've avoided touching as though it would scald, I now want to grab with both hands and cling to.

"How about this for your mom?" Lila offers me a leather planner embossed with pine trees on the front, unaware of the chaos ricocheting inside me.

"Perfect." I would have walked through this entire store and settled on a scented candle.

She crosses to the back of the shop. "I'm thinking one of these for Eliza. I'm biased, but my sister's art sounds like her whole vibe."

She gestures at a small painting of abstract flowers. It's a tumult of joyful color and will suit Eliza to a tee.

I lift it off the wall. "You're good at this."

"Yup. And I was thinking this—" She moves to a small wooden jewelry rack and carefully removes something. She holds it up to me, revealing three green stones on a delicate gold chain. "For your grandma. Kind of representing you and your brothers."

She thought about my grandma? I don't deserve this generous woman.

"I don't know if she likes jewelry though..."

"She'll love it, princess." I swoop in to give her a brief, heated kiss on the mouth, then kiss my way over to her ear. "Thank you."

"Aw, PDA." Wren leans in the pass-through archway wearing a purple apron like she wore when she barged into the bike shop last week. "Are you guys coming to the lake with us?"

"They're in," Hope confirms.

"It's been a long time since I had an ex worth getting mad at, but my new life's goal is to pull a Lila." She gazes up at the ceiling with a dreamy expression. "Maybe I'll save it for Callahan."

Lila ticks her head to the side, swaying a touch so her shoulder presses against mine. "What does 'pull a Lila' mean?"

"You know." Wren's enormous grin reminds me of Rhett's. "Throw up on some jerk's shoes."

Groaning, Lila spins to press her forehead against my chest. "Does everybody know about that?"

Hope meets my eyes. "Uh, there might be some talk about it."

That's small-town speak for *everybody knows.*

I run my free hand up and down Lila's back. I wouldn't expect the witnesses to keep quiet about her run-in with her ex, but I didn't think it would come back to haunt her so quickly.

"This has been fun." She tilts her head to look up at me. "Can I stow away in your luggage and go home with you?"

Yes, please!

"You're my new role model," Wren says. "We're proud of you."

Lila turns. "It wasn't premeditated."

"When I tell the story it was." A bell rings somewhere on the bakery side of the building. Wren points at us as she backs away. "I'll text you the details for the lake day."

"Do I move?" Lila asks. "Do I change my name? What's the protocol here?"

"You own it," Hope says. "I saw Ada and Isabel in Delish yesterday, and they said you're their new hero. Amy and Jodi can't get enough of the story."

"It's not really how I wanted to be recognized in this town. 'Hey, aren't you that girl who puked on a guy?'"

"You can always explain that you told him off first," I tell her. "It was impressive in context."

"Not helping."

"That's something to be proud of," Hope says. "He needed telling off."

Lila takes the things she picked out for my family and sets them on the counter. "When I give my presentation, everyone on the town council will be thinking about how I threw up on a tourist on Maple Street."

"It was for the greater good."

"So satisfying to watch," I add. Hope high fives me.

Lila glares. "That's deeply disgusting."

"It's true, though. That dumb—" I bite my tongue on what I really want to call her ex. "The most valuable thing he ever had to lose was standing right in front of him, and he couldn't think past his shoes. Yeah. It was satisfying to see."

"Aw," Hope says, turning away from us. "Let me just send a waffle emoji to my man real quick."

Lila stares up at me, her eyes soft and hazy. "I didn't know mountain men were so romantic."

"I've been reading up."

***

I stretch out on the Adirondack chair on my porch, listening to the river while I whittle. Lila lost a lot of time while she was sick, so now she's making some of it up, putting the final touches on her presentation for the town council. Ever since she discovered that her puking on Josh's shoes has become the hottest gossip in town, she's stepped up her efforts.

As if they had anywhere higher to go in the first place.

When I took her home, it was on the tip of my tongue to ask if I could hang out with her while she worked, but she'd been eager to go through her website mock-up again. The promotion is too important for me to risk being a distraction, so I left her to focus.

The restless itch just beneath my skin is no longer nameless. Its name is *Lila*. I want to talk to her, touch her—just being near her would be enough. I try to console myself I'll see her soon, but *soon* has never felt so uncertain.

My phone rings on the little all-weather table, and I check the face that fills the screen. Interesting.

"Hi, Mom."

"Grant, I'm glad we caught you. Your dad's here, too."

Dad says his own hello on speakerphone. "How are you enjoying Oregon?"

"It's a scenic little town. I'm having a great time."

That's a terrible description for my time here—*great*. But I don't know how to explain the invisible string tying me tighter to this place. More specifically, to one particular woman in it. So I'll stick with an easy answer. I can grapple with the trickier parts later.

"Your photos are just gorgeous." Mom has a soft spot for landscape photography.

Hey—one more item I can add to the list of things she likes.

I've texted them pics when I think to. Mostly scenery or a few of the shops. Nothing of Lila. Now that feels like it's been a mistake all along.

"I looked up that hike you did on AllTrails," Dad booms. "Didn't seem up to your usual style."

"He means it was a molehill instead of a mountain," Mom adds.

"I wanted to relax this time around."

"And have you? Have you relaxed and enjoyed yourself?"

She sounds so eager, I regret telling Lila my parents don't check in with us much. They have their own ways of showing affection, but that doesn't mean they don't care.

"I have." My emotions are more tangled than when I first arrived, but I've never enjoyed myself more.

"We're glad to hear it. We were going to wait until you got back to talk to you in person, but we decided it would be the perfect cap to your time off."

I still, the hoot of an owl in the distance strangely ominous. "What would be?"

"We're ready to make you CEO." Dad's voice takes on the serious tone reserved for Irwin family business meetings, as though this is their official job offer. "Effective immediately."

I register it...and I don't. I knew this day was coming—they made Dean the Chief Financial Officer almost two years ago, and they've dropped plenty of hints they wanted more for me, too. But here? Now? I feel like I've lost a handhold and am scrambling down a cliffside.

"We want you to lead the company, son."

I'm glad they've never caught on to video calls so they can't see the look on my face.

"We're thinking we'll hire on a new store manager and a new General Manager so you can dedicate yourself fully to being the CEO."

It sounds like Dad's shuffling papers. Does he already have a contract written up? A five-year plan for the business? A five-year plan for *me*?

"You can focus solely on the company's future rather than worry about the day-to-day tasks in the flagship store."

Interacting with coworkers, helping customers—almost everything I told Lila I enjoy about my job involves the day-to-day tasks in the flagship store. As much as I want the CEO position, I never thought about giving up my current job to get it.

"You've wanted this for years."

I can't tell if Mom is congratulating me or reminding me.

I finally find my words. "Yeah. I have. Thank you. I'm just...surprised."

"Go out and celebrate." Even this feels like a command from Dad. "Then, when you come back Sunday, we'll talk about moving you up to the executive suite."

Mom laughs. "He already has an office."

"Now he'll actually use it. Maybe a new desk is in order?"

The line goes silent, and I realize he's actually asking. "I'll think about it."

"Enjoy the rest of your vacation," Mom says. "You've earned it."

We hang up, and I slump against the chair back. I thought my emotions were a mess before, but my parents just set off a grenade inside me. Everything's raw and exposed.

I shouldn't be this stunned. The promotion was always somewhere on the horizon. I would take up my mantle and become the new head of Irwin Outdoors. Everyone knew it, nobody doubted it. I've expected it and even looked forward to it.

So why does the news I finally have it make me want to bolt?

THIRTY-TWO

LILA

I AM A GROWN WOMAN. A few days ago, I put on an incredible Fourth Fest—so I've heard. Today, I'm at a pristine lake with stunning mountain views, surrounded by my closest friends. Tomorrow, I'll give my presentation to hopefully secure an important job promotion in my hometown. I have *a lot* going on.

Yet, all I can think about is the fact that Grant's walking around without a shirt on. The shoulders on this man should have their own fan clubs. He's a raging distraction and completely oblivious to it.

Well, okay. From Wren's many unhelpful compliments, he can't be totally oblivious. Still.

I can be strong. I'll just have to look at him exactly never.

"This is gorgeous," Grant says.

I make the mistake of facing him. He gestures at the water and the three mountains that loom in the distance. Caldera Lake is so clear, it's practically a mirror reflecting the scene down to the last rock and tree.

I lean closer to him. "No leeches, right?"

He leans even closer. "Every lake has leeches."

My whole body shivers as if they're already on me. "Why is the wilderness like this?"

We set up Tess's sunshade and lay out our gear—beach blankets, a cooler full of drinks and snacks, at least a dozen bottles of sunscreen, and an assortment of inflatable loungers to float around on. August's hopping on one foot while Tess slathers any skin not covered by his swim shorts and long-sleeve rash guard.

"But why couldn't Ian come?" he asks, squinting as she rubs lotion on his face. "You said it's a friends day. He's our friend too."

"I know, buddy." Tess tries for a smile. "Maybe another time."

She doesn't sound very hopeful.

"Look what Griffin got ready for you!" Hope pops around the corner of the shelter with a purple hippo float that's even taller than she is.

August's grin reveals a missing tooth. "I want to ride that!"

"Gotta wear your life jacket, my guy," Griffin says.

I know the man wasn't actually born wearing jeans and flannel, but it's weird to see him in board shorts and flip-flops. Like coming across old pictures of The Rock when he had hair. It doesn't look right.

Grant, on the other hand, looks amazing in his board shorts. But no. I need to show some restraint here.

August wiggles into his red life vest, but as soon as he steps off the beach blanket onto sand, he pulls back. "Too hot."

"I'll help you." Tess grabs both his hands and hops him down the beach, lifting him in the air in giant, giggling jumps.

Hope takes a few cautious steps across the sand. "I should have brought my water shoes."

"I've got you." Griffin tosses her over one shoulder and churns sand as he runs down the beach until they both splash into the water. My sister shrieks the whole way, but man, is she happy.

Wren grabs the purple hippo. "Looks like it's you and me, pal."

She darts down to the water, throwing herself onto the hippo when she reaches the lake.

"Are you ready?" Grant asks.

Not really. To be honest, the last time I came out here with them was at least five years ago, and I don't remember actually getting in the water. I spent my time oiled up in the sun or huddled in the shade with a book. But I made it this far—might as well go the last fifty feet.

I pull my knee-length cover-up over my head and toss the teal fabric onto the rest of my things. A gusty groan comes from Grant's direction. I try to look shocked, but really, I'm just glad my retro red two-piece is as distracting to him as he is to me.

"Sorry." He grins at me, ruining the repentant act. "You look incredible."

"This old thing?" I put a hand on my hip. "I only wear it when I want to stun mountain men."

"Done and done."

I start to head out across the sand but backtrack to the blanket as quickly as August did. "It really is hot."

And rocky. It's probably as close to a sandy beach as we can hope for, but it's covered in pebbles, too. My poor feet ache already.

Grant moves in front of me, facing the lake. He squats down, looks at me over his shoulder, and gives it an inviting pat. "Hop aboard, princess."

"Really?"

He drops his eyebrows in silent challenge. "Don't make me order you to get up here."

His stern threat zings through my belly. I'm tempted to see

just how in charge Grant can be, but a lake busy with families probably isn't the place for that kind of test.

I step closer and set my hands on his shoulders.

He dips even lower into his squat. The thighs on this man...whew.

"You'll have to jump up."

I can see about three ways this could go where we wind up in a heap in the sand, but I jump anyway. Miraculously, his hands close tight around my thighs, and I rearrange my hold so I don't choke him. Cargo secured, he strides across the beach to the lake.

I pat his chest. "I wouldn't mind being chauffeured around like this all the time."

"You've got a deal."

He wades slowly into the water but doesn't put me down.

"Are you going to let me go?" I ask.

"Nope."

It *is* pretty cozy. I actually like—

I shriek when the cold water hits my feet and calves, but he keeps stalking deeper. I cling even tighter to him, as though the heat from his back can offset the chilly water. Thankfully, the shock doesn't last. Soon, we're shoulder-deep, swaying in the waves.

"This isn't bad." Understatement, but I'm stuck to his back like a level-five clinger. Not a lot could be better.

His fingers lightly squeeze my thighs. "I'm fond of it."

We watch Tess and Wren tread circles around August's hippo float. He's grinning and shouting something about pirates. Hopefully the distraction is working.

"What do you know about that Ian guy?" I ask softly.

"Only what's publicly available. I met him a couple of times through his old guiding business, but we don't know each other. Seemed like a good guy."

"I hope he'll fight for Tess and August." She needs somebody who'll step up and show her that he wants to be in their lives, no matter what.

"If he's smart, he will."

I think for another minute about this supposedly famous climber. "Think he'd be willing to be involved in a future event as a special celebrity guest?"

I can already imagine scenarios to put his fame and expertise to good use. Maybe we could partner with Horizon Hikes somehow.

Grant laughs. "Pre-injury Ian would have done it in a second. Now? Hard to say."

"Sunshine doesn't have many celebrities to choose from. We've got Leo Dalesandro, but I don't think he lives in town."

"Leo Dalesandro's from here? The NFL center?"

"Yup. Although, he got injured, too." That bone-snapping injury was the talk of the town for a solid month. "Maybe our celebrities are cursed."

"Probably best not to include the curse on your tourism website." He aimlessly moves us around in the water, taking in the views. "Are you ready for tomorrow?"

"I hope so." I've done everything I can expect to do short of giving the presentation.

"You're going to do great. Just be yourself, and I know you'll get it."

"If I don't, I'll look like a dummy in front of everyone." The whole town knows I'm trying for this job, and half of them expect it to be handed to me with a bow on top. I don't know how I'll show my face in Delish or Perk Me Up if they opt to give the job to someone else.

Grant turns his head but can't look at me when I'm clinging to his back. "Hey. You refer to yourself as 'dumb' a lot. Maybe

I'm wrong, but I have some guesses why. Don't let him stay in your head. He doesn't deserve the real estate."

I lay my cheek against his shoulder. I've let Josh live in my head way too long. He's the kind of "genius" that needs everyone around him to look stupid in comparison. Even with me, he had to come out on top over the smallest things. I hate that the self-talk I learned from him is still hanging around in my brain.

"You are smart, dedicated, and capable. You've got this down, princess."

"Thank you." I rest my chin on his shoulder and hug him tighter. "I'm nervous. It has to be perfect."

"You don't have to be perfect. You just have to be... genuinely Lila."

I hold out two whole seconds before bursting into laughter. "That was so cheesy, it hurts. How do I like you so much?"

"I'm serious."

Oh, I love it when he gets firm with me. My tough cinnamon roll.

"I know you think you need to have this perfect veneer for social media, the job—maybe even around town."

Hmm. I'm rethinking my praise for his toughness. He doesn't have to see me quite so clearly.

"May I suggest people will love you more for who you are on the inside than anything that isn't really you?"

This annoying, wonderful, beautiful, persistent man.

"You may suggest it," I concede. I rest my head against his. "I thought I learned that lesson last year when I left Josh. But then I moved back here, and it felt like everyone had such high opinions of me...I don't want to let people down."

"If being yourself lets people down, they were never worth your time in the first place."

"Do outdoor store managers double as therapists or something?"

He chuckles. "It probably drives us to therapy. I've seen some things."

"Like what?"

"Walked in on my brother making out with his future wife in the stock room."

I giggle against his back. "Did you learn anything?"

He slips his hands higher around my thighs. "You're naughty."

We're quiet for a while, my hands wandering along his upper chest and collar bone. I've never thought about chest hair a whole lot, but I have to say, I like it. I think I'd like anything on him.

"Only a few days before you go back to Texas." We've avoided dealing with this reality for a while now. It's a lot easier to bring it up now that we're not making eye contact.

He holds my legs tighter to him. "True."

"Do you ever think...maybe you could be happy here?" Can he even hear me over my pounding heart? "Sunshine's kind of grown on you, and we have a lot of mountains for you to climb. Maybe some of the people here could grow on you, too."

If he can't hear my heart, surely he can feel it hammering against his back.

"Princess, you have grown on me. More than you know."

He reaches around to pull me into a front carry position with his arms bracing me at my back. I keep my legs and arms around him because now that I've asked, I don't want to let him go. It doesn't seem possible we could be so right together only to know each other for a single month. How is that fair?

As I suspected, this is much more difficult when I'm staring into his eyes. They hold too many apologies for me to cling to hope.

"My parents called yesterday."

I do not like this preface.

"They offered me the CEO position."

My heart that's been beating so wildly cracks. I try to tape it up with empty reassurances, but it's splintering too fast. My patch job is just temporary anyway—any minute now, it will crumble.

"I'm happy for you." It's a whisper, but it's true. "This is what you wanted, isn't it?"

He watches me for long seconds like there's no right answer. "It is what I wanted."

I nod once, shoving down the ache in my ribcage. I cup his face in my hands and smile as bright as I can. "Then you go and lead that outdoorsy business. You love the company so much, you'll make a wonderful CEO. I want you to have the life that will make you happy."

And I do. I want all the happiness and love possible for Grant, even if I can't be the one to give it to him.

Realistically, this doesn't have to be goodbye. We could try to visit each other. Weekends, holidays, vacation—the world is our long-distance oyster. But I can't think about flights and travel times when I'm nestled in his arms.

He leans in to kiss me, soft presses of his lips that feel achingly like the goodbye I don't want to hear. But then his hands splay against my back, bringing me closer. His kiss becomes more insistent, deeper. I run my fingers through his hair at the nape of his neck, holding him to me as if I never have to let him go.

Grant's kisses are a thing of beauty—the perfect slide and caress of mouth, lips, tongue. I could let him direct me all afternoon, but I like to be in charge sometimes, too. We wrangle just a little, and I take control. Slow the kiss down. Indulge in the tiniest bit of torture. I nip his lower lip, and he groans against my mouth.

One of his hands comes up to skim through my hair and cup the back of my head. It's a good thing because I feel like I could float away on the waves. I've lost my *in charge of the kiss* privileges, but it's still a win.

"All right, all right!" Hope shouts. "This is a family lake!"

Grant releases me enough to break the kiss—but no more. I don't know which of us looks more smug. Clearly, we're both winners here. Or, maybe the kiss battle was a tie. We could always go in for a tie-breaker...

"Family lake!" August shouts.

Grant and I laugh and allow a breath of space between us. I turn to August. "Better?"

He makes his fingers into a vee and points them at his eyes, then at us. I fall into a fit of giggles.

"We have a five-year-old chaperone," I tell Grant.

"It's probably for the best. I can't be trusted today."

"Can you be trusted tonight?"

His eyes heat. "No."

"Do you want to come over anyway?"

"Always."

THIRTY-THREE

LILA

I CHOSE my blouse in "power purple" for the presentation. The color gives me an extra boost of confidence, even if silk is overkill in a room where only Mayor Martinez is dressed above business casual. But it works—I slip into a zone of unruffled poise as I go through my notes.

I explain my plan to expand Sunshine's local events calendar and make the town more readily available to host other organizations' events. I illustrate broad ways we could enhance our infrastructure to add more visitor-friendly services. And I cover the importance of highlighting our best selling point— close proximity to all things outdoors.

The mayor and half a dozen council members nod along, even though I'm guessing they already know all this. It's not so much that they never thought they needed someone focused on tourism before, it's that they never gave it the budget. I need to make what I think I can achieve—and what that, in turn, can do for our community—so vital they beg me to expand my hours.

Finally, I get to my website mock-up and a potential town-centric social media account. Sunshine's current website isn't much more than the chamber of commerce pages, their events calendar is a year out of date, and their social media presence is nonexistent. I click through the pages I made highlighting local events, small business spotlights, and local clubs and organizations.

Then, I open my favorite tabs: *Stay, Shop,* and *Dine.* I probably went overboard, highlighting more of my favorite local lodges, restaurants, and stores for this imaginary website than necessary, but it was the easiest part for me.

Finally, I click open *Play.* This breaks down into smaller categories like *Bike, Hike, Swim,* and *Float.* Plus the sidebar I added last night in a burst of inspiration.

"Sunshine is an ideal location for mountain biking, rafting, hiking, and snow sports. We can increase tourism by making our attractions better known. But what about people who have very little outdoors experience—like me?"

I'd rather sit on another ant hill than admit my deficiencies, but Grant's right. I need to be myself. Whether I get this promotion or not, I need to be comfortable in my own skin. That includes accepting I'm not Queen of the Outdoors. And I don't have to be.

I click open the sidebar "I pulled together a variety of entry-level suggestions from businesses like Horizon Hikes, Get in Gear, and Wildwater Rafters featured under a heading I'm calling *Beginner-Friendly Activities to Get Even the Most Indoorsy Person out in Sunshine.*"

Because if it can work for me, it can work for anyone.

———

I stop by The Painted Daisy on my way home. My poise and confidence have fizzled somewhat, and now I just want to see my sister. And maybe a slice of Blackbird's pie.

Hope is all smiles the second I walk through the door. "Well? How did it go?"

"Good, I think. Maybe even great? Some of the council members are hard to read. Mayor Martinez was enthusiastic." The actual interview portion was more like a Q&A at the end, but I think I handled everything well. Even the ones I'd pin as skeptical seemed to appreciate at least one thing I put forward.

"Did he give you a timeline for when he'll call you?"

I shrug, even though I'm already tempted to check my phone. "In a few days. They need to consider everything."

She looks at me like I'm covered in leeches. "You know this is just a formality, right?"

"No? They advertised the position and have an applicant pool."

"None of the other applicants put on the best Independence Day celebration this town has seen. After that, the job was yours."

My mouth hangs open for a second. "You don't know that."

"How do you *not* know that? Griffin's mom is on the council, and she told me the only real concern is if they can afford you."

I'd been relieved to see Kat McBride in the council audience, but I would have been a whole lot more relieved if I'd had this information at the beginning of the week. "Nobody told me that. My hair's been falling out from stress."

Of course, I spent half the week after the Fourth Fest sick in bed, so I didn't have a lot of opportunities to find out.

"I'm sorry. I thought you knew they weren't going to find anyone better than you."

I laugh, but it's half sob. It's been a while since I've truly had that kind of confidence. I've been freaking out for weeks that I needed to be some kind of expert in the wilderness to get the promotion, and now she tells me it was a lock the whole time? "You mean I've been doing all this outdoorsy stuff for nothing?"

I know it's wrong the moment it's out of my mouth. Every activity I did, no matter how reluctantly, helped me improve my plans for Sunshine's website, social media, and calendar of events. They gave me more ideas for expanding our local services and how we might attract new residents and businesses. I wouldn't have had the idea for half the presentation I gave today if I hadn't stepped outside my cozy comfort zone.

"I don't know if I'd call it nothing," Hope says. "You came away with a pretty good souvenir from that first hike."

My heart squeezes. If I hadn't signed up for that five-day nightmare, I wouldn't have met Grant. Trying to picture the last month without him...it's impossible. I wouldn't be in the same place I am today. By far, I wouldn't be as happy. Even if that happiness comes with a giant question mark.

"I just wish I could keep my souvenir."

"You've still got a few days left. Mom's going to try to get you guys to come to dinner, so be prepared."

"I figured." I just want to hide out with him until he has to leave on Sunday. Make a blanket fort and tuck ourselves away from reality like we did last night. Pretend none of this has to end.

Maybe I should face the fact that pretending never worked very well for us. Starting now.

"I need to tell you something." I shore up the last reserves of ego boost left in my purple power blouse. "Grant and I didn't come back from that trip a couple. I ran into Josh as soon as we got to town, and he was doing like Josh does, and Grant stepped in as my fake boyfriend. Or, I stepped in as his fake girlfriend. It's fuzzy. Either way, the key word there is *fake*. I'm sorry I lied to you."

She blinks at me for a second. "You tried to fake date Grant? What in the rom-com scenario?"

"I know. Josh was being so humiliating, and I thought the lie could be contained to just him, but then *Mom* was there, and it spiraled."

"Huh. When did you realize it's real?"

I love that it's not even a question for her.

"For me? It was gradual. For him...I wasn't sure until maybe a week ago. And now..." I draw in a deep breath as though my lungs can never fill enough. "I don't want to let him go."

She rounds the counter and wraps an arm around my shoulders. "So tell him."

"I did." Pathetically, and while I was hitched to his back, but it counts. "But he's got his family business back home, and I can't compete with that."

I can't be the kind of person who asks him to give up his life's dream for me. I'm a lot of things, but I'm not that selfish.

"Lila, you had to compete for Josh's attention, but I don't think there's any competition when it comes to Grant. Josh wanted everyone to look at him. Grant never takes his eyes off you."

He sees past the ideal image I try to put forward in a way no one ever has before. I can just be myself, and he's still right here with me. The good, the bad, and the violently ill. "I've never felt so seen. It's annoying...and so immensely comforting. I want to be *seen* by Grant all the time."

"Like *naked* seen?"

Hope and I turn to find Wren standing in the pass-through. Of course. The open doorway is a brilliant marketing move and an ongoing source of irritation.

"Not exactly what I was going for."

She smirks. "Your blush says I was right, though."

Wren Krause is also an ongoing source of irritation, no

matter how much I love her. I release Hope and smooth the wrinkles in my blouse.

"I should go change. I'm meeting Grant for a late lunch, and then we're going to..." Possibly indulge in my blanket fort plans, but I'm not ready to be that transparent yet.

Except, apparently I *am* that transparent. Wren slow nods and Hope utterly fails to hide her smile.

"Enjoy each other's company all weekend?" Wren prompts.

I turn my nose up, but I'm pretty sure it's too late to try to save face here. "I was going to let him decide."

They both break down into giggles.

"Oh, yeah," Wren says. "It's time to get biz-zay."

She hits me with finger guns like a sassy desperado. I exhale a laugh. Screw it. I'd rather be honest than save face.

"Yes." I stand a little straighter and square off with my mouthy friend. "I'm going to spend the rest of the weekend with my hot mountain man doing whatever we please because if this is all the time I get with him, I'm not going to waste a minute of it."

They give my little speech a standing ovation. These two can be so exasperating...but I wouldn't want them any other way. I leave on a high note of wolf-whistles and applause. Striding down Maple Street, I feel like I could hike to the top of McKenzie Peak and actually enjoy it.

Halfway back to my apartment, an idea hits. Buzzing with excitement, I take the stairs two by two and rush through my door to sit on the edge of my bed. I pull out my phone and sift through pictures until I find the right one.

A rare selfie I took on the hike. One of the Three Sisters mountains is behind me, the sky is unbearably blue, I have zero makeup on—and it's absolutely *real*.

I type up a caption for my Instagram.

Seven months ago, I thought I'd lost everything. I ended my relationship with my fiancé, I lost my job, and had nowhere to live. I moved back to my hometown of Sunshine, Oregon to start over at thirty. I'm rebuilding my life, little by little. My content might change its focus, but in my heart, I'm still me—genuinely Lila.

THIRTY-FOUR

GRANT

I'M in sight of my cabin and in desperate need of a shower when my phone buzzes. I can't help the eye roll. Rhett's timing could be better.

"Yeah?" Not the warmest greeting I've given him but probably not the worst. I spent the morning hiking the trails behind the lodge to distract myself while Lila gave her presentation. I've got enough time to catch a breath and shower before I need to head into town to meet her. Unfortunately, Rhett's a pro at sidetracking people.

"Good vacation then?" He laughs, completely unfazed by my irritation. "You sure sound relaxed."

I drag a hand down my face. I don't need to take my impatience to see Lila out on him. "It is a good vacation."

In fact, it's the best, for reasons I won't go into.

"Sounds like it. Mom and Dad told us about their surprise promotion. Congratulations. You've been waiting for this."

Everyone keeps saying that. I've even said it. I'm just not sure that means much anymore.

"Thank you. It was...unexpected." I can't say when I

thought it would happen, but mid-vacation never occurred to me.

"You've never been away from work this long. I think they want to make sure you're coming back, so they had to give you a little incentive."

"They weren't wrong," I say before I can think better of it.

His laughter dies out. "What?"

I don't know how to begin to explain. So I don't.

"You like it there that much?" This laugh doesn't come quite as easily as the first one. "Did you meet someone?"

Meeting someone doesn't remotely compare to the reality of it. Finding the person I want to spend the rest of my life with is the truth of it.

"Wait." He drags the word out, trying to catch up to everything I'm not saying. "Are you kidding me? Who is she?"

Is there a point in keeping this secret? Do I even want to?

"A woman I met on the hiking trip. She's...radiant sunshine. She's all heart and spirit and drive. She can be soft and gentle one minute, and the next, she's ready to burn the world to the ground to defend her people. She's like...coming home to a place I've never been but knew all along was waiting for me."

Lila fills my thoughts, photos overlapping in an endless montage: Exhausted but laughing on the trail. Sweetly snuggling with August. Going to battle to protect me from my parents and Kelsey. In my arms in the lake. In my arms last night...

"I'm in love with her." Saying it out loud is like a bird released from a cage, finally able to soar. Hmm—bad analogy for Lila. But the *free* sensation doesn't fade. It grows until it presses up against my ribcage with an aching longing.

Because Rhett's not the one I really want to tell.

"Wow, man! Congrats! That's the best news."

His enthusiasm has the opposite of his intended effect and brings my feet back to earth.

"She's building a life here, and my life is in Magnolia Ridge." A truth I've been only too happy to avoid looking at straight on for weeks now.

"I know my advice is suspect. I don't have the best romantic track record. My exes would say I'm the last guy you should listen to."

"You're really selling it." I've talked with some of his exes—he's barely scratched the surface of what they say about him.

"But if I felt about someone even half the way you sound when you're talking about her, I would risk anything to hold onto her."

A tiny spark of hope lights up inside me, searching for something to cling to. "I want to, believe me, I do. But everyone's counting on me. You need me there."

"*We* need you? Since when?" He coughs. "Uh, respectfully."

I sigh as I barge through my cabin door and storm around the tiny space. "You'd be surviving on granola bars and beer if I weren't there to check up on you. And Dean..."

"This will be good. Please explain how our happily married, home-owning, ultra-responsible sibling would be lost without you here to big-brother him."

"Fine. I can't." If anything, Dean's taught me lessons these last couple of years. He's found what's most important to him and built his life around them.

"And for the record, I like granola bars and beer. I get it. You had to step up a lot when we were kids, but I'm thirty, man. Don't use me as an excuse not to chase your own happiness."

Lila's voice echoes in my mind, telling me to create a life I don't have to take a vacation from. If I could lay out the plans and make it happen, what would that look like? Easy—being with her. The rest—where I work, where I live—isn't nearly as vital as that one all-consuming point.

"She is my happiness, but I've worked too hard at the business to just walk away without a second thought. I don't know if there's a way to have both."

"We're two reasonably smart guys," Rhett says. "I'm sure we can figure something out. There's a solution here somewhere. You could work remotely. Do something else entirely. Enact a hostile takeover of the closest outdoor store and raise the Irwin flag. Whatever it takes."

"If only it were so easy. There isn't anything like that in town. The closest one is—" Wait. *Wait.* Did Rhett really just solve my problem? I've been so stuck on this idea that it could never happen, I couldn't see the solution right in front of me. "You're a genius."

"Finally." He sounds like he's puffed out his chest to receive a gold medal. "Some long-awaited recognition."

"We can revisit the recognition later. I need to make some calls."

"Nope. First, I need a name."

"Lila." It's a sigh on my lips, and I do not care a bit.

"Pretty. Second—it was the shirt I sent that won her over, wasn't it?"

THIRTY-FIVE

LILA

I CHECK out my reflection in the peach minidress and spin to watch it twirl. It's probably too much for a late lunch at Magnifico, but I want to dress up a little for Grant. If these are our last few days together, I'm going to *Live, Laugh, Love* the heck out of them. That includes wearing cute dresses and doing my hair because that's just how I am.

My phone buzzes on the dining table. It's gone crazy ever since I posted my Instagram update. It turns out *a lot* of women can relate to having to start over. I've received hundreds of comments and DMs with a similar theme:

I've been there.

I'm cheering for you.

You can get through this.

Yes, I've also had quite a few saying my ex is probably better off without me, I'll never find anyone better, etcetera. My follower count has dwindled some, which I expected. But for the most part, the people who interact with me are encouraging and supportive, and I'm a tiny bit embarrassed that I felt like I had to keep up the big city girl act for as long as I did.

Like my cheesy boyfriend said—I just had to be myself.

My phone rings, and I peek at the screen. Mom. Probably gunning for that family dinner Hope mentioned. I would appreciate the way she's wholeheartedly welcoming Grant if that dinner weren't going to cut into our *do whatever we please* time.

"Hi, Mom."

"Lila, I've got great news."

Hmm. Not a family dinner push then.

She sounds out of breath like she's been running somewhere. Makes no sense because she's the one I got my anti-athletic genes from. "Henderson's finally got a taker."

"Really? That is great news. What's going in there?" She hasn't mentioned showing it to anyone lately. Oh. "Is it another thrift shop?"

Not that I have anything against them. I'm just holding out for a little more variety downtown. I'm not naive enough to think my Sephora wishes will come true, but a business we don't already have would be ideal.

"Not a thrift shop. Come down and see for yourself."

"I can't, I'm meeting Grant for lunch." I check the time. "Actually, I need to leave right now."

"You can swing by on your way."

"It's not on my way. Just tell me who it is." Usually, she crows about new business tenants the minute she's able to. Her urge to surprise me is weird and poorly timed.

She makes a giddy humming sound. "It's much more dramatic to see for yourself. I know you'll be thrilled."

"I'll be even more thrilled if you just tell me so I'm not late for Grant."

"Lila Kathleen, if you don't come down here right this minute, you will be disappointed you weren't first to hear the news. I would think as Sunshine's tourism coordinator, you would want the inside scoop on who's moving to town."

I sigh but grab my purse. "*Probable* tourism coordinator. I'll be there in five minutes. But you'd better make it quick."

"Oh, I don't think you'll mind a delay," she says before hanging up.

Okay, that's not cryptic at all.

Five minutes later, I stroll up to Henderson's. Mom's out front staring up the block and clasps her hands as soon as she sees me. She's absurdly happy for something as simple as a commission and a new business moving into Sunshine.

In fact...the last time I saw her this happy was at Hope's engagement party.

I slow down as I close in on her. "What's going on?"

Mom shakes her head, but I swear she has tears in her eyes. Are Hope and Griffin pulling a surprise wedding or something? Seems unlikely, but nothing else explains her reaction.

"Go inside and see for yourself."

A frisson of nerves skates through me. I stare at the glass door I papered over with Fourth of July themed wrapping. The window next to it still shines in all its patriotic glory. I've been in here half a dozen times. It should be no big deal to walk through that door. But Mom's acting extremely fishy.

"Go on." She nods at the door. "It's a good thing. And if you don't agree, well, that's okay, too."

I peer at her, trying to make sense of this, but she's too giddily mysterious for me to make sense of her. So I pull the door open—

And find Grant walking around the empty store. His smile eases the worst of my nerves.

"Hey, princess."

"Hey." I meet him in the middle of the store. "What's going on?"

"I have something for you." He reaches into his gloriously bulky cargo shorts and opens his hand in front of me.

A wooden dahlia bloom rests on his palm. Its layers of petals are rustic and uneven, but perfectly smooth. I reach out a hand to trace one finger over the delicate points.

"It's beautiful."

"I still need to stain it and seal it, but I wanted to give it to you now."

"You made this?" I take it from him and clutch it to my chest.

"I've been working on it since I saw your tattoo. Well, I was working on it before then, but that's when it started to take shape."

"You *whittled* it?" Doesn't seem the right word for such a beautifully carved little piece.

"I hope you like it."

"I love it." I love it so much, I'm struggling not to cry over it. "But why are you giving it to me in here?"

The heavy-duty cleaning solution still fills the air inside the old department store, and our words echo around the big, empty space.

"Because I'm taking your advice. I want a life I don't need a vacation from." He takes a step closer to me, his hands going to my waist. "And I want that here. With you."

I suck in a breath. I've been telling myself for weeks not to wish for more than what we have right now, and it's hard to let his words sink in.

"I always thought my parents' story of love at first sight was exaggerated. Then I met you, and I realized it was possible. I started falling in love with you from the first time I saw you."

I laugh, but my heart feels like it could fill this whole store. *Grant Irwin loves me!* Nothing ever sounded better. "In all my hiking chic at Horizon?"

I wasn't exactly at the top of my game during our first few days together.

"You were in your hiking chic, but not at Horizon." He flexes his fingers against my waist. "I saw you at the coffee shop earlier that morning. Something right here—" He taps two fingers over his heart. "Unlocked when I saw you. I was immediately attracted to you, but *hope* glimmered there, too. I hadn't felt that kind of hope in years."

I know exactly what he means.

He takes my hand and laces our fingers together. "Lila, I'm in love with you. We haven't known each other long and I'm not asking for promises today, but there's no way I'm leaving Sunshine without trying for something with you."

I throw my arms around his neck, clutching my flower tight in one hand. "Something?"

His smile tilts to one side. "*Everything* would be even better."

Oh, this man. He leans down and presses his mouth to mine. I'm not sure which of us grins harder, I only know this is a kiss made out of happiness and light. And a little tongue. But my brain buzzes with one important fact I forgot to tell him, and I pull away.

"I'm in love with you, too. You're so good and kind, and you have the sweetest heart. And sexy? Hoo boy, you knock me out. I don't want you to leave, either. But what about your family business and becoming CEO?"

I still don't want to keep him from his dreams, even if his dreams keep him from me.

"I've heard that Sunshine is a thriving town drawing in outdoor enthusiasts year-round. But the nearest outdoor gear supplier is in the next town over. I figure this space is the perfect location for a new Irwin Outdoors store."

I freeze. "Are you serious? You're going to open one of your stores here?"

His smile quirks. "I thought you would have seen through that already."

"I hoped, but I didn't want to assume."

He pulls me closer to him. "I talked to my parents. I told them I love working for our business, but I want my life to be here with you. There's a lot of logistics to work out, but they like the idea of expanding into a new state."

I make a sound of disgust. "They didn't say anything about you being happy?"

His grin hits me straight in my overloaded heart. "I love how quickly you jump to my defense. They're thrilled that I found you and want to build a life here. They asked me to bring you to Texas soon so they can meet you."

"I'd love to." I smooth my empty hand over his chest. "These are big changes for you. Are you sure about this?"

He slides one hand into my hair to cup my head, looking into my eyes so intensely my stomach dips. "For the first time in a long time, I'm not doing the next thing I think I should do, or the next thing that's expected of me. I'm following my heart. *You* are my happiness, Lila. In every possible way."

"Really?"

"Genuinely."

EPILOGUE

GRANT

SEVEN MONTHS *later*

Irwin Outdoors in Sunshine, Oregon is officially open for business.

Our grand opening weekend went better than I'd dreamed it would. I've been around for some of our store openings in Texas, but this one felt more significant. Maybe because I helped remodel the space from the ground up. Maybe because Sunshine's residents rallied around to welcome us into the community. Or maybe it's because opening this store has been an important step on the path to making my happiness here a reality.

As great as the high of seeing the old department store fully transformed into an Irwin's crowded with customers was, nothing compares to tonight. I might never come down from this.

In fact, I hope I don't.

Moonlight Lodge's converted barn glows with old-fashioned string lights and the happy faces of all of our closest friends. My entire family flew in from Texas to see the new store, and they mingle with Lila's relatives in the rustic-chic space.

I catch sight of her across the room talking with Eliza and Dean, and my breath stops in my lungs. I'll never get over how utterly perfect she is. Not because she doesn't have flaws or never has a bad moment, but because she's so completely herself. And that, to me, is perfection.

She meets my gaze and grins so wide I have to mirror her joy. We're not being very subtle, but I don't think anyone expects what's coming next.

A hand wraps around my arm, and I look down to see Grandma Gloria beaming up at me.

I lean down to kiss her cheek. "You look radiant tonight, Grandma."

"You always were a sweet talker." She makes a show of looking over at Lila, and her smile widens. "Whatever you're planning for tonight, I approve."

I freeze, hoping my face looks neutral and innocent. "What do you think I'm planning?"

Her gaze turns arch, like she's sifted through my secrets and knows them all by heart. "I couldn't say. But this lovely party in this beautiful space? How you're watching your pretty fiancée like you're waiting for a signal? The way your happiness shines brighter than all the stars in the sky? Makes me think you're up to something more than just celebrating a store."

I lower my head closer to hers. "How do you see right through me?"

"I've had practice. I've watched you your whole life." She pats my cheek. "I'm happy for you, honey. I couldn't be prouder of the man you are and the life you're creating for yourself."

Gratitude, love, and admiration clamor around in my chest. I wrap her in a huge hug. "Thank you, Grandma."

She pulls back and gives a stout nod. "Make me some great-grandbabies soon, won't you?"

I swear, this woman's seen every last hope and dream in my head.

"Dean's news isn't enough for you?" I tease. They announced their pregnancy at Christmas. He's had his arm around Eliza since they arrived in Oregon. It's like he thinks she and that baby are his good luck charms.

They probably are.

Grandma Gloria just smiles. "There's always room for more."

Rhett loops his arms around each of our shoulders, managing to hold her much more gently than the crushing grip he's got on me. "Room for more what?"

"More happy couples in this family." Grandma pokes him in the stomach. "Wouldn't you say, scamp?"

He wrinkles his nose. "Pretty sure we've maxed that out."

She *tsks* at him, but he just laughs. He'll figure himself out in his own time.

Lila joins our little group, and Rhett releases me so I can focus on her.

As though that's ever been a problem.

She slips an arm around my waist. "Have I told you lately that I'm proud of you?"

"It's been a few minutes."

"Then I'm overdue." She turns to Grandma and Rhett. "Is this guy the best or what?"

"I'm standing right here," Rhett says with a pout. "If you keep this up, I might start to think you like him more than me."

Grandma pokes him again. "Find your own woman."

"Pass."

"Come on." She steers him toward the laughing crowd behind them. "Leave them be. Lila needs to change anyway."

Grandma winks as they walk away. And she wonders where Rhett gets his mischievousness.

Lila's hands tighten on my waist. "Did you tell her?"

"Nope. She just has mysterious grandma ways."

"I love her. And she's right. I should go."

I lean down to press a soft kiss to her mouth. "Hurry back."

She grins up at me. "You're never getting rid of me."

"Promise?"

Her grin falls away, totally solemn. "I do."

"Tease."

"You love me."

I mirror her seriousness. "I do."

With a giggle, Lila slips through the crowd. My heart rate kicks up, ready for what comes next. I scan the mingling people and spot Leo Dalesandro off to one side. I nod, and he finds Ian Vaughn to get to work setting up chairs. Crazy to think two famous athletes have become some of my closest friends in the last few months.

Then again, most of my life these last few months has been completely unexpected. In all the best ways.

Mom and Dad head over to me, smiling brighter than ever.

"You pulled it off," Dad says.

"We knew you would," Mom adds. "It's a beautiful store. You chose a perfect location in town."

"And you chose a perfect fiancée. We're glad to see you settling in so well here."

"I don't think I could be happier." Except maybe in ten more minutes.

Mom gives me in a quick hug. "Seeing your joy makes *us* happy. You deserve every bit of it."

"Thanks, Mom." I won't get choked up. I can't spoil the fun that's coming.

Charlie Callahan waves at me from the back of the room. *It's showtime.* Also, it's probably not safe for my heart rate to go any faster.

"If you want to see a little more of my joy, why don't you sit here in the front?"

I gesture to the chairs Leo and Ian hastily set up in two rows down the center of the converted barn. Mom and Dad probably have questions that go along with their curious looks, but I just steer them closer until they sit. Leo ushers Grandma over while Ian guides Lila's parents to the other side of the aisle.

"If I could get your attention." My shout into the small crowd results in a hush. Everyone turns toward me. "If you could all take a seat, please."

I give them a minute to shuffle into chairs while Jodi Ellison joins me at the front of the room. Who knew the diner's co-owner was also an ordained minister? My beautiful fiancée who knows every last detail about this town, that's who.

Eliza gasps like she just figured out why I'm overdressed in a suit for this casual party.

"On behalf of the whole Irwin family, I want to thank every one of you for coming out to mark the opening of our first Oregon location." Applause moves around the room, along with a few wolf-whistles from Griffin. "But I have something to confess."

The room goes silent.

"When Lila and I realized all of our friends and family would be here with us tonight, we wanted to take advantage of the opportunity. We decided we've been engaged long enough." Two months has never seemed so much like an eternity. "We don't want to wait to start our life together. So we're getting married tonight."

Excited whispers fill the space, along with an "I knew it," from Eliza. Charlie pushes open the back doors, and an instrumental version of *A Thousand Years* plays on the air.

Lila appears holding a bouquet of orange and red dahlias, her long-sleeve white dress making her look more ethereal than ever. A thousand years would never be enough to love this woman, but I plan to cherish every single one I get with her. Starting right now.

My gaze is locked on her grin I can't get enough of. She draws closer too slowly and somehow too quickly. I want to savor every precious moment, but I also want her in my arms right this second. Every beat of my heart confirms she belongs with me.

Today. Tonight. Forever.

When she finally reaches me, it takes superhuman strength not to jump to the end and kiss her. I don't think our audience would mind. But I call on all my patience, and take her hand in mine.

Her eyes fill with tears, but she shines even brighter. "Are you ready to marry me, mountain man?"

I lean in close. "I thought you'd never ask, princess."

BONUS EPILOGUE

TESS

EARLIER THAT SUMMER...

Wow. That is one big scowl.

I park my car in front of the duplex Amy Ellison showed me two weeks ago, my gaze locked on the surly man standing on the porch with her. AKA, my new neighbor. AKA, my project.

Behind me in his booster seat, August gasps. "Look at the dog!"

Naturally, my son would focus on the most innocent piece of this puzzle. Not the man with the wild mop of shoulder-length red hair and matching scraggly beard. Not Amy, grinning at me like nothing in this arrangement could possibly be uncomfortable. But the giant, mottled-brown dog with its tongue lolling out, zero thoughts in its head.

"It's so cool," August adds.

Right now, he thinks everything is *cool*. The sports car that cut us off on our way here was cool. His blue shirt he's worn for three days straight is *cool*. Even the old scars on my forearms from oven burns have been deemed *cool*.

At least August is enthusiastic about our move out of my mom's house. *So far.* I need to keep that positive attitude in place for as long as I can. Soon, he's going to realize his grandma and aunt are across town instead of across the hall, and I expect his excitement to crumble like an over-baked cake.

But I can't keep living with the rest of my family anymore. I'm thirty-two. I need to create a little space for August and me. And maybe get out from under my mother's increasingly smothering wings.

I turn to face him. "Do you want to see your new room?"

His wide grin reveals two missing teeth. "I want to meet the dog!"

"Let's wait to see if he's friendly." The dog looks a whole lot friendlier than the man, but you never know.

We climb out of my car, and Amy steps off of the porch to greet us.

"Good morning, you two!" She offers an open hand, and August slaps it in a high five. "I'm glad you're here. Are you ready to get settled in?"

"I want to meet the dog!"

His little brain's just got the one track this morning. Actually, mine does too: the scowl on the man watching us. He's not exactly doling out warm fuzzies. I knew he wouldn't be, I just wasn't expecting a level-five glare in greeting.

Amy chuckles. "It's good to have priorities. The dog's a sweetheart. Let me introduce you to your neighbor first."

We clamber onto the porch the two duplex units share. I gently hold August's shoulder to prevent him from launching at the dog in a full-body tackle, but he'll only wait so long.

"Tess and August, meet my nephew, Ian." Amy gestures

between the three of us. "Ian, these are two of the best people in Sunshine you'll ever know."

I flash a brilliant smile at Ian. In my experience, a little sweetness goes a long way. Whether in the bakery when the line is long and customers get twitchy or when August's grumpy and doesn't want to do his blood sugar tests, a warm smile and cheerful attitude can be infectious.

Ian seems to be immune. His scowl is a sweetness-repelling shield. He's giving off strong *Keep Out, No Trespassing* vibes. Which is a little awkward, considering we'll be sharing a duplex for the foreseeable future.

"It's nice to meet you, Ian." I use my customer service, *This is the best day ever!* voice. I get crickets in return.

"Mister, can I pet your dog?" August's squirming at my side, but instead of the potty dance, he's doing the *I need to meet a new dog* dance.

Ian drops his gaze to my son. Something inside me goes hard with the fear his unfriendliness will spill over onto August. The quickest way to kill my good nature is to be rude to my child. All my people-pleasing instincts evaporate, and Mama Bear takes over.

But by some miracle, Ian nods. August carefully holds out a hand for the dog to sniff. Once he gets the lick of approval, he moves on to gentle pets. He's had a lot of practice meeting dogs at Sunshine's parks.

"I don't have much time today." Amy holds out a Delish diner keychain to me. "Here are your keys. Trash and recycling pick up is on Wednesdays. If you have trouble with anything, you know where to find me."

She steps off the porch and toward her sedan, but turns back, pointing at her nephew. "Ian, why don't you help Tess and August carry their things inside? That'd be neighborly of you."

She winks at him, hops into her car, and drives away. Leaving me here with the least-neighborly guy I can imagine.

See, this is where my optimism and positivity sometimes bite me in the butt. When Amy offered me this apartment, I'd been too focused on the steeply discounted rent to ask much about the solitary nephew she'd mentioned. I'd only clarified that her request I try to befriend him didn't have any romantic notions behind it. Now, I've got nothing but questions.

Like, *Does he ever smile?*

Is he trying to zap me into oblivion with his ice-blue eyes?

How long does he plan to give us the silent treatment?

"Come on, August." I can't spend all day on the porch working up anxiety about my neighbor. "Help bring your things inside."

I unlock the front door and push it wide. It's a simple, two-bedroom apartment filled with modern furniture with clean lines. We're lucky to get it. I won't let anything ruin this chance for us—including the man next door.

"Your bedroom's the blue one," I tell August. "Go take a look and then come help."

I head out to my wagon, his "This is so cool!" echoing through the apartment. I open the hatch, and my heart jumps straight into my throat when Ian appears at my side like a lumbering bear.

I do *not* scream, but it's hard to spin the awkward sound I make into a friendly greeting.

"Amy said I should help." His voice is deep and gravelly, like he doesn't use it often.

"Thank you. That'd be great." I don't care if he's being neighborly or simply following through on duty to his aunt—we brought a lot of stuff. "Do you mind getting the biggest luggage?"

He hefts the giant bag out of the back as if it's empty instead of stuffed to bursting with my clothes. His biceps flex beneath his short T-shirt sleeves like the guy never skips arm day. Which is not something I usually notice, but this close, they're hard to miss.

I take a couple smaller bags and go into the house. My room is cozy and bright, with spots of orange and blue in the bedspread and rug giving it a sense of cheer. I love it.

I set my bags by the dresser, and Ian does the same with the bigger one. He glances around, looking out of place in the feminine room.

"Is your apartment pretty much the same?" I ask. I'm pretty sure Amy and Jodi used to let them out as short-term rentals.

His gaze cuts my way, skating over me in a quick assessment. "No."

He shuffles from the room. Okay. This is going...not great. But I can do this. I've dealt with plenty of grumpy customers at my family's bakery. Of course, those grumps don't usually live next door to me.

I go out to the car for the next round, passing August, who's already given up on unloading in favor of snuggling up with the dog on the porch. Ian's at the back of my car like he's waiting for his next instructions, so I try again.

"This is a great place out here. Do you do a lot of hiking on the trail?" Hiking seems like a good topic for small talk. A trail starts just past the duplex's backyard.

"No."

I suppress a sigh. Is this going to be like when August was three and "no" was his favorite word? At least when he got especially cranky, I could put him down for a nap. I don't think my new neighbor would handle the suggestion well.

Ian drags a big box to the edge of the hatch, but I stop him.

"That one's a beast." It's got my extremely expensive, extremely precious, extremely *heavy* mixer in it.

He cuts me a look like he and his giant biceps don't appreciate the warning. He scoops it up without a struggle. *Impressive.* When I carry it around, I do a lot more grunting and sweating.

I grab the much lighter box of August's Lego bricks, and trail Ian into the house.

"Where do you want this?" he asks in the living room.

"On the kitchen counter, please."

I tuck August's toys into his room and join Ian in the kitchen. "Amy says you haven't been in town very long. Where did you live before?"

"Colorado."

I wait for more, but he doesn't offer more. "How do you like Sunshine?"

Apparently, my only goal in life is to smother this man with smiles and get him to talk to me in more than single sentences. We don't have to become BFFs, but I have to hope we can reach some level of non-glaring social interactions one day. Otherwise, guilt over my too-cheap rent will crush me.

He hitches a shoulder. "It's changed a lot since I was last here."

"When was that?" I don't remember ever seeing this man before. You'd think a guy who looks like he'd fit right in on a Viking boat ready to plunder a village would stick out more in my memory.

"About fifteen years ago. I worked as a rafting guide one summer."

My triumph over him saying two sentences together pauses. Freezes. Slips away entirely.

Ian Vaughn. My heart somehow speeds up, slows down, and sinks into the crawl space beneath the duplex all in one go.

This can't possibly be the same Ian. Amy never told me his last name, but now that I've connected the dots, it has to be him.

Maybe the red hair should have sparked a memory, but he's just so *different*, in every possible way. Back then, he'd been all breathtaking boyish good looks, and handed out wide smiles to everyone. I'd never seen anyone half so charming or enthusiastic. He'd effortlessly turned the summer before my senior year of high school into a twisted knot of unrequited infatuation.

My hands go clammy and my stomach floods with anxious moths, even though this Ian is nothing like the twenty-two year-old version I'd once crushed so hard on. I need to get it together.

We're neighbors. The charm, smiles, and enthusiasm that used to make him sparkle have taken a back seat to frowns and dirty looks. And...I promised Amy I'd do my best to befriend him.

Cool. Cool, cool, cool.

Keep an eye out for Tess and Ian's story, Make Mine Sweet!

ALSO BY GENNY CARRICK

The Love in Sunshine series

Mad About Yule

Standalones

The Loch Effect

The Magnolia Ridge series

Say the Words

Have a Heart

Stay this Christmas

Make it Real

A NOTE FROM GENNY

Thank you for reading Grant and Lila's story! I've been wanting to give Grant his HEA ever since he first appeared all handsome and jilted in Dean and Eliza's book, Have a Heart. When Lila appeared similarly heartbroken in Mad About Yule, I knew what I had to do!

To Claire, & Amanda, thank you for your wonderful feedback on this book! You brought me out of a slump when I wasn't sure if this little romcom was any good. (I will wonder this about every book, apologies in advance.)

To my editor Cindy, thank you for your notes on clarity and always knowing where those pesky commas go. I swear I'm taking notes.

As always, Melody gets all the praise for this wonderful cover! It's like you pulled them straight from my imagination. Everything's there, from Lila's skepticism to Grant's chin dimple! I love them!

And today, tomorrow, always—I'm constantly grateful for my family. You're my whole world, and I'm lucky to have you. Maybe we should go camping??

ABOUT THE AUTHOR

Genny Carrick is a fool for happily ever afters, especially if there's a whole lot of laughter along the way. She writes rom-coms about sassy women, the cinnamon roll men who fall for them, and swoony moments outdoors whenever she possibly can.

When she's not lost in romantic reads, she's probably up to something crafty or trying to get her dog and two cats to love her.

After a quick detour in Texas, Genny recently returned to her true love, the Pacific Northwest, and lives with her brilliant husband and two hilarious kids.

Stay up to date with book news at gennycarrick.com

www.ingramcontent.com/pod-product-compliance
Lightning Source LLC
Chambersburg PA
CBHW061637190726

48289CB00006B/1635